William Joseph Roberts

Presents:

Tales of the Apocalypse

Three Ravens Publishing
Chickamauga, GA USA

Credits:

Cover art by: J.F. Posthumus
Edited by: Alyssa Casto & William Joseph Roberts

William Joseph Roberts Presents: Tales of the Apocalypse
by William Joseph Roberts /Three Ravens Publishing – 1st edition, 2023

Ebook ISBN: 978-1-962791-22-9
Trade Paperback ISBN: 978-1-962791-23-6
Audiobook ISBN: 978-1-962791-24-3

Table of Contents

Opening Words of Wisdom

By: William Joseph Roberts

Post Apocalyptic anything has been one of my top favorite genres to read, play, and to write most of my life.

I've devoured most everything I've found in the genre that I could get hold of, with some of my favorites being A Canticle for Leibowitz, The Postman, The Mountain Man series. I'd also be a complete poser if I didn't mention the Fallout Game series that I fell in love with after the original game hit the shelves back in the late 90s.

I've even managed to pen more than a few of my own titles in the realm of Post Apocalyptic. From short stories in the Last Brigade universe, and novel in the Fallen World universe, to several one offs of my own taking place in the greater fLUX Runners universe with more currently in the works for the upcoming year.

For me, the draw to the genre is simple. The challenge of survival. Whether it be an alien invasion, nuclear winter, jacked up natural disaster, or zombie horde, the challenge of keeping the characters alive through whatever messed up scenario I've tossed them into is fun and exciting to me.

It allows me to dive down research rabbit holes that I enjoy, and admittedly have a hard time pulling myself out at times because I love to learn interesting and new things. Even better if I can put that information to practical use or get some hands-on experience with whatever the skill or task is that I'm making my characters go through.

Maybe I'm just a glutton for punishment?

My number one word of advice to anyone writing in any genre, and doubly so for Post-Apoc, is do your damn research. Read, ask questions to content experts, get practical hands on experience in these things you're going to talk about. Hell, go down to your local Army-Navy store and pick up an older generation MRE (Meal Ready to Eat), so you can accurately describe the flavors and the experience of preparing one of those meals.

If you don't get the facts correct, (i.e. one two guns in the world use a *clip*, all others use magazines, Glocks don't have a manual safety, yes you can make antibiotics at home, etc.), those who do know the facts will tear apart your work and possibly never come back to it. Those folks in the survival/conspiracy/homesteading communities thrive on facts and practical knowledge and from my experience, are a good percentage of the readers who enjoy this genre.

So, my advice to you is to step away from the keyboard as much as possible when researching and get your hands dirty. You'll gain knowledge and have a new experience to draw from when adding *flavor* to your works.

William Joseph Roberts (aka Hillbilly)

In Praise of Beloved Elders

By Anthony H. Roberts

The Lizard Girl

Tammy peeked around the dead transpo laying her eyes out for the Elders. She reckoned she was about 30 throws from their hunkerdown. The previous night's signal meant they were close enough to knock on the Citadel's door. As a top stealthie, it was her duty to bring back the Elder's Last Words. Her Granpa, Jimmy Eyesfront, was the topman so it was a bloodhonour crawl for his Last Words. Tammy knew she'd be trekking soon too—moving on up from lizard to trekker—but first, she had to be careful and keep herself from gettin' dropdead good'n'gone.

The girl skittered across the crusty hardbake. She was outta touch of the Citadel's Reapers—at least she hoped so—for if she weren't then she'd be dropdead for sure. She paused after each forward movement and listened for the rat-a-tat-tat of the Reapers or the fuzzybuzz of a Skeeter's wings. But there were no sounds beyond the swirlin' hoot of the hardbake, so she stewed like a good little lizard. Just because she didn't see nothin' didn't mean there weren't nothin' there— 'specially this close to a Citadel where there was all kinds of nasty to drill'n'kill you.

A Citadel meant Swells and Swellsof goodgrub, and wherever there was goodgrub, there were heaps of ways to get good'n'gone. The Swells had all the richie toys - Reapers that could lop you in half and Skeeters that would slice'n'dice you into bloody biddy bits before you even felt the first laz burnin' up yer backside. Reapers and Skeeters were meckoes and had eyes too - not as good as her eyes, but they could drop'n'chop you if you weren't careful true, and Tammy was the carefullest and truest of all the lizards in The 99.

Papa said the meckoes were dumber than a can digger at midday and they was all gettin' old'n'obso meanin' they couldn't see like they did back when they was hooked up skyways and was hunting folks down right, left, and wrongways. Elders like her Granpa Jim called the skyways *SaddyLights*. She didn't understand the tecky talk of it but the *SaddyLights* had all burnt up because of *rear-entry* so there was no more skyways to tell the meckoes how to creep up on you. Nowadays, a meckoe had to be right on top of you to burn you down. Granpa Jim said it was due to a slow *sis tommy fail ya* but Papa said that it was just *our damn good luck*. Tammy didn't know nothin' 'bout luck, good or damned, she just knew to stay low and go slow, and if she was true to the waze, she had a good chance of not windin' up in a can digger's coffin.

Tammy scanned left'n'right then moved ever so tipsily ahead. She had a wild hare to rile up and run it straight at the Elders just to show 'em how good she trekked, and slow and stupid the meckoes had got, but such a brainbaked play would only anger her Granpa, and it might get her dead'n'done too if there was sandmecks still deep down in the hardbake. She didn't think there were any left - Papa said they'd all got sunburnt and sandblasted—but it weren't no way to present yerself for Last Words neither. And this being a bloodhonour crawl, she would do it rightways with all the proper respects. Those was the waze of The 99. She wanted her Granpa to be proud of her and know that Tammy Eyesfront was tightwired and rightways, always.

EyeSpys

Terry Teabags was fifty-nine years old, which made him the oldest man of The 99 - two years older than Jim - and damn near obso in these Fallen Times. Three weeks of night creeps had placed them within a couple of throws of the Citadel. He and Jim had mapped every throw 'round the perimeter and probed its defences a wee bit, but not without losses. Ratcatcher John and Sally Bowlegs had both bought it from some damn pop'n'choppers. *Remember and Praise Them.*

The risky business fell to the Beloved Elders. They got the tricky work and would die for the good of The 99 if that's what it took, and it took a damn lot. Nothin' was more important than the survival of the tribe, otherwise, you're livin' for nothin' and you might as well be dead'n'done already, or holed up and hunkered down like the Swells.

This bit of risky business was bustin' into a Citadel to hunt down goodgrub. Times was hard (they was always hard) but The 99 had grown and there was lots of bellies to feed. With any luck, they'd do'em right once they got inside the walls. Swells always had damn goodgrub. Always.

Terry pulled his battered EyeSpys from his pocket and glassed the horizon to the southeast. After lighting the fire last night, he knew a lizard would come—it was the waze—Last Day, Last Words, all that holly jolly rot. But there was no movement out there. He scanned the glass again, and then… yes, there she was, the wee little lizard girl. A slight puff of dust and then another. Damned good crawlin', rightways always.

"Jimbo, I've spotted either a muttie rat creepin' toward us for a sniff or a smallish lizard. Somethin' on all fours anyways, flat on her guts and headed right and tight. A pretty good creeper to these old eyes. I reckon it's your boy's girl, that slippsy one—Tammy."

Terry handed the glasses over to Jim who placed them to his eyes. At first, he saw nothing, then there was the smallest puffs of earth. No meckoe could spot such a fine little creeper. Good on you, Tammy girl. With the devil's luck, she might make it to be an Elder one day herself.

"Whatcha think? Should we call her out and save her a few ticks of the tock?" asked Terry. "I'd bet that girl's virginity there ain't no prowlers in this vicinity. We been movin' about for days now, practically waggin' the dingus at God himself, and outside of John and Sally's damn badluck with those Poppers, this bit of blast is ghosty."

Jim handed the glasses back to his comrade and replied, "Nah, it's best for her to crawl it in. It's good practice for the girl and there could be more Poppers out there too. She should slow go it and feel her way—besides, it's her virginity and not yours you'd be risking. If you want to skip on out there and lead her in, you have my permission to get all squatty and hump yer big ass out there."

Terry clapped his friend on the back and shook his head 'no' in rebuttal.

"You don't live to my ripe old age by pokin' your ass up around a bloody Citadel. I'm content to wait for the girl to arrive in her own sweet time. I've put back a few nice plump rats for the occasion too. Some nice fatties I'll roast up to welcome her in proper. Good eats before Last Words, and we'll be right to march up to the gates, pearly or otherwise."

"The only gates I wanna see are the Citadels openin' wide for us."

"Amen, Brother, but now it's time to cook us some finger' lickin' rat."

Last Words

The roasted rat was the best Tammy had ever eaten, but then, nobody flamed a rodent-like her Uncle Terry Teabags.

"Enjoyin' that bit of vermin, are you girl?" asked Terry.

"Yes, it's plenty good, Uncle," answered Tammy between crackin' tender rat bones between her teeth.

Terry glanced over at Jim and winked, "Nothin' better than Rat Ala Terry for a growing young girl. It's all about the spices. People make fun of me for rootin' around like a can digger in the old grocery digs, me and my old spice bag, but nobody makes jokes about my rat. It's the envy of The 99, more beloved than any Elder, I reckon."

Jim laughed at his old friend and revelled in the joy of a good meal with his grangirl and best mate. There was a time when cats and dogs were plentiful and made for goodgrub, but the cats were mostly gone now, and eating a dog was deaddumb and against the laws of The 99. There weren't many dogs left and them that was left were more valuable as sniffers and watchers than as grub. A good dog could save your life a hundred times but you could only eat him once, but a cat - when did they ever save anyone? Terry kept a cat for many years. Mr. Whiskers was his name. Jim never understood that—better in the pot he thought—but Terry said the cat was damngood company and paid his way with all the rats it caught. Anyways, Terry would have killed anyone who laid a finger against Mr. Whiskers and so no one ever did. When the old cat finally died, Terry made a damngood stew out of him and shared it with the most hungry children of the tribe, so maybe Mr. Whiskers done some good after all.

When Tammy finished her meal the old men sat down beside her. As a lizard, it was the girl's job to relay any orders from the Er Lord and to bear witness to the Elder's Last Words.

"Tactics first, then we'll get to the Words. Remember what I say and share it with the Er Lord. You got your ears open?"

"Yes, Granpa. I got my ears wide open, both of 'em."

Jim chuckled and tousled the girl's bright red hair.

"Righty then, let's begin. We started this trek with six Elders. There are only two of us left—me and your Uncle Terry. Ratcatcher John and Sally Bowlegs—*Remember and Praise Them*—got dead'n'done creepin' up on a half-buried Reaper three days ago. They thought it was gonebustup and were gonna snatch the battery pod out of its guts but it was boobied-up with pop'n'choppers. Badluck as all deadluck is. That was the only meck we've seen outside of the perimeter. We haven't seen any swells so we don't reckon there's any eyes peakin' over the wall. They've either bunkered down or buggered off."

"Or they're waiting for us to come in numbers so they can flip the switches and cut us down all at once," offered Terry.

"That's a possibility, but I don't think so," said Jim. "Something else is going on in there. Now, to the other two: Bingo Tailsman and Godfree Hunter. They found a vent pipe off to the East—that was more than a week ago. Protocol states that lost mates stay lost and an open tunnel is a poor man's trap. But they decided to go in Big Risky. I advised against it and so did your Uncle."

"I begged 'em not to go," said Terry, "but they thought it was worthy, and Elders are allowed the Big Risk, and that's what they did."

Jim nodded in agreement, "They hung their stars in the sky and I reckon those stars fell hard. They could be deep in the bowels eatin' canned beans but I reckon they're dead'n'done. So… two dead, two lost, two remaining to give it a go."

Jim Eyesfront drew a large circle in the dirt and scratched six boxes on its perimeter. "Here's the lay of the land. Two reapers fronting three gates. The gate in front of us is our best chance as both of the other gates are at full ops—still sweeping with the occasional test fire to lock in their sights. This one in front looks like the main entrance, which means it's likely seen more action down the years. More wear and tear leads to meckfailure. The left turret is scanning on the reg but it's not test firing. We sent in some windups and they went right up to the wall with not a shot fired—that's a dead. I'll bet my life on it."

"And mine too, though I agree with the judgement" said Terry.

Jim continued, "Unless there's eyes on us, which I don't think there are, this gate is approachable. The gun on the right appears to be jammed—it's hot but it only fires in a 10-degree arc and straight ahead. That's why we lit the signal fire last night. We're ready to give it a go. If the Swells left any scraps, we'll eat well tomorrow. If it's all boobied-up, then look for us dancin' in the campfires."

"There you have it, Young Tammy," said Terry Teabags, "Any final words from our dear Er Lord? Bet he didn't think a couple of mangy old goats like your Granpa and me would make it this far, eh?"

Tammy was confused. Of course, the Er Lord had complete faith in the Beloved Elders. Who knew more about breaching walls and skipping past mecks than Granpa and Uncle Terry?"

"Never mind your Uncle's foolery," said Jim. "You can start the Eulie now."

The girl cleared her throat and began, "These are the words of the Er Lord, I mean, these are the Final Words from Grey. The Er Lord… Grey Gory."

"Take your time, girl," said Jim, "there's no hurry."

"Slow and breezy, Tammy," added Terry, "We've known Grey Gory all our lives and it's hard to muck up whatever nonsense tumbles out of his mouth."

Tammy drew a calming breath and began again, she so wanted to get the Eulie done right and proper, "I bring you, Beloved Elders, a message from the Er Lord Grey Gory. In faith, We of The 99, know the names of James Eyesfront, Terry Teabags, Bingo Tailsman, Godfree Hunter, Ratcatcher John, and Sally Bowlegs. We will Remember and Praise your names should the Pearly Gates fall hard on you. May your access be easy and the grub be damngood. Protect and Feed The 99, Rightways Allways."

"There you go," said Terry. "I reckon we're toes up for sure now with a grand send-off like that. Nothin' left for us but to waltz on up to that Gun Gate and knock knock on Heaven's door."

Jim was proud of his grangirl, proud of her crawl and for the words she carried. She had become a strong and fearsome young woman. He took pride in The 99 too. They were still human and better than the Swells who hid behind walls and cut down the hungry. And far better than the desert trash who would eat their own children when times got hard. The 99 would survive, Rightways Allways. Just looking at his grangirl, he was sure of that.

Jim leaned over and gave the girl a hug before speaking, "These are my Last Words, Tammy, should I fall hard. Carry them with you and keep them close to your heart as I keep you ever close to mine."

The old man saw tears well up in his grangirl's eyes but that was alright, this was the time for such tears.

"I've lived a life longer than most, more years than I deserved. I've loved a strong woman who held my heart for many good years. I've starved and I've fed well, but most of all, I have kept the faith and remembered all those who have sacrificed for The 99. Janey Goodnight, my dear wife, your Granmam, who died hungry in childbirth but damnwell delivered the child—your Papa—before she departed this blasted earth. Remember and Praise her Allways. My only brother, Bobbybill Eyesfront, who broke the Four Seasons Desert Inn wide open and fed The 99 for sixteen full months. Bingo and Godfree. Ratcatcher John and Sally Bowlegs. And I remember Ovey Maria and Heysuess Zeus too, and Jericho Jenky and Martha Maynott and Little Biggie Hassan. I remember the charge of Anton Delarge and

Annice Patrice on the Grand Hilton Towers and how Pietre the Lame was laid low at the gun gates but not before taking out three mecks that got us inside. So many good people lost so that others might eat. I Praise them all, not one is forgotten by me. If I go toes up tomorrow, I go in faith. So be it. I will Protect and Feed The 99 until my deadgone day for I know that I am Beloved."

To finish the ritual, the girl wiped away her tears and spoke in her best voice, "And should you fall hard, I will remember the names of my Beloved Elders, Uncle Terry Teabags, and my Granpa, Jim Eyesfront. And I will never forget you. If there is no signal within three nights of this one, I will return to The 99 and see you dancing in the campfires of the dead gone bye. In Allways Remembered, Beloved and Praised."

The girl wiped her eyes then gave them each a hug before crawling away into the darkness.

"I guess she didn't want to hear what I had to say," said Terry.

"She's young and a bit upset," said Jim. "Should I fetch her back for your Last Words?"

"Nah—let her crawl away and find a nice hidey hole. There's been enough tears for one campfire and I've never been one for all that holy whatnot rot. Let's get a good night's sleep then find out what prizes lie in that goddamned Citadel."

Knock Knock

Jim and Terry stood a stone's throw from the Gun Gate. To their right, the West Gun remained silent. An acrid smell filled the air around it and the men were certain it was dead'n'done. The East Gun was very much alive but straining to sweep back and forth. A grinding sound emitted from its motor every time it tried to sweep and a small wisp of smoke leaked from its greasy guts.

"Whatcha reckon, should we try to disarm it or slip on by?" asked Terry, "Might be boobied-up like that meck that got John and Sally."

Jim looked it over and replied, "Best to leave malfunctioning mecks be. With any luck, it will burn itself out soon enough. The bigger question is, 'Is there juice in this Gate or not?' Do you see any laz lights around?"

Terry gave the gate a once over paying special attention to the frame and the locking meckanism in front. He got ever so close and took a deep breath through his nose to sniff out any evil intent.

"I reckon she's open and ready for business," said Terry as he stepped back and kicked the gate as hard as he could. To their mutual amazement, it swung wide open for them.

Jim shook his head at his friend's audacity and then followed him into the compound.

"I thought we were gonna play it safe," said Jim.

"Sometimes a kick in the guts is the safest option."

There was a long boxy corridor just beyond the gates that the Elders referred to as the *Turkey Shoot*. Here's where the devil's business was done and where many a trespasser came to a bloody end. Terry reached into his bag and pulled out a hefty wooden ball.

"Let's see how she rolls," said Terry as he threw the ball straight down the corridor. There was no response other than the sound of the heavy ball bouncing its way down the boxy corridor.

"It could still be weight triggered or lined with heat sniffers," offered Jim searching the walls for signs of traps, "I don't see any gunsights or trip plates. The ground looks level, but that doesn't mean trouble won't rear its ugly face once we're halfways across."

"The Few, The Chosen, The Old Meat Sacks," said Terry. "You take the west, and I'll take the east. Hug the walls and creep the edges - at least that'll minimise crossfire. If there's guns in there, we'll be dead before we know it anyways."

But there were no guns and it was no turkey shoot. The two men cleared the corridor and entered the compound proper.

As they entered, they were treated to an expansive view of waist-high grasslands leading up to a large central building surrounded by hundreds of smaller homes done up in the same ornate Mediterranean style. Ropey vines had crawled up the sides of the building clawing it back for the wild. Grass and weeds came up through cracks in the road and the trees were as overgrown and untrimmed as the grass was tall and long.

"Doesn't look like anyone's home," said Terry.

"But they've got the power goin'," said Jim. "Somethin's keepin' the water pumpin'. Or someone."

Terry pulled out his eyespys and gave the building a good glassing, "Gun turrets on top. Big Boys but not sweepin' and their eyes look dead'n'done. No electro-lights in the building either. The front door is wide open and it looks welcoming enough… *MOVEMENT!*"

Terry and Jim hit the ground at the same time. Terry held his glasses up again, "I'll be damned… a big fat ginger cat just walked out the front door. I haven't seen a cat since Mr. Whiskers. I'll take that as a good sign."

Jim looked around and tried to piece it all together, "Nobody is taking care of this place. Not man nor meck. It's all overgrown—there's years of growth here and lots of good water. Must be a well. We're in the middle of a Citadel and there are defence turrets all around us but no shots have been fired. This doesn't make any sense. Where are the mecks? And where's all the goddamn Swells?"

"Looted and scooted? Or met with darker ends. Ravengers?" asked Terry.

"Who then? Ain't nobody but The 99 around these parts," said Jim. "The Blood Red Scavies are dead'n'done and Big Ugly Dave's lot are out in the blast somewhere scratchin' cans if they ain't dead'n'done yet. Nah, mate, this is the prime cuts. First in, but to what?"

"I reckon this building holds all the answers," said Terry. "And we might even see another cat! Imagine finding a whole colony of them purring away inside there. What a treasure that would be!"

"Your feline fantasies aside," said Jim, rising up and giving his clothes a quick dust-off. "The door is open. Let's see who's home."

Rat'n'Spats

Carved in stone above the entryway to the building were the words, "WELCOME TO THE GRAND EXCELSIOR RESORT AND SPA". As Jim and Terry walked inside, they felt as if they were entering a tomb. The air was stale and musty. The marble floors were scattered with leaves and rat droppings. A bird flew across the skyline giving them both a fright, but there were no mecks to be seen and no Swells.

Jim gave a questioning glance to Terry then cupped his hands and shouted, "HELLO. IS THERE ANYBODY IN HERE? COME ON OUT YOU STINKIN' SWELLS!"

But the only sound they heard was Jim's voice echoing down the long dark hallways. They proceeded to the main foyer where a great room opened up for several stories. A huge skylight lit about half of the interior space, the other half was cast in shadow. There was a central garden area where a fountain still flowed. Tropical plants had overrun the ground floor and were climbing their way up, floor by floor, reclaiming as much of the building as they could. The fountain bubbled away and Terry was delighted to see more cats prowling through this makeshift jungle. A large map covered in moss and lichen stood before them, and as they got closer, Jim searched the titles.

"I'm not seeing anything that looks like a kitchen, but look here," said Jim pointing at a box on the map, "EXCELSIOR GRAND BALLROOM & EPICURIOUS GRILL. Grill? That sounds like a place for goodgrub? Good as any to start."

"And look at this," Terry said as he pried a mouldy placard off the floor and showed it to his comrade.

"WE INVITE YOU TO A FEAST LIKE NO OTHER!
EXOTIC FOODS OF THE OLD WORLD
A GRAND TIME WITH WONDERFUL FRIENDS
TONIGHT ONLY IN THE EXCELSIOR GRAND BALLROOM!"

"Looks like a Swell time," said Jim. "Let's trek it out."

Long before they reached the ballroom they could smell the stench of decay and rot. Coming down a long and dimly lit hallway, the smell only grew stronger. The hallway ended at a set of brass doors coloured a dull turquoise with smears of tarnish that read like bruises on an Elder's legs. The carpet leading into the room was squishy underfoot and smelled of loamy earth.

Jim tried the door. The latch clicked but the door only moved a few ticks. The two men pulled hard against the door, and then they pulled harder still, until it gave way enough for them to slip inside.

The ballroom was dark as nightfall. There were no skylights and both men feared venturing too far from what little light leaked through the door.

"The turrets at the gate had power," said Terry. "Just because the electros are off doesn't mean there's no power in here. Let's look for a switch. I'll go right, you go left."

Jim found a bank of switches to the left of the brass doors and flipped them all up. Sparks showered down from the ceiling in a few spots but enough lights winked on to reveal the room in a ghastly pale glow. The stink came from bodies. Seated around hundreds of tables were Swells in advanced stages of rot. All of them sat in front of mould covered plates, some staring through bone and leather faces, others slumped over having become one with their fungal meals. Bottles of wine were scattered across the tables and on the floor. Rats scurried here and there paying little notice to the lights or the intruders.

"The rats are well fed," muttered Terry, "Cats too, I reckon."

"Let's see if they left us anything worth eating beyond rats and cats," said Jim.

The men made their way cautiously across the vast ballroom. There was a stage at the far end of the room and something on it that looked like a large pyramid. As they got closer, they saw a corpse seated at a small table next to the pyramid, which was constructed of thousands of tins of potted meat.

"This is so wrong," said Terry. "We're in a room full of rotting Swells and I'm looking at a mountain of potted beef? That's enough to feed The 99 for weeks. What the hell's it doing up on this stage in front of this rotten lot?"

"It's either bait or a sick joke," said Jim. "The Swells came here for a party. Look at them, all dressed up in their finery and they sure as hell weren't eating potted meat. Whatever happened to these bastards happened fast. That meat up there isn't for them—it's for any scavenger stupid enough to make a grab for it. Pick up a can and BOOMBYE Brothers and Sisters."

"And look at this bloke," said Terry pointing to the man slumped over the small table next to the pyramid. "He's got a gun in his hand - not a lasgun neither but the old-fashioned type. Ledshot revolver. And if I'm not mistaken, that's a hole in the side of his skull, what's left of it anyways. This Swell punched his own ticket."

Jim climbed up on the stage steering clear of the pyramid of meat tins. He walked over to the man and began to gingerly inspect him.

"There's something on the table here. A writing pen and a letter. His Last Words, eh Teabags?"

"Be careful there, Jimbo. Could be boobied up too. Last Jokes on you."

"Nah, it's just a letter. I think it's for whoever finds him."

Jim pulled out a pair of well-worn reading glasses from his inner pocket and perched them onto his long nose, "Let's see…" said Jim, as he reached down and carefully picked up the stained piece of paper. Across the top in big block letters were the words, TO WHOM IT MAY CONCERN followed by the main discourse.

"Welcome to the party!

What a Swell time to die! That's what you call us—Swells—right? Well, as you are not dead (yet) you can see that the party is clearly over. I killed them all and then I killed myself. I poisoned their food and shot those who didn't die fast enough. I shot some of them because I didn't like them (most of them weren't very likeable), but don't worry, I was merciful in my murders. You see, I was their doctor. My last medical service to them was to pronounced them all dead by my own hands. Oops, so much for the Hippocratic Oath! No great loss. They only lived for parties and killing Rats like you. It was sport for us. Something we could bet on, something to shake us out of our perpetual boredom. How many Rats would a mech wreck if a mech could wreck Rats? And yes, that's what we called you people out there beyond our gates—The Rat People—Rats eating Rats. After I killed everyone, I shutdown most of the power systems and mechanical units. I left the gate turrets on because I didn't want to get near them. They're all DNA encoded and snipewire protected to keep you Rats away. I don't mind putting a bullet in my head but I didn't want to lose a hand trying to shut off a mech to save a few Rats. I do apologise for the inconvenience. I hope they weren't too much trouble for you, and if they were, please forgive them - we all have our jobs to do, even the mechs.

The tinned meat is for you! It's so pedestrian but then that's right up your alley. I'm sure you're wondering if it's rigged, well, rest easy—it isn't. As my guests lay dying face down in their dinners, I took the time to stack it up all nice and pretty for you! It's my gift to your Rat Nation. You see, I knew you'd come here one day—Rats are always drawn to death, aren't they? Death and decay are your bread and butter. Well, enjoy the meat while you can! Tinned or otherwise, we all rot in the end.

Bon Appétit!
Dr. Robert Hershel Townsend III
PS: Today was my 60th birthday, and what a Swell party I had!

Open Bar

Jim finished reading the letter then laid it back down on the table. Across the ballroom, a whirring sound came to life and Jim and Terry dropped to the floor.

MECK!

The men remained still so as not to draw the meck's attention, Jim flat on the stage and Terry on the floor. Security mecks were known to have motion sensors. The best thing to do was to lay low and wait for it to make the first move.

"Honoured Guests! Please do not fear me. I am a hospitality service unit. I am only here to serve you. I am not weaponised nor can I hurt you. Is there anything you desire? Can I get you a drink from the bar, perhaps?"

Jim looked across the room at a heap of glowing metal coming out from around the bar. Security mecks shoot first and don't take drink orders. This was a servant meck—a waiter and a long-time waiting at that.

"Why were you hiding, meck?" shouted Jim, "Why didn't you announce yourself the moment we came into the room?"

"Excuse me, Sir, but I had gone into a deep sleep to better preserve my failing batteries. My wake-up protocol required photosensitive cells to charge before activating my system reboot. Once the party was over, I turned out the lights and powered down. By my rough calculations, I have been asleep for 4 years, 3 months, 22 days, 16 hours, 33 minutes, and 36 seconds. When you turned on the lights, that triggered my photosensitive cells to begin recharging. Once charged, they initiated the reboot that brought me back online. Is there anything I can get you? I am only here to serve. You have nothing to fear from me."

The men rose to their feet and made their way over to the hospo meck. The meck was a little over two meters tall and made of a chrome-like metal, posh in its day but now covered in layers of dust with a vine from the floor creeping up the side of it. It was equipped with serving trays around its middle and rubberised treads for movement. Retractable arms jutted out at all angles for pouring drinks and delivering food.

"What are you doing here, meck? Can't you see that all these people are dead'n'done?" asked Jim.

"Affirmative, Sir. My previous guests are all deceased human beings. Dr. Robert told me that he had poisoned them for their own mental health. The Doctor then shot himself before giving me any further instructions. My protocols are to make sure the guests are all well served. I did what I could for them but the problem of their mass demise exceeded the parameters of my programming. After a time, I decided to shut down and go into a deep sleep, and that is where I have been until your arrival. Is there anything I can get for you? Is there anything you need? Our bar is fully stocked, or it was when I powered down."

"Yes, indeed, we need service and lots of it," said Terry. "Do you have any food around here—food that is not rotted away? Stores? Pantries? Boxes? Dry goods? Dog food? Cat food? All the food. Liquor in sealed bottles? Lots of liquor. We'll have all of that, everything you got, meck."

"Certainly, Sir, though I cannot bring you all the items you desire. However, I can show you the route to our food storage units and gardens. But first, drinks are in order—what would you prefer, Sirs? We have many fine wines and top-shelf whiskeys. Perhaps a lighter beverage like a soda or a canned juice? All of those should be fine for human consumption."

"What's your name, meck?" asked Jim.

"I have no name, Sir," answered the robot. "I am Hospo Unit 501-32B-6069X."

"Can you respond to a name?"

"Of course, Sir. I can respond to any name you wish. It is within my programming to do so. Humans often feel the need to personalise their—"

"Yeah, nah, enough of that," said Terry. "You're *Rusty* now. Got it? Rusty the Rust Bucket - that's you."

"Yes, Sir, I am Rusty the Rust Bucket, a very good name, Sir, as I have been in deep sleep for—"

"Rusty, can you access the weaponised meck protocols?" asked Jim, "The Reapers—the big guns at the gates—can you shut'em down?"

"No, Sir, I do not have access to modify their behaviours but I can tell you the location of the security control facility. We are all tied into the same central processing computer. If you will give me a moment… Yes, there are 36 weaponised mechanicals on the property. Only three sets are still functioning and they are all at the gates. You see, the defense mechs are designed for extended use and to draw power from all other units should they require it, but they also need human maintenance at regular intervals, and since all the humans outside of yourselves are deceased, the weaponised mechanicals-"

"Can we shut them down? Can Jim and I do it from Security Control?" asked Terry.

"If you do not have the proper access codes, then you cannot, Sir. I am sorry, but I can not access those codes either."

"Good old Rusty is just a hospo unit, eh?"

"Are you sure you do not want something, Sirs? Perhaps just a glass of cool refreshing water?"

"Are the guns running on battery power or off the mains?" asked Jim.

The meck paused for a moment then responded, "They are all running off the main line. Their emergency batteries normally last for 72 hours. I would estimate that being far less now as they are all well past their replacement dates. Their batteries may be completely depleted at this stage—I do not know for certain. Are you hungry at all, Sir? I can check to see if any of the kitchen mechanicals are still operational? If they are, they could make you anything you desire—that is—anything that is not spoiled or rotten."

"Rusty, can you shut down the mainlines?"

"No, Sir, I cannot. Shutting down power systems is beyond my protocols, however, I can show you where the main power room is, and perhaps you can do it. The power grid has no security protocols. Are you sure you would not like a drink? I know the room is in quite a state, but given a little time I may be able to wake some of the cleaning units to make it more presentable. Perhaps if you come back later this evening I can-"

"Two whiskeys—the best you got," said Terry. "And bring the bottles. Hurry along, now, little Rust bucket. We don't tolerate no lolly-gaggin' from our mecks."

"Yes, Sir!" the meck exclaimed, spinning on its wheels, and zipping off toward the bar dragging an uprooted vine behind it.

The two men looked at each other and then over at the meck who was pushing dead bodies out of the way, struggling to get at the bar and the shelves full of liquor bottles.

"What do you think?" asked Jim.

"I think we cut the mains and lay low for a couple days to let the batteries bleed off—that should shut down the reapers, and then we set off the signal fires and move the whole 99 right in. We're no Swells but I reckon we'll show this place more love than they ever did. It beats wanderin' around the blast and I have a hankerin' for some of that good tinned beef."

"No more Rat Ala Terry?" asked Jim.

"I don't know if I'd go that far but a little variety in the diet is always welcome," answered Terry. "And here come the drinks."

The meck whirled up to the men with two dust-covered bottles and two equally dusty cut-crystal glasses.

"I hope you'll find this to your liking, gentleman," said the meck as he presented one of the bottles, "The Macallan single malt was a favourite of many of our guests here. It comes highly recommended and was first distilled-."

"Yeah, nah, that's great," said Terry, grabbing the bottles and leaving the glasses with the meck. "Now, my Rusty new friend, why don't you shuffle off to the pantry and make us an inventory of everything the rats ain't been into? After that, we'll talk about shutting the mains down."

"*Rats*, Sir? I'm sorry but you are the only Rats that have penetrated this facility. Are there others here? Would the other Rats like something to drink? More whiskey, perhaps?"

"From now on, *Rats* means rodents only," snapped Jim. "You will refer to me and mine as The 99 or The Beloved. Got that, Rust bucket?"

"Yes, Sir. Updating. Rats are rodents and all humans associated with you are The 99 or The Beloved. I'll be back soon with the inventory, Sir," said the meck who departed sluicing his way across the sodden carpet.

Terry put one of the bottles down on the nearest table and then opened the other.

"In Praise of Beloved Elders," he said before taking a long pull and passing the bottle to Jim.

"For Those Who Came Before and After," answered Jim, taking several hard pulls himself.

Terry stared at a couple of finely attired corpses sitting in their chairs waiting for the brandy and cheese plate that would never come.

"I'm hungry. Let's go find something to eat, Jimbo, then get after those mains. I reckon there's a better place to drink than amongst these mouldy dead'n'dones and I have a hankering to scratch a cat or two."

Terry took the bottle from his friend and drained it off before tossing it away.

"They're gonna write songs about us," said Terry, wiping the burning whiskey from his mouth.

"They may at that," said Jim, "and they'll be some left to sing them too. Now, how about that other bottle? It's been a long time since you and I got on the lash, and I think we've earned it."

Jim twisted the top off of the other whiskey bottle and offered it to his friend.

"In Praise of Beloved Elders."

"Rightways. Allways."

The ginger cat they saw earlier sauntered through the door and looked at the two men. It meowed loudly then walked over to Terry and began rubbing up against his legs.

"That's a good kitty," said Terry, lifting the purring cat into his arms. "Well hello there, Mr. Gingerbread. Do you fancy a nice long scratch?"

Jim smiled and wondered if cats weren't so bad after all.

Valentina's Run

By Al Hagan

Valentina Mendez Hernández watched the target location patiently through the binoculars, writing down who came and went and when. Her bolt-action rifle was right beside her, loaded up and on its bipod. She had only to slide it into position, push the safety off, and acquire a target in the scope.

Sitting at a dusty desk in an abandoned office building was boring, and her mind wandered. She thought of the moment two years ago when she put her phone down for the last time. Her parents had died a couple of days prior, along with almost everyone else, but what she remembered, what made it all real to her, was the phone.

It was dead. The Internet was dead. The television was dead. The cars were dead. Everything electronic had stopped working. The lights. The microwave. The cooktop. All of that death, all of that disaster, and what stuck in her mind was the stupid phone.

Maybe it was all just too overwhelming to that sheltered little sixteen-year-old girl, and she hung onto something that was traumatic, but only a piece of the big picture. Maybe that was the only way she could handle it.

And then I spent the next two years growing up, she thought. *Two years of more hell than anyone should see in a lifetime.*

It was getting too dark to see the target location, so she eased back from her sniper's nest on hands and knees, the rifle cradled in her arms. She had broken the window out, that one and several others, to not draw attention to a single window. That meant that the mirror finish was gone along with the glass, and people could see in just as readily as she could see out. If someone could see you, they could shoot you, hence the caution, especially in this neighborhood.

She went downstairs to check the ground-floor fire doors, which she had locked down with rope tied between the crash bar and the metal pipe banister. Then it was up the fire stairs one floor above her lookout and over to the opposite end of the building, to an inner lunch room, where she had her pack and blanket. No one had hit any of her tell-tales, so it seemed safe.

She pushed a table against the lunchroom door and stacked a pyramid of ceramic coffee cups on it. If someone came through the door, the crashing cups would wake her up and she would start launching bullets in that direction.

Supper was bread, beef jerky, and water. Breakfast and lunch had been the same thing the past couple of days that she'd been here, and would be for another couple of days until it was all gone.

She didn't feel like burning a candle to read or do a crossword puzzle, so she just sat and thought. Remembered the life she had had, and didn't appreciate at the time. It was too late now. Hexen had taken all of that away forever.

It was probably a bioengineered virus, but no one had the time to fully analyze it before it killed them. That meant that the CDC hadn't even fully named it before it just didn't matter anymore. They had assigned the temporary name HXN2. Some wit created the name "Hexen" out of that. It raced around the world in a matter of weeks, killing ninety percent of the world's population. As if that hadn't been bad enough, something had happened at the end to kill all of the electronics. Some people speculated that it had been nuclear weapons hitting China. Some said it was a deliberate EMP bomb. It didn't really matter, either. It didn't change the result.

And Valentina had come into being, the Valentina that existed now, not the teenager that had lived before Hexen. That innocent child had been born under a proud Latino name that reflected both her father's and her mother's last names. That child had had her *quinceañera* at age fifteen, as all proper Latinas do, a combination of birthday party and entrance into womanhood. Her family was upper-middle class, she was destined for college, she was tall and beautiful, and there was a bright future ahead of her.

Now she was a gun for hire, a security guard, a private investigator, and occasionally a temporary but legal deputy for local law enforcement. Whatever paid the bills. She wasn't an assassin, but she had killed when necessary. This particular job was surveillance, with the possibility of supporting a raid with long-range rifle fire. Maybe someone was going to be arrested and they wanted to make sure his friends didn't fight back. Whatever. She'd lost interest in asking her boss who the client was.

And I live like a pig, she thought sourly, looking at her bed.

She had cut cushions from office chairs to form a pad and placed them under a table. Her mosquito net was draped over the table, to hang down to form a tent around the bed. There was a light blanket because the nights were still a bit chilly, and a sheet to wrap herself up completely, head and all. She really, *really* hated it when spiders and roaches walked across her face.

She was up before dawn, opening one of the fire doors and checking for a sign. She found it. During the night, a messenger had spray-painted a symbol on one of the lobby windows, her symbol. Below, there was the abbreviation "RTB". Return To Base.

Base meant an actual bed and bath and clean sheets and better food, but it also meant she was not working. She was feeling low and the rain shower that wetted her down on the walk back didn't help her mood any.

The block of townhouses looked the same as always, tiny overgrown yards and stray kids hanging around with their bikes. They were runners, message carriers, doers of small tasks. They were the modern cell phones. If you wanted to call Valentina in from her current duty, send one of the strays to paint a message. They were also guard dogs. Chihuahuas, not German Shepherds. They didn't have anything much in the way of teeth but they'd make a hell of a noise if a stranger came into the area.

They all liked Valentina because she was a pretty girl and she didn't yell at them to go away. The whole gang clustered around her, wanting to tell her something or riding circles around her on their bikes, or just walking beside her.

Her heart went out to them as always. They were all orphans. Virtually every kid was an orphan once Hexen finished with the world. Hell, she had been one. Tony fed them and put them up in one of the townhouses and did what he could. He had lived in one of the units and simply started using the whole row of them when the owners died or disappeared. That was how you got real estate now—you stood on it and said it was yours. If you needed to, you had a rifle in your hands when you did it, and a bunch of friends with you, all with their own rifles.

She dragged into Tony's place, not bothering to knock since one of the strays had run ahead to announce her arrival, and then held the door open for her with a stately bow.

"Valentina!" Tony smiled at her through the pain. He'd been Army and left some fingers and most of a leg in Iraq. He didn't start medicating with alcohol until after three in the afternoon—"five o'clock be damned"—so he was hurting. He thought he didn't show the pain. He was wrong, but she wasn't going to tell him.

"What's up?" she asked.

"They think that guy is somewhere else, so forget about him. But I was going to call you off anyway because I have something much better. Have a seat."

She looked at the chair, uncertain, and replied, "I'm wet."

He opened his mouth to reply, closed it, and opened it again. She caught the gleam in his eye.

"Not like that, asshole," she growled.

He laughed. He could take an insult. What would genuinely hurt him would be for her to pity him for his disability. She was secretly pleased to amuse him, but she wasn't going to let him know that. Instead, she blew out an exasperated breath as she dropped her pack and set her rifle down gently on it. Then she grabbed a towel from the bathroom and folded it in the chair to sit on.

"Okay, so what's your big news?'

"Have you ever heard of Marten Oilfield Security? Or any of the Marten companies?"

"I don't think so."

"They're big in Texas. Very big, very well-connected. Did you hear about that gang getting artillery dropped on them in Dallas? That was them. They have armored vehicles, machine guns, grenade launchers, the works. They're as serious as a heart attack. It wouldn't surprise me at all to see them moving here, into Oklahoma. But they're not here yet, they don't have the connections, and they have reached out to me for a job."

"Or they don't want to risk any of their own people."

"Don't be so negative. It's a good thing to be recognized and hired by them. It may lead to a lot of bigger and better things for us."

That's how Valentina found herself on the road to Wichita the next day, to transport a prisoner back. Tony had provided a truck, a crew cab complete with a steel bar with loops to lock a prisoner's handcuffs around. She didn't have much experience driving, but there weren't that many vehicles on the road. It was actually kind of fun. Kind of an accomplishment to drive.

Tony had told her to wait another day and he could get someone to ride along, but she had scoffed at the implication that she couldn't handle it.

"You want to impress these Marten people? Then let's get it done as quickly as possible," she had argued.

He really tried to get her to wait, but she could be pretty hard-headed.

She found the police station and presented the signed and notarized documentation that would allow her to take custody of the prisoner. There were a couple of hours wasted, waiting for the chief to return, and then to check out her paperwork, until finally, he called her into his office.

"Chief Hartmann," he introduced himself. "Am I to understand that you are here by yourself to transport this prisoner?"

"Just me."

"Really? That's unusual. Normally there would be two people. But it is rather late in the day now. I assume you're going to spend the night and then depart in the morning?"

She wanted to make a snarky comment about how she could have been two hours down the road if he hadn't dinked around with the paperwork, but pointing out people's failings usually didn't make things go smoothly.

"It looks like that's what I'll have to do," she went with, instead.

"Well, then allow me to buy you dinner at one of our local fine dining establishments."

"Um, I don't know about fine dining. This is all I have to wear. I didn't even bring anything else."

Her clothing was practical, without a thought of fashion, with layers that would allow her to accommodate heat or cold, plus a leather coat to ward off the wind and rain. You couldn't rely on any restaurant, house, or anywhere else to provide a cool atmosphere in summer nor a warm one in winter. You had to be ready to make yourself comfortable.

"Oh, I was joking. We don't have any fine dining. It's basically home cooking and home-brewed hooch. I'll bring some of my deputies. You'll fit right in, dressed as you are."

"Then I accept. Thank you."

The food was good, chicken that was grilled to perfection and delicious bread. She loved homemade bread. The beer that she nursed was a bit bitter, but she wasn't going to drink much. She rarely had too much to drink, and never when she was on a job.

The conversation was nice, mainly sharing what was going on in her corner of the world since the flow of news had been severely stunted. Radios and telegraph and some phone services were coming back, but of course, all of those needed electricity to function, and that was rare and small-scale at present. Print, as in newspapers, was also coming back and also faced the same issues with power.

Suddenly a big, burly man thrust himself into the group. He leaned across the table and grabbed Valentina's wrist.

"You?" he growled, then snorted in disgust. "*You* think that you're going to take our brother away in chains? You'll never make it."

Her eyes were locked on the man's and she was starting to breathe heavily, adrenaline flooding into her system.

"And why not?" she replied.

"Ha! Because we're going to stop you and free our brother."

"So you are conspiring to assault me and free a legally arrested prisoner?" She glanced to each side to draw the other men into the conversation.

"Oh, they're not going to help you. No one will. They have to live here."

A cold spike of fear went down her spine. All of the other men were just sitting there, watching the drama unfold. No one was lifting a finger or uttering a word to stop the man. It was all going to be up to her.

"Why don't I just twist your little arm until it breaks?" The man dug his thumb into the underside of her wrist and started to twist.

She struck as quickly as a rattlesnake, a lightning-fast in-and-out that tapped him on the neck and returned. He saw the movement and swung his arm to block, intending that his forearm would sweep hers aside, but he was far too slow. Her arm was back where it had started before his block had even gained any momentum.

"What was that supposed to do?" he sneered. Valentina's little sleeve knife was razor sharp and had severed one of his carotid arteries without him feeling much more than a tap. The man sitting to his side suddenly pushed his chair back and jumped up, stepping back, and wiping his face. The big man looked at him, up and down, and then deliberately turned away. It was an insult. He had evaluated the man's potential as a threat, found him lacking, and dismissed him. He never realized that the man had gotten sprayed with his blood and was trying to get out of the way of the jet.

He turned his attention back to Valentina. They locked eyes and he was going to twist her arm some more, but his demeanor abruptly changed. He wavered, let go of her, and straightened. That just made things worse. His knees gave way and he fell, slamming his chin on the table hard before collapsing to the floor.

She turned to Hartmann and asked, "Is there anything you need to tell me?"

It came out loud and harsh, through gritted teeth, and with Valentina pumped up on adrenalin. She was ready to fight, fight like a barroom brawl, punches and kicks and action. What she'd done to the big man was almost delicate and didn't satisfy the raging animal he had awakened in her.

Later on, she'd feel guilty about her behavior. She always did. She'd be surprised that she could do such things. She'd question her own sanity. But right now, she wanted to kill someone violently, like with a baseball bat, starting at the feet.

Dully, almost lost in the background, she could hear one of the men at the table shouting in amazement. He'd been on the other side of the spurting blood and had been fairly clueless until now, seeing the big man collapse and the other side of the table, chairs, floor, and pretty much everything painted in fresh blood. To be fair, it was after sundown and candles were the only illumination in the place, so it was pretty dark.

Hartmann looked shocked, but then she could see the gears starting to grind in his head, trying to figure out what to tell her. She reached a hand around to grab the back of his neck and drew it to her, rattlesnake-fast again, and then the other hand had the sleeve knife at his throat.

He couldn't do anything to defend himself. She was too close to him, inside his arms, past his defenses. He couldn't punch or push or grab her quickly and forcefully enough to stop the blade.

"Talk!" she shouted, their faces close together. "This is the same knife that I just used on that big, ugly bastard. Do you want to go the same way?"

"Wait, wait!" he stammered.

"Let go of him!" came a shout from behind her.

She looked around to see one of the cops aiming a pistol at her. She met his eyes and shouted back "Fuck you!"

Turning back to Hartmann, she said "First, do you trust that asshole to hit me and not you? And secondly, I don't care. I wish I'd died from Hexen like everyone else. This world sucks. Tell him to shoot if you've got the balls. Tell him! TELL HIM!"

He had been transfixed, staring into her eyes. He could imagine the blade against his neck as if it was under a microscope, the lethally sharp blade looking rough and jagged at high magnification, his skin cells flaking off and falling away as the knife cut in and then the blood spewing out. Her final shout broke that spell and he raised a hand to wave the cop off.

"Okay, okay, just ease up on that blade. We're in a bind here. There's not a lot we can do against that crowd. You know what it's like. There are all of these little kingdoms. We can't fight them all. If the state police hadn't arrested Baker, they'd have already busted him out of jail. It's just that they don't want to make trouble with the state guys."

"So the plan was to hold him until I took custody of him and then ambush me once I got out of your jurisdiction. That way, everyone here has clean hands. You cowardly bastard, I ought to cut your throat as a favor to civilization!"

That brought a fire to his eyes and he started to say something until he moved his head and caused the tip of the blade to dig in a little. That calmed him down rapidly.

Valentina slowly swung the knife away from him and made it disappear into her sleeve again. She drew back from him and smiled.

"We're going to your house," she announced.

"What?" the chief sputtered in openmouthed astonishment.

"Yep. Me, Baker, and you. Call it a sleepover. Hey, you as much as admitted your criminal buddies aren't going to make a move until I get out of your jurisdiction. It'll be perfectly safe. And I need a place to sleep tonight."

The chief looked skeptical for a moment, then nodded, his lips pressed tight together. He told his men that everything was fine and waved off their offers to go along. He figured that everything would be good in the morning and the problem would be out of his hair. The quicker and easier that went, the better.

They stopped by the station and pulled Baker out, handcuffing him to the bar in the back seat of Valentina's truck, then out to the chief's place. It was semi-rural, just outside of town but not deep in the country. As far as she could see in the truck headlights, it seemed to have a little bit of acreage, a chicken coop and barn, and a surrounding of woods.

The chief was first through the door, letting Valentina escort Baker, but he didn't resist.

They came through the door and Valentina saw that the chief had a little honey, younger than him by probably fifteen years.

"Get out," she immediately ordered the honey.

The woman looked like she had been slapped, and looked at the chief in confusion.

He looked pissed, but he nodded.

"Yeah, just for tonight."

"Where am I going to go? Where's your truck?"

"Just . . . go over to Mary's house for the night. You can walk that far."

The honey drew in a couple of breaths, about to burst into tears.

"Get out!" Valentina was considerably louder this time.

The chief looked daggers at her, but he took his honey's arm and guided her to the door, where they had a whispered conversation. That was fine; Valentina was busy casing the place, dragging Baker along with her. The chief found them in the living room.

"You're a hunter," Valentina mused, looking at the mounted heads of deer, ducks, and a bobcat that adorned the walls. "Got a muzzleloader?"

She knew that states frequently had a deer season in which only muzzleloading firearms were allowed. That meant that an avid hunter could hunt the muzzleloader season, plus the regular deer season, and potentially a bowhunting season, too.

"Yeah, I do."

"Let's take a look. Gun safe in the bedroom?"

He looked confused, but she already had an AR rifle strapped on her back, a weapon that was light years more effective than the ancient single-shot, so he went along. It's not like he was putting a more lethal technology in her hands.

The thing was too long to fit in the gun safe, so he pulled it out of the corner of the closet and held it out to her.

"Show me how to load it," she said, not making a move to take it from him.

"Well, you just pour a measure of powder—"

"Which powder?"

He hesitated, but again saw no real objection to telling her. He grabbed two cans from the closet.

"This gunpowder goes down the barrel. Then you use this ramrod to push a bullet down it. And this other can is a finer gunpowder that goes in the pan right here. Pull the hammer back until it locks. When you fire it, this flint that's clamped in the hammer opens the pan to expose the priming gunpowder and shower sparks into it, which then shoots fire into the gunpowder in the barrel and ignites it to fire the bullet down the barrel."

"Great, just put it down. I want to fire it later. I noticed a barn and stuff. Do you have chickens and cows? Do they need to be fed?"

"Well, they—" He stopped and she could see the gears turning in his head again. "Uh, yeah, yeah, they probably are getting hungry. I ought to go feed them. I'll be back in about a half hour."

"Oh, before you go, do you have any gasoline in the barn? I want to top off my truck. You know how spotty it can be, trying to get gas on the road. I'll pay you for it."

"Yeah, there's ten or twelve five-gallon cans full in there. Don't worry about pay. It's on the house."

Before Hexen, Valentina had known absolutely nothing about farms and cows and things like that. She was no expert now, but it had been dark for a couple of hours and she knew that the animals had been fed in daylight. The little honey had likely fed them several hours ago. She'd bet money that the chief would start running as soon as he got out the door. That was fine. He was excess baggage now.

She didn't need him around for what she had planned.

The first thing was to get Baker under control.

She looked him over and wasn't impressed. Not favorably, anyway. He was a skinny little white dude, balding even though he looked no more than 35. To make up for it, his hair was long in the back like it was sliding off his head. His mustache did some weird thing where it continued down to his jaw, then along the jaw until it met the sideburns.

"We haven't had a chance to talk yet, but I wanted to let you know that my contract is dead or alive. That means if you piss me off, there's no reason for me to keep you alive. Or maybe I'll be nice and just break your legs. Now, you think that your guys are going to come save you. Maybe they will. But until then, you belong to me, and I can do anything I want to you. So there's no reason for you to try to escape since your buddies are going to free you, and every reason to keep me happy because I can hurt you very badly. Understand?" She smiled sweetly at him.

She was also stretching the truth. She was supposed to bring him back alive. If she shot him, she needed to have a good reason. But then, if it was just him and her, alone on the road, and he was no longer alive to tell his side of the story, then her story was the only one.

At any rate, he didn't answer. He just stared at her. It didn't intimidate her one bit.

"Now, the chief being a hunter, I'm certain he has some camouflage clothing, which you are going to borrow."

She rummaged in the closet for a moment before throwing a shirt and pants on the bed.

"I am going to toss a handcuff key to you. Unlock the cuffs, take that orange prison stuff off, and put the camo on, and then we'll get you cuffed again. I'm going to stay here on the other side of the bed and consider whether I should just shoot you." She swung her rifle up to point at him.

He stripped naked and turned to face her full-on.

"Is this what you wanted to see?" he sneered.

She wasn't embarrassed at all. In fact, she started openly at his crotch.

"Oh, that's adorable!" she exclaimed, feigning delighted surprise. She looked him in the eye. "It's like a penis, only smaller!"

He clenched his jaw and reddened, then opened his mouth to reply. She beat him to it.

"Get dressed before I take my knife and shave that stubby pencil off. There's nothing that says I have to deliver you with that still attached."

"There will be a reckoning," he said through gritted teeth, breathing hard.

"Yeah, I'm worried, Short Round. Get dressed."

She got him cuffed again and they went on a tour of the house, picking up a roll of duct tape along the way.

Next, they headed for the barn. Valentina stayed on the lookout for the chief. He might be waiting in ambush, but that would be pretty stupid. If he was smart, he just took off. Baker's boys were probably headed this way right now. No reason for the chief to get involved.

She had an old Maglite flashlight, a non-LED type that survived the EMP, and flashed it around the barn. There were the gas cans, and a wheelbarrow caught her eye.

"Stumpy," she said, looking at Baker. "Load those cans into that wheelbarrow and push it into the house."

He looked sullen but complied, and then she duct-taped his ankles together. When she returned a short time later through the back door, he looked at her, confused.

Then she sliced the tape.

"On your feet, Sleeping Ugly, and back out to the barn. I noticed it had a hayloft. I've always wanted to take a boy up into a hayloft. And considering the equipment you showed me earlier, you're definitely a *boy*."

He cursed her for that, and she just laughed. Once in the barn, she gagged him with duct tape and then taped him to a support post, with tape at his ankles, knees, forearms, biceps, and neck. He couldn't move. He couldn't make any noise by screaming or by knocking anything against the post, and the barn was far enough away from the house that no one there could hear him grunt through the gag.

She figured that's where his boys would look for him, the house. Her truck was still parked out front, so it was logical that he was still there. And if they found the chief, he would confirm it.

It only took about an hour.

There were four of them, surely more than enough men to overpower one girl. They parked their truck a quarter mile away and walked in. They knew where the chief lived and eased into the little strip of woods that divided his property from the neighbor's. He wasn't a farmer, so the woods came in closer to his house than if he had been. He didn't have to plant a crop on every possible foot of land.

Once close to the house, they split up, with one guy at the back door, ready for anyone who came running out. The other three looked in the windows but couldn't see anything. They did have a front door key, courtesy of the chief, so they turned the lock and quietly walked in.

Immediately, they were hit with the smell of gasoline.

"What the hell?" muttered one, looking at the leader, Cade.

"Don't shoot," he said. "She must've poured gas on the floor, thinking that if we fired a shot it would set it off. Holster your guns. Dave, run around to the back. Tell Mike no shooting. Tell him to run back to the truck and get his bow. For us, it's knives only." He pulled his own, a huge Bowie, and waved it around a little.

They stood there quietly for a few minutes until Mike returned with his bow and broadhead arrows. They had four blades coming out from a central, pointed shaft and were intended to slice a devastating wound through an animal. Or a human, in this case.

With Mike at the back door, the other three went through the house room by room, with their knives and a couple of old flashlights. Eventually, they ended up at the chief's bedroom, which was locked.

Cade backed his men off to coordinate.

"The door's locked so she has to be in there. It only locks from the inside. I want Mike and Dave at the bedroom window, Mike holding the flashlight for Dave to see so he can shoot his bow. If you hear me say, 'I promise', then break the window out, turn on the flashlight, and scan the room. If he sees her, have him shoot her. I'm going to yell through the door and try to get her to show herself."

He gave them a minute to get in place at the window and then called out.

"Valentina! That's your name, isn't it? Just give up Baker and you can go home. We got nothing against you. I don't even care that you knifed Joey. He was a drunk and an idiot. He messed with you and he got what he deserved. No harm, no foul on that one."

No answer.

"Valentina, look, just unlock the door, and send Baker out. Then we'll be on our way."

No answer.

Cade stepped close to the man beside him and whispered, "When I say, 'I promise', you kick the door. We'll hit her from two sides at once."

He stood back a little to let him get in position.

"Valentina, no one's going to hurt you. I promise!"

There was a crash of broken glass and a thump as the guy kicked the door, sending the bolt smashing through the little bit of wood that held the door in place.

The door pulled a length of heavy-duty string as it swung open. The string pulled the trigger of the chief's muzzleloader. The hammer fell, showering sparks onto gunpowder, and igniting more gunpowder in the barrel. Flaming gunpowder was thrown out of the barrel, straight into a house full of highly explosive gasoline fumes.

For those at Ground Zero, it may as well have been a nuclear weapon going off.

Most of the roof was launched upwards fifty or sixty feet in the air. The interior and exterior walls disintegrated and shot out in all directions at high velocity. The roof halted its ascent, wheeled in midair, fell over to one side, and crashed back down to earth.

Valentina was in the barn loft the whole time, second-guessing her choices.

It's better to ambush them than to have them ambush me, she told herself. *If nothing happens, then I can cut Shorty loose and have him out the back door of the barn and heading towards the woods in a heartbeat. If he slows me down, well, then he gets the knife. Or maybe I should just leave him here, alive, and give myself a head start now.*

Undecided, she started down from the loft, which meant walking to the back of the barn to get to the stairs. Just as she started down, the house blew up. She had no idea that a bit over fifty gallons of gasoline had that much explosive power.

When it blew, her feet went out from under her and she slid down half the stairs, screaming in surprise. She ended up sitting on the ground floor, legs splayed out. "What the hell?" she swung her rifle around, looking for the threat.

The barn was metal, designed to look like an old-fashioned wooden one, and a huge number of pieces of the house smashed into it. It sounded like being on the inside of a drum being pounded by a thousand giant drummers. After the initial impacts, there was a pause, and then the drummers started up again as the airborne debris came crashing down.

Valentina jumped up and ran around under the stairs. That was a lot of metal in a small place, and should be pretty durable if anything hit them, she figured. Once under them, she rolled up in the fetal position and covered her head and face with her arms. She just had to trust her backpack to protect the rest of her.

The roof exploded. Chunks of wood and steel panels rained down into the barn, thumping or clanging off of the metal stairs, followed by fluffs of pink insulation drifting down.

Valentina started counting when she heard no more debris or other impacts, counting and coughing from the cloud of dust that seemed to be everywhere. She got to sixty and decided to count to another sixty. When no more noise occurred, she slowly crawled out from under the stairs, shined her flashlight around, and said "Jesus H. Christ" under her breath.

The end of the barn facing the house looked like a car after a high-speed crash. The metal was badly crumpled and crushed and there seemed to be some pretty big holes. The double doors were bent and one was barely still hanging. Debris had sliced into the barn like a cleaver and what looked like part of the roof was wedged there, sideways. Rafter boards had speared down from it and impacted the floor. They would have gone right through anyone standing there. The floor had been fairly clean and was now littered with debris, plus the dust that had come out of every nook and cranny and was now drifting down.

She started to walk out to look at the house and finish off any of Baker's men, but just as quickly she thought, *Nobody survived that. We almost didn't survive it. Or maybe "we" didn't.*

When she touched Baker's arm, he jumped, as much as he could jump, as tightly as he was bound, and screamed inside his gag. She ran the light up and down him and didn't see any blood flowing.

"I'm going to cut you loose," she told him and realized for the first time that her ears were ringing. It sounded like she was underwater, trying to hear someone who was out of the water.

They went out the back, her indicating the way he should walk with her light. She had no intention of walking through that debris field, probably full of nails that she didn't want to step on, so they made a wide circle around the whole mess.

And my truck was parked closer to the house than the barn. It couldn't have survived, either. But those men got here somehow.

They ended up on the county road very near the truck that Baker's men had parked. It had been an easy guess. They had come from town and stopped, rather than driving past the house and then stopping.

She headed for the vehicle, rifle at the ready, but no one was around. After tying her prisoner's ankles together, she checked it out more carefully, specifically to see if she could start it. Since the EMP had fried the computers in all of the vehicles built in the last thirty years or so, any ones that were running had been built before that time, or had been extensively reworked.

This one had likely been up on blocks in someone's yard for years before it suddenly became worthwhile to get it running again. In cases like those, very few people still had the keys, so the ignition switch was typically removed and replaced with a simple switch that required no key. Sometimes they also put a hidden kill switch in, but this truck fired right up the first time she tried it.

She breathed a sigh of relief.

Working quickly, she got her prisoner's hands switched from being cuffed in front to cuffed behind and added a long strip of duct tape to the handcuffs. He'd have to peel it back to get to the keyhole even if he had a key, and peel the rest of it off to get the cuffs to open. He ended up trussed pretty thoroughly, in the bed of the truck, and tied down with cargo straps.

Valentina pulled her map out, a rare item that had gone out of style years ago with GPS on everyone's phone.

They expect *me to head south, so I won't. East, then. Joplin. Fayetteville. Fort Smith. Then maybe Broken Bow and I'll figure out the rest from there.*

Most of the trip was a blur. She drove for a few hours before stopping to catch a catnap. She woke up and drove, stopping for gas when and where she could find it, and pouring clean water down Baker's mouth like a mother feeding a baby bird. But she drew the line at helping him go to the bathroom.

At that first gas stop, she had ripped the duct tape off of his mouth and was surprised at how much lip skin had come off with it. He bitched and cussed for a while, until she told him he could bitch or drink water, but not both. He chose water. Then he said he had to pee.

"So pee. If you think I'm going to pull your pants up for you, you are badly mistaken."

He stared at her for a few seconds until he remembered that didn't bother her a bit.

"I guess you blew up the chief's house with my guys in it?"

"Damn right."

"How many?"

"Hell if I know. I saw two outside and there had to have been at least one inside to kick the bedroom door. But your boys are going to have to do a roll call to see who's missing. I'm betting they pretty much got vaporized. Oh, and there was the big moron in the restaurant that came right out and told me your guys were going to ambush me and free you. I gave him a little jab in the neck and watched him bleed out. You ought to thank me for getting rid of that idiot."

He didn't thank her. He swallowed hard and didn't say anything.

The technology just didn't exist to put out an alert to all of the police forces in a multi-state area. There was no rapid, reliable communication, and the police forces themselves were severely lacking. When most of the population died, that included law enforcement officers. The ones that survived needed to eat, so many turned to farming and ranching, with maybe an arrest made here or there if the perpetrator was obvious. But there was no network of officers waiting to scan the traffic for some fugitive.

She didn't know what the consequences of blowing up the chief's house would be, but she thought that there was a possibility of him simply covering everything up. Not pursuing charges or anything. He had turned Baker over to Valentina, a legal procedure done properly, and she had transported her prisoner as directed.

She had a delivery address in Marshall, Texas that was a bank. She'd never delivered a prisoner to a bank before, but the manager knew exactly what to do. There was a nearby strip mall and he had the key to an empty storefront with some heavy metal shelving units. She cuffed Baker to one of the units and cooled her heels for a couple of hours until somebody could take custody.

That somebody arrived in a big SUV, a big black woman. Big as in a tall and muscular Amazon warrior. She strode into the store and glanced around.

"My name is Brennan," she said to Valentina, offering her hand.

"Valentina Mendez," she replied, giving the short version of her name, which dropped her mother's maiden name.

"Did you bring him in alone?"

"Yes, I did."

"Any trouble?"

"Well, there were some guys that wanted to free him as soon as I took custody. I stabbed one of them to death and blew up the police chief's house with some of them in there. So yeah, trouble. But nothing I couldn't handle."

Brennan laughed heartily.

"Oh, girl! I have to hear this story. And some other people would love to hear it as well. It's getting late. I assume you don't have a place to stay?"

"No. I was just going to sleep in the truck."

"No. No way. You're coming with us to the ranch. You've earned yourself a good meal and a nice bed at minimum. I imagine you're tired of driving. Isaiah here will drive your truck. Excuse me a second while I check the prisoner."

She walked over to Baker and he shrank back from her as much as he could.

"It's good to see you again," she gushed. "Not so good for you. Did you crap your pants when you saw me? Because you've definitely crapped your pants."

He turned his face away from her.

"That was me, actually," offered Valentina. "I wasn't going to take his cuffs off and I sure as hell wasn't going to wipe his ass."

"Entirely reasonable," Brennan remarked. She waved her two men to come closer, then reached out and took Baker's jaw in one hand, twisting him around to face her.

"Isaiah and Lawrence here are going to take you around behind this building. You will remove your soiled clothing and clean up to the best of your abilities. You will discard the soiled clothing in a dumpster. They will then handcuff you and place you in the back of my vehicle. There is a blanket there that you will use to cover your naked body. If you resist or attempt to escape, these men will use any and all means necessary, including deadly force, to subdue you. Do you understand me exactly?"

"Yes, ma'am."

She looked at her men.

"Clear," they said together.

They made one stop, at the bank, for Brennan to send a message. Apparently, they had a ham radio network of their own, which didn't surprise Valentina, considering what Tony had told her about this operation.

Brennan wanted to hear every detail on the drive back, saying she was going to be busy once they got there. She loved it.

"Although I'm afraid you'll have to tell the whole thing again to Dani and Taylor, and Eric is back in town also."

"Who are they, exactly?"

"Eric Marten and his wife, born Daniela Angelina Ruiz Vasquez. She goes by Dani. I'm sure Taylor will be there. They're all young. Dani is 20. Taylor's 16, but don't let her beauty-queen looks and youth fool you. All of them have used deadly force on multiple occasions. Eric and Dani gathered refugees from the cities and put them together with farmers and ranchers for training. He hired me to head up security. In this world, if you build up something like a nice ranch, people want to steal it from you."

At dinner and afterward, Valentina had more fun than she'd had since Hexen. It was the first time she didn't feel scared, dirty, depressed, or some combination of all three. It felt normal, the old normal. She ended up telling of her adventures, of Tony, and her life. Eric went to bed late and the three women stayed up even later, drinking wine and laughing and sometimes crying.

When Dani learned that Tony's truck had been blown up, she asked if the truck Valentina took was comparable.

"Probably not. It was reliable enough to get me here, but the body is not in as good a shape."

"I see that as a business expense," Dani said. "The truck was lost through no fault of your own. We'll replace it. And I want to meet Tony. Maybe in a month?" She looked at Taylor, who was already pulling a leather-bound notebook from her pack.

They put their heads together for a short conference and marked out a date with travel time on each side.

"Give Tony that date and he should be able to get a letter to us if he needs a different one. But we are going to be providing security for some oil and gas operations in Oklahoma and it would be great to have some good locals that we can trust. You know that's why we contracted with you in the first place, because we'd heard good things about you."

"Well, it's Tony, not me. It's his operation."

"You said earlier that you and him were not a thing. Are you a partner? Or is it all Tony's business?"

"I am just an employee of his."

"*Chica*, I think we're going to change that." Dani crossed her arms. That meant business. "I understand that Tony can't get around too easily with his leg gone. That's fine. He can keep doing what he's doing, but his operation is going to grow and I want a field manager. I want someone out there, onsite, anywhere. I want someone I can trust. I want you."

Valentina looked at Dani, wide-eyed. The thought of being responsible for other people, for managing things, for keeping disasters from happening, scared her. It scared her worse than a cop pointing a pistol at her.

"You can do this. I have confidence in you."

Valentina got choked up and tears came to her eyes. She never cried in front of people. Never! But she couldn't stop. Nor could she stop the swell of pride in her chest. Somebody *believed* in her! Sure, Tony did, too, but he didn't have many people. Dani was big-time. Seriously big-time. She was on a first-name basis with the governor of Texas. She and Eric owned a quarter-million acre land grant, banks, substantial percentages of oil companies, and God knew what else.

Dani could have just about anyone. And she wanted *her*.

Valentina was trying to wipe her tears away with her hand and keep from bursting into full-on boohooing when Dani came over and hugged her. And then Taylor joined in hugging both of them.

"We're going to rebuild this world," Dani promised. "You're going to help. I need you."

All The World Was A Stage

By Jon Fain

With the Great Collapse and the Great Silence came a sudden darkness in which one could no longer plug in and sample the world. The dial was stuck, no more channels to choose from. Of course, that was only the first layer to be stripped away.

Who knows what part of the ongoing turmoil finally caused it? It didn't matter, root cause, spark to the inferno. After a scant six days, the food supply—once so fat and happy it too could entertain and distract—went belly up.

At first, cooler heads tried to lead others through this new challenge, only to be outnumbered and outgunned by a ravenous, spreading mass.

With this Great Scream, old myths, and the rules they carried, rotted on the vine.

One had to accept. Or not. One had to participate. Or become participated upon.

Because some took to the taste.

Monte, for one. Monte, who sometimes had a bit of gristle to share.

Sounds smashed together—banging, orders shouted to the slave-like troes, moans and whimpering from the dwindling Stock. The cacophony looped every day, into and throughout the night. It was a churning accompaniment to the fear that had stolen sleep.

Like a repeated nightmare he was unable to shake, each night the moment came. Cold hands gripped for phantom legs before grabbing his arms. Quint got dragged off his bedding of rank rags, yanked across the hard planks, and handed to the troe waiting on the ladder to take him down. Cold hands held him immobile.

Then he was passed along again. A pair of troes pungent with the fresh stink on their flesh and rags, pungency riding their breath, fondled and rubbed him as they carried him across the cavernous room. To keep from retching, Quint focused on the big man.

Like a boulder in a dry riverbed, long black hair shadowing his shoulders, draped in stitched-together skins of indeterminate origin, he loomed in the dark corner of the Barn; tonight, his seconds, Cesar and Petra, were nowhere to be found.

"Ahaah… Quint! Come here and give me what for."

Monte liked it on the lips. The troes lifted Quint onto the wide table. Served up like this, he had no choice but to match his mouth with the fat man's, slick with rancid, foul grease.

The first time this happened, he'd been tongued a wad of punished flesh, Monte pushing it from where he'd had it tucked at the back of his maw. It was the first meat Quint had had in months and at the blooming taste, his revulsion gave way like a weed from sandy soil.

Now the Stock had grown putrid. Monte licked the corner of Quint's mouth at the end of their now routine exchange, the fat man's tongue slippery like a clam. When it was finally over, Quint held up the hollowed-out knuckle, tied through the joint, and hung by a leather loop around his neck. It too had been tongued smooth.

The troe at Monte's side waited for the big man's belated signal then pulled the stopper on the jug. Someone dripped the Brute out from whatever could be found nubbing up in the Field. It was nothing like the taste of home, fruit fermented from what dropped or was lovingly picked ripe from the trees. Quint struggled to keep memories alive of that better time. Foolishly, recalling the Orchard and the rush of sweetness its beautiful, life-giving fruits could provide, he tossed back what he hoped would be the first of many.

The burn down his throat made his fingers spasm. The tiny receptacle tied around his neck slipped from his grasp. It flopped back against his chest like a hanged man.

Monte's deep laugh gurgled as if from a fetid puddle at the back of his throat.

"Ah, Quint… Quint, you wretch! Whatever will we do with you?"

Sometimes the troes brought him down early like this. Especially when the Brute was plentiful and Monte needed the diversion of a reduced drunken man. Quint had learned to amuse. Like the famous girl who told nightly tales to her captor to stay alive, he rambled about one-eyed giants, and—well, he'd forgotten the rest.

He couldn't help but think of the One-Eyes, in a spastic half-vision of what might be taken from him next.

Quint's salvation—if that's what it was—had been one of chance. Someone in the Stalls, long gone to Stock, had mistaken him for someone else. The story started that Quint had been a teacher. In truth, in the Orchard, he was only a humble cook. But like a virus, this higher status worked its way through the Stalls, grew stronger in the Loft, and became so virulent that even Monte was not immune.

In those first days, still drugged by whatever it was Cesar and his band of troes had shot into him on coated arrows when they'd descended off the Hills, Quint was addled enough to believe he'd been fully consumed. Eaten beyond the extent of the left leg, which they'd taken off on the way in. So when he was saved, of a sort, chosen by Monte to become not just a Story Teller, but the Critic—why was that? What a cosmic joke?

No.

No joke.

Rather the collected run-off of all the most heinous, fear-sopped dreams that everyone had ever had and been unable to purge out, an overflow that came together like tributaries to flood over everything good, decent, and hopeful, which were weak opponents to what replaced it.

Quint closed his eyes.

In the natural cycle of things, like the seasons that came to bring the buds, the blossoms, and then the fruit, it would all have to reach the resolution of a final fall. The unnatural stream would have to dry up at some point.

Wouldn't it?

Monte angled his mammoth head. While Quint's mind had wandered, the fat man's good humor had evaporated. His face morphed into the frosted mien that chilled troe and Stock alike.

He raised his right hand. Moved it and held his palm just off to the side of Quint's head.

The sounds of the troes' labor dropped in volume. With the massive chunk of flesh beside his ear, it was as if Quint had gone partially deaf.

His temple pulsed. He wished dully for it to end.

During the Play, Monte's nonsensical pantomime and gestures were meaningful to him alone. But the set-up for the nightly performance had just begun. Hard-laboring troes moved weathered chairs and lumps of tattered rags meant to set the scene, recreating the Hills between Here and There.

This was something different. Some play before the Play. Only the rare well-fed maintained the wherewithal for that.

Monte raised his left hand and positioned it on the other side of Quint's head to bookend how he had placed his hand on the right. In the muted pause, Monte blinked slowly, with crocodile calm. He flexed his forearms, drew back, and brought his hands together.

Then *clapped!* Like leading the applause after the Play, Monte clapped again, again, and again!

Until Quint's close-to-shattered head throbbed from the fat man's oh-so-personal ovation.

Somehow—ears ringing, brain crawling like what was left of a smashed insect—he remained upright. After a moment, while the room continued to spin, the ringing stopped.

"Tell me, Quint, now that I have your attention… because I have forgotten... what is the Thing?"

"The Play," Quint said, his dry lips parting around the words.

"What? What was that?"

"The Play's the Thing!" Quint said as loud as he could, his voice cracking, and then fading, with the effort.

The Stage was set.

Troes brought up that night's Stock. As it got sorted out, the commotion intensified—the grunting, slapping of flesh and high-pitched cries indicated the troes continued to have their way with what remained of the food supply before it was otherwise used up.

Quint held out his stringed bone for another taste, but Monte ignored it. His head still aching, Quint let the receptacle swing back on its loop of leather.

The Stock had not been replenished in quite some time. The Stalls underneath the Barn were nearly barren. Rumor spread that in the Field and beyond, over the Hills into the Orchard, babies were no longer being born.

In the Loft, among those few like Quint who served some alternative function, limbs got lopped, tastes taken, but enough remained for them to be of continuing utility as sexual receptacles, for idle torture, and as endpoints for other nefarious use. Quint—sequestered, isolated until needed each night—had no close contact with the others. For whatever sick reason, he was deemed special.

Troes led by the cunning, witch-haired Petra, and the ox-broad Cesar—Quint shuddered to remember the first sight of him leading the others over the Hills, his legs churning, racing at the forefront of the whooping marauders waving nets, spears, and quoits—now headed out on a regular basis. Not all returned. Doubtless, the savvier among them sought better fates than to become replacement Stock as had come to happen, slowly consumed by the collective appetite Monte had created and which now circled back on itself.

Besides his two lieutenants seeking ever-more sustenance, Monte's most favored troes—an ever-shifting designation—stayed in the Barn, close ranks. They kept the fat man fed—fat, if never fully satisfied.

And they performed the Play.

Their variable, ever-changing supporting roles were made manifest in a hodge-podge of recitation, violence, obscenity, real coitus, and fake tears. Monte directed his players with hand gestures, bark-like grunts, and finger thrusts. It went on for hours each night, on occasion outlasting the darkness, dragging itself into the other side of the next day. The troes, who sat as the audience, took note of the fat man's cues as well, missing or misunderstanding his arcane prompts at their peril.

Confusion was tantamount. Monte spoke in tandem with the performance, to guide it. He recited an ever-fluid spontaneous dialogue, trying different voicing for each character, but his festered projection was incapable of much range. Frustrated as his actors tried, usually unsuccessfully, to repeat his nonsensical words, he would wipe off the harsh Brute from the sides of his mouth as it drooled down his chin and shout out again and again.

It was never clear what it was besides diversion, although it had something of the creation story to it, a recurrent theme of how Monte had come to lead such an unrelenting and evil band. There was otherwise never any *why* to it—the Play was a fever dream, lines lifted from old texts either found or remembered, regurgitated sayings set free of forgotten meaning. Quint knew that some came from the faded labels of the receptacles of long-gone foodstuffs, empty metal cans, and drained glass bottles that Monte pulled with uncharacteristic care from oily rags. And when the fat man ran dry of such corporeal inspirations, he had his dependable overflowing source—the insanity that rushed through him. Troe and Stock alike were trapped in the foul spend oozing out of that hideous brain.

The troes assigned to roles put on their nightly, raggedy garb and assumed positions on the Stage.

Monte called out—and taking turns, following some unspoken process, his collective tried to repeat after him:

"A toss for poor Corky!"

"Oh, too brutal!"

"Takes one to no one!"

"Sun-ripened tomatoes packed with pride!"

Quint felt woozy as if suffering aftershocks from Monte's earlier blows. He wondered if he would maintain his wits long enough to recite his review on this night. As Critic, on signal from Monte, it was Quint's role to end it.

Very quickly over the initial stretch of the nightmare, playing along, doing what he had to do to survive, Quint realized Monte wanted a different, equally compelling but always positive interpretation for each performance. Very quickly Quint was no longer the humble hard-working cook from the Orchard, with his sharp knife work and knowledge of ingredients; he became by necessity, the quick-witted purveyor of meaning where there was none— otherwise he was finished.

But perhaps. Perhaps it was time to stop fighting, of doing whatever it took to survive.

Perhaps it was time to let Monte have his final, lip-smacking way with him. The cook's final meal.

But then—

"I need you to travel," Monte called and they all thought it was the next proffered line.

"I feed you to travail!" yelled one of the troes on the Stage above them, trying to translate the fat man's garbled spew.

Quint realized Monte was staring at him. Talking to him. He remembered the bit of gristle that Monte had passed to him earlier, mouth to mouth, the way it worked a sour taste through him, and tried to focus on that bit of unpleasantness to stay sharp.

"Shut up, you!" yelled Monte.

"Buck up too!"

"Intermissile!" Monte bellowed. "Take fie!"

As the ever-dwindling handful of troes that made up the audience cracked into spastic applause the fat man turned again to Quint and showed a harsh cavern of cracked, mustard-brown teeth in what passed for a smile.

What was so funny?

"I need you to travel," he said as if it was the most casual request. "You with Petra. Meet up with Cesar and his band. Help them find that old school of yours and bring me back some tasty snacks. Young treat."

Not yet resigned to what might be a final fate, Quint did not think he'd heard correctly.

What did he say?

They were to leave at dawn.

Quint was asleep, or as close to it as he dared get, when finally, for the first time in ages—he dreamed. Scenes came staggering at him, trying to escape from the wizened empty place that had smothered his spirit.

As with many dreams it shifted in focus, but the clear theme his equally drifting essence yearned for was escape. But as that proved futile, his path became less wish fulfillment than a full-on remembrance, the replay of what had happened.

One morning, it rained poison. It became delirium to drink. Spared by some quirk, he joined the first group that would have him, and in that way ended up in the Orchard, the valley of strong trees and flowered meadows that had somehow survived and would remain as such for longer than its denizens should have expected.

An image of a woman and a child, both long gone now, came and went. The shadow of his second-chance family floated half-sensed, like a tentative last wisp of a dying cook fire—away. Replaced by the memory of the tumultuous assault down the Hills by Monte's minions.

Quint shuddered in sleep, and a feeble sound came out of him. Still searching for salvation, however unlikely, while his damaged, hacked-at body balled up under a thin covering of rag, his subconscious, set free after so long, journeyed on.

Somehow, he had found his way to an ocean.

In a truncation of dream space, instead of a half continent away, it was over the last of the Hills bordering the Orchard—he heard the faint hiss of the waves blistering onto hard-packed sand—but he was confused. He stood under what seemed like a green canopy of trees; he looked up, trying to find the sun. It was dark as the pitch that painted the sky before a storm.

"With which do you wipe?" came the wind's whisper, gusting into a harsh laugh.

With it, came the stench of a rotten sea.

As he came awake Quint struggled for air, his nose and mouth buried into moist gummy folds and matted, wiry hair. Petra straddled him. Her full weight pressing against his face, she yanked his arms, spread-eagled him, and forced his wrists down against the Loft's splintered floor.

"I'll leave you one… you choose… you choose," she taunted, high-pitched, a sadistic child at play.

"Brerfuss!" urged another shrill voice, and chorused another troe, on the other side of Quint. "*Brerfooos!*"

The preference remained for flesh fresh off the body—and as there were fewer bodies to choose from, there were fewer prime parts extant. He'd feared this moment, known by the odds it would have to come. He would be reduced one appendage, perhaps one digit, at a time.

"Ah, Quint… Quint, Quint," Petra sing-songed, mimicking Monte. "Whatever will we eat of you?"

Blinded, panicked by the smother of her loins, he couldn't breathe. He heard hacking laughter somewhere around him. He managed to work his mouth free, bit hard on something rubbery, salty, and foul—arched his neck, rocked his head, and went back for more.

His assailant yelled and lifted her body off his head. Quint, spitting hairs, tried to get free. But without legs, and with his arms pinned to the floor, he had no leverage and she had him by fifty pounds.

"Take it!" she cried. "Take the damn thing off!"

He shouted against the sharp blade gouging into his left shoulder. When they'd taken his legs he'd been unconscious, waking from the sizzle and stench of his cauterized wounds. Not this time. Now he'd be—

"Seed and the twist!" shouted Monte, from down below them.

Hands released his arms as if they had caught fire. At least one troe sucked air in surprise.

"Stop in the name of glove!"

Salvation, however temporary and doomed not to last, took many forms.

The Play was the Thing.

Petra twisted, kept her fist against Quint's windpipe as she rose, with her other hand tugged her tunic down. He couldn't fully breathe, but now he could see. The troe who had been ready to saw into his arm slinked into the gloom in the back of the Loft. Two other troes had not yet deserted Petra, but he could sense they were distracted by their fear of the fat man, gauging their odds, calculating their moves.

The knife that had been started into him lay close by. He made a move and went for it, but his left arm and hand couldn't respond; his upper body had gone numb from Petra's pressure and the tight grip of the troes.

"He tried to escape!" she shrieked. "He can't be trusted!"

"You don't decide! You do what I say!" Monte yelled back. "You troes! Troe her to me! Troe that rank and filey crunt!"

"You fat stool! No one talks to me like that!"

"Troe her to me!"

The remaining ones that Petra had recruited to help her get a morning meal re-calibrated loyalties and re-chose their side.

One went low and one went high, but she kicked the first one between the eyes with her heavy boot. Quint heard the crack, the groan, and the thing fell with its full weight onto Quint's chest; he had the wind taken from him and saw stars.

Pinned down again, he tried to clear his head and look around. The troes, de-balled upon their recruitment and kept undernourished and mentally whipped after that, were generally no match for Petra, but the one remaining, urged on by Monte's savage bellowing, fought like a demon. Smaller than his commander, he stayed low and wrapped his arms around her lower legs. Petra flailed punches unable to land. The troe kept down, scooted behind her, and hung on. Quint heard him whimper, and smelled fresh piss and shit; it would end soon.

Petra kicked back viciously and got him off her left leg. She spun to finish the job but must not have realized how close she'd come to the edge of the Loft. When she kicked her right leg out, her momentum and the troe's attached weight sent them flying off together.

Sounds smashed—thuds like wet sacks of grain, a loud crack, a lingering groan.

But then?

Monte's voice rose to its highest pitch: "Quint, Qua-int you did this! Look what you diiiid!"

The tumultuous stretch he'd endured felt like it had emptied the blood from his head, made Quint feel like he might float off. But his surviving so far on this hell-ash morning in spite of Petra's surprise attack spurred him. Strength came from knowing he had nothing, *nothing!* left to lose. He braced himself on his left hand, in which the feeling had returned, pushed off the wooden floor, pushed with all he had left to get the immobile troe off him.

He heard deep grunts. The gnarled wooden ladder laid against the Loft lifted and cracked back against the beam. Lifted and cracked, lifted and cracked, steady on, steady on. Like the beat of death, came the wet wheeze.

Came Monte.

Quint balanced on his hand, hopped, and had to do it again to get closer to the edge where Petra and the troe had fallen. Quint hopped a final time and reached the ladder. He jabbed his hand down, spun himself, hurled forward, and shot out his right stump. He hit the ladder but it didn't move. Monte was on it and his weight held it down.

With a bellow, Quint charged the ladder, head-first, like a rutting animal. He butted it and butted it again.

The ladder didn't move. Quint dared look down and Monte's dead black eyes came up to meet his and with that exchange, all final hope was extinguished.

Intent on this frontal assault, Quint failed to sense anyone was behind him—and then it was too late.

Strong hands yanked him back.

Dragged quickly across the Loft, Quint did not know how many there were who held him, how many had out-flanked him, and he didn't care. He was finished. Worse, he would no doubt experience every excruciating moment left to him, every instant of a life once, long ago, so precious—now dreaded, now poisoned, now to be extinguished at last.

They were taking him further back into the Loft than he had ever been, into a deep dark space where he would die. He assumed this was the place of some special torture.

Those who held him on either side paused.

Quint barely perked up when heard the creak. Something had been opened, a door perhaps to the final chamber. Or perhaps they would be tossing him out of the top of the Barn; the better to crack his head open on rock-strewn, hard-scrabble ground. A quick end would be welcome. He dared to look up, expected to be beaten down for his insolence, his disregard for his decided fate. Instead, he blinked as bright light dashed across his face.

Before he could react, more hands and arms were there, and like every evening when he was taken him down from the Loft, he was passed along.

But this was different: the fresh air outside the Barn, pungent with the smells of lush vegetation and thick soil, made him gasp. The heat from a forgotten sun washed over him. He heard bird-call on the wind. It stirred a faint hope and he began to struggle against his captors, a doomed animal's spastic dance at escape.

They held him tight. The next thing he knew they were running him up the slope behind the Barn. Any moment he expected to hear Monte coming too, directing and demanding his players at his bidding, as always.

At the top of the rise, they placed him down in the roughly hewn bed of a wagon of some sort. The others already there, emaciated, thin, covered in rags worse than his, missing limbs too, were too feeble to make room. The pair of dull dark eyes of a woman beside him seemed to flicker once, then re-close. Quint knew he had been brought to join the sour-smelling dregs of the fat man's Stock. And that as much as he wanted to separate himself from it, he was a part of it too.

Someone reached over the wide planks of the side of the wagon and caressed the top of Quint's head. Despite his innate, long-ingrained fears, he leaned into the touch.

What he'd come to realize was that those who had him now were different. No Stink came off them. They were healthy, strong. Bearded men and sweet-scented women, dressed in matching red and green colored garb, all carrying metal poles or wooden sticks and clubs, came around the sides of the wagon.

Quint murmured words suddenly remembered.

"No Play. No Thing other than thankful Prayer."

The numbers grew around them. Dozens of people, silent, purposeful, rescuers now redeemers, surging toward the Barn for rightful revenge.

Many reached out to touch those beaten down in the back of the wagon, who tried to respond in kind, but were too weak. With the others, Quint lay back and let them restore his human soul.

A voice called out and the wagon Quint and the others were in started to move. It did not have wheels; it had runners like a sleigh. It glided over the Field, through pastures dormant and unseen, rocking gently, sliding on.

Exhaustion claimed Quint during the journey. Once he opened his eyes and found himself in the high white light of a new dawn.

Later, startled awake, Quint stared at a large structure, a fort, or some other bulwark of defense with plank-board walls that rose twenty feet above the wagon as they passed through its gate.

He did not know if this was real. He still couldn't shake the fear. Was it just another motley stage set? Something collected and constructed to confuse him, test him, tease him with a bastardized version of the Truth and Meaning of it all, torture him to the point of no return?

And tell me… what is the Thing?

High in the air, it was the smashed face of Cesar, his head impaled on a long sharp pole stuck in the ground. A warning, a statement. A triumph gained at last.

Because as they moved on, beyond this totem spread orderly rows of heavy-leaved trees. If not exactly as he remembered it—when he saw the apples, he knew.

The remains of memory, the dried bed of his dreams, did not do it justice.

As they came closer, as the others around Quint stirred and began to silently take it all in, he could not believe how many there were. They filled the trees so that the red lushness overwhelmed the green of the leaves. Where they'd fallen, they covered the way, so that his saviors had no choice but to pull the makeshift sled over them.

Quint heard the popping of the ripe fruit underneath. He smelled its fragrance, the suddenly familiar sweetness. A mist of juice came up between the boards of what had brought him home.

He felt the light rain from a world turned upside down, rising against his face.

A Long Year

By JL Curtis

"Rocking C, Rocking C, this is Johnny, how copy?" A burst of static followed then the call was repeated, "Rocking C, Rocking C, this is Johnny, how copy?"

Old Tom, pulling his suspenders up over his shoulders, limped into the parlor come radio room, grumping, "Can't even take a piss in peace…" Flopping into the chair in front of the desk and propping his cane against the wall, he punched the microphone bar, "Sheriff, this is Rocking C, go head."

"Rocking C, you've got fifteen, maybe twenty shamblers heading down fourteen sixty-nine toward your north forty. I can see some steers up in the corner of that pasture," the sheriff said.

Old Tom cussed under his breath, then keyed the mic, "Gonna take me fifteen, maybe twenty minutes to get up there. Me, Tommy, and Olivia are the only one's here." Spinning the chair around, he bellowed, "Tommy! Olivia! Muster!"

Sheriff Coffee answered resignedly, "I'll come in behind them. We can pincer them between us. How you folks sitting for gas?"

Spinning back around, he mumbled, "Damn kids. Never can find 'em when you need 'em." Keying the mic he said, "We've got a couple hundred gallons left. Sure wish you had a diesel. We're good on that, probably two thousand gallons left in the tanker."

"Where is everybody else?"

"Micah, Dot, Jose, and Eric are up on the rail line by Panhandle, trying to get some propane out of that tanker you spotted last month. Mrs. C, John, Bruce, and Tammy are up on two eighty-seven with Box H and Diamond J, they're trying to hit that warehouse, if they can get in and out without setting off a bunch of damn zombies. They want to see what's in it. Might be food."

Tommy, thirteen, gangly, with a shock of straw-colored hair sticking out in all directions came sliding in the door, "What's up?"

"Where's Olivia? We got shamblers coming up on the north forty."

"She's feeding the goats. We gonna go?"

Old Tom levered himself up, "Yep, go get her. ARs only. Two mags only. We're gettin' low on ammo." Tommy grinned, scrambling back out the door, as Old Tom limped into the library and now armory. Looking out through the barred windows, he noticed some rust on the welds and shook his head, "Damn shoddy work. Shoulda taken more time on them."

Reaching up, he took down two AR-15s, checked they were unloaded and safed, and pulled four magazines out of the filing cabinet. He stumped down the hall to the bedroom he and Bruce shared, reached into the chest of drawers, and slung his old single action around his hips. Old Tom buckled the gun belt, pulled a box of 200gr long Colt wadcutters out of the drawer, and opened the box. He loaded one, skipped one, then loaded four more and slipped the single action into the holster, flipping the thong over the hammer to keep it tight in the holster.

Limping back to the library, he found Olivia, also thirteen and blossoming into what he was sure was going to be a beautiful woman, if she lived that long. Black-haired, sloe-eyed, and dusky-skinned, she'd definitely gotten her beauty from her mother, Juanita, God rest her soul. Thankfully, she hadn't seen her mother turn, since it'd happened in town. Sheriff Coffee said he thought she'd died in the fire that burned half the town that night. Old Tom glanced up at the calendar, thinking, *that was exactly a year ago today. Which means I broke my leg six months ago. Shit… At least I'm still alive.*

Olivia smiled shyly as she racked the bolt on the AR, rolled it, and confirmed the chamber was clear, "We're it?"

Yes, we are, Ollie. Ain't nobody left but us. Sheriff Coffee is going to meet us up there. You got your eyes and ears?"

Olivia pointed to the bag sitting on the chair, "Mine and Tommy's too. He never remembers to bring his. Are we taking the wagon or the truck?"

"Truck. It'll give y'all some height, and once you're in, ain't nobody getting in there with ya."

Olivia replied ruefully, "But it's going to be hot and noisy when we shoot."

"I know. But I'd never forgive myself if anything happened to either one of y'all. Now let's go! Move it!"

Olivia slung the AR, picked up her bag, and ran out the door, "I'll give Tommy his stuff and we'll be locked in by the time you get there."

"Smart ass kids," Old Tom mumbled under his breath, as he grabbed the keys off the board, limping out behind her. Tommy was standing at the back of the truck, AR at low ready, as they walked out. Olivia had also loaded her

AR and was scanning back and forth as she walked slowly across the yard. Old Tom slipped the thong on the single action asking, "Truck clear?"

"Truck is clear, sir."

"Okay, y'all mount up."

Tommy swung the plate steel door open and waited until Olivia had scrambled in, then climbed in pulling the door closed and Old Tom heard the bar clang down inside as Olivia slid both firing ports on the right side open. He wrestled the driver's side door open, cursing the weight of the plate added to it, along with the bars over the window. Sliding into the seat, he started the truck, waiting for the oil pressure and temps to come up, then turned on the A/C, making sure the duct was tight on the center vents and looking back to make sure it hadn't fallen down where it went into the bed.

Peering out through the bars over the windshield, he put the truck in gear, yelling, "We're moving," and hearing the kids yell back they were strapped in. The truck rumbled over the cattle guard at the first fence, then he picked up speed as he turned the radio on. Three miles up, he turned into the cattle guard at the north forty and keyed the mic, "Sheriff, coming into the north forty from the south now." He glanced up toward 1469 and saw a small plume of dust, and a quarter a mile ahead, six or seven longhorns milling around the feeder.

Yelling back, he said, "Almost there. Sheriff is to the right." He made sure he could get to the single action as he eased up the pasture behind the cows and finally saw the shamblers. The fence had them slowed down, and apparently, a couple of them were hung up as the steers looked on curiously. Finally, one made it over and headed toward the steer they called Brisket as he pulled the truck in behind them, yelling, "Off your right. One to three o'clock, nothing further back than that!"

He heard a mumbled reply and keyed the mic, "Sheriff, we're gonna light them up." Static then a pair of clicks sounded, as he heard measured fire coming from the back of the truck. Putting the truck in park, he slid over and looked out the right window, seeing the sheriff pop the plate lid that replaced the sunroof on his Chevy, and stand up, unlimbering his old bolt-action rifle, he yelled again, "Sheriff is up and shooting."

Ten minutes later, all the shamblers were down, heads exploded like melons by the rounds, except for one head that was stuck on Brisket's left horn. He yelled, "Cease fire, cease fire!" Hearing the kid's reply, he yelled, "Moving." Putting the truck in gear, he eased behind the cows and steers, drifting them out of the way, as he pulled up to the fence.

The sheriff had dropped back down into his truck, pulling up on the other side. Getting out, the sheriff confirmed they were all dead outside the fence, as Old Tom confirmed the one that had made it over was dead. Of course, since he was missing his head, that was pretty obvious, but procedures were procedures. Once that was done, he banged on the plate door, "Y'all can get down now and get some air."

Sheriff Coffee leaned on the fence, "I count twenty-two. Dunno how they made it out this far." Nodding to Tommy and Olivia, he continued, "Good shooting."

Olivia smiled at the sheriff, "Thank you, but Tommy got more than I did. I only got six of them."

Tommy scuffed his boot, "Well, I had a better angle. But Olivia was more accurate. She didn't miss. I missed one."

The radios went off, interrupting them, "Diamond J calling Sheriff Coffee, Diamond J calling Sheriff Coffee!"

The sheriff went back to his truck to answer the radio and Old Tom said, "Okay, police up the brass and let's get back to the house. Don't enjoy leaving it unoccupied." Tommy and Olivia picked up what brass they could see, then played rock, paper, scissors to see who got to ride in the cab back to the house. Olivia slumped in the seat, the butt of the AR under her chin, "Tom, what was wrong with them? They moved even slower than that last bunch."

Tom shrugged, "Dunno, maybe that guy up in Eaton Rapids is right, maybe they don't eat enough, they get slower and slower, then just mummify where they are."

"Well, I'll be glad when I don't have to shoot any more of them. I know they're not people any more, but I still don't like it."

"I know, Ollie, I wish you didn't have to either." *Dammit, it's wrong that we have two thirteen-year-olds who are having to kill people. Maybe Ollie uses that philosophy, but they used to be people. Thankfully, they haven't had to shoot anyone they knew!*

Old Tom glanced up at the cameras as he heard Tommy yell, "They're back!" He counted the trucks, seeing one extra one that didn't have any kind of protection, and wondered who that was.

Grumbling, he got up slowly, grabbed his cane, and limped to the back door, telling Olivia, "You're on radio monitor. At least until I can get back."

"Yes, sir."

Limping out the back door, he rubbed his shoulder ruefully, when the barred outer door banged into him in the wind. He automatically scanned the people, Mrs. C, John, Bruce, and Tammy were there, and an old white-haired, stooped man he didn't recognize, along with two thin, traumatized kids. *They look about the same age as Tommy and Olivia, give or take. Scared shitless? Or what?* Limping over to the trailer he whistled, "Wow, that's a haul!"

Cherie Crane nodded, "Turns out that was a restaurant supply warehouse. We're good for six months now, and we're going to go back for more. Everybody loaded up everything they had space for. Lots of number ten cans and big bags of staples."

"Any problems with Zombs?"

"Not till the very end. Dunno whether they smelled us, or the movement brought them, but they were real slow. Only a coupla' dozen. We took 'em down and skedaddled back here. You heard anything from Micah?"

"No, ma'am. Not a word, which is probably a good thing. Who are the newbies?"

Cherie nodded toward the old man and kids, "They apparently lived near the warehouse, watched us until we started to leave, then came hell for leather down the road, plowed through the last bunch of zombs, and begged to be allowed to follow us back here. He's named Sean, the kids are Billy and Bonnie. Apparently, they are his grandkids."

Old Tom winced, "Oh, damn."

"Yeah, damn. Who's on the radio?"

"Ollie for now. I needed to get up and move."

"Okay, send her and Tommy out, maybe they can get the kids to unwind a bit."

"Will do, ma'am. Just out of curiosity, where we gonna put them?"

Cherie looked around, "Ah, damn. Uh, the old man in the bunkhouse, the boy in with Tommy, the girl in with Olivia. And we're out of beds aren't we?"

"There is one folded-up hide-a-bed still in the bunkhouse, so that'll have to do, but yes, we're out of beds."

They both turned when they heard trucks growling up the road and across the cattle guard, heralding the return of Micah and Dot in the armored 3500, followed by Jose and Eric in the old Miller's Propane truck. Eric stuck his hand between the bars, holding a thumbs up as they swung into the parking area in front of the barn.

Tom limped over to Micah as he stepped down out of the cab, "How'd it go?"

Micah bent over, groaning and stretching, "Oh, damn… Bad backs suck. Good, once we figured out how to jury rig a hose to the truck. The tank car had bled down, but I figure we got probably three-quarters of a truck full. Stopped off at the Box H and filled them, then the Diamond J. We'll fill our tanks tomorrow, getting too late now. Anything happen around here, other than the shamblers?"

"Nah, pretty quiet. But Brisket has a head he took off one of them stuck on his left horn, so if you see it, don't be surprised."

Dot came around the back of the truck, "Head on horn?"

"Yep, one of 'em made it over the fence and went after Brisket. He objected, to the point of stomping the Zomb in the ground and hooking him a few times. Took his head, literally, and it stuck on his left horn."

Dot rolled her eyes and shuddered, "That's an image I didn't need stuck in my head."

At dinner, everyone ate quietly, the three newcomers huddling together at one end of the table, with tiny portions. Finally, Cherie said, "Y'all can get more than that to eat. We're not going to starve out here."

When she said that, Sean broke down. Tears streaming down his face, sobbing into his hands, he kept shaking his head, as the young girl, Bonnie, hugged him and cried too. The boy, while not crying, sat with his head down, hands in his lap. The old man finally looked up, wiped his tears, and said softly, "You don't know how much that means. This is the first food we've had that didn't come out of a can in almost nine months. And the first time we've seen lights too. We were down to nothing, other than what we snuck out of that warehouse. Oh, God…"

Micah asked softly, "Bad?"

Sean nodded, "Real bad. Billy and Bonnie stayed with us while Rob…" Fresh tears poured down his face, and both the kids teared up this time, "Robert, my son, and Jean, his wife, worked downtown. They never came home that night. My Bonnie, she died… Well, she didn't make it but three months. Diabetic. Ran out of meds. We buried her in the backyard."

Scrubbing his face, he pushed back from the table, "I've been out of meds for six months, just trying to hang on for the kids. Y'all saved our lives, or at least their lives."

He got up and stumbled out of the dining room, wiping his eyes. As the kids got up and followed him, Cherie said quietly, "Billy, Bonnie, please give your grandpa some time, okay? *All* of you are as safe as we can make you, and you both need to eat some more food."

Billy asked quietly, "How come you have lights?"

Bruce smiled from across the table, "Well, we've got solar panels and batteries. We don't flaunt it, you saw us pulling the blackout curtains, right?"

"Yes, sir."

"As soon as dinner is over, we'll be turning off the lights and everybody goes to bed, except for the watch. With the blackout curtains, there isn't any light to attract bad things."

Bonnie asked in a high-pitched voice, "Watch?"

"We have cameras to watch the perimeter of the ranch yard, and the road to the ranch. They run off those batteries, too. And we maintain a listening watch on the Ham radio. If one of our neighbors has problems, we go help them, like we helped y'all today."

Bonnie glanced at Olivia, "What do you do?"

Olivia smiled at her, "I do whatever I'm told, but I can man the radios and do the watch. I help cook and clean too. We take turns, except for Old Tom, 'cause he burns everything to a crisp. We don't let him cook."

Everyone at the table, including Old Tom laughed at that, even as he turned red, "I cook good enough for myself, kid. Just because you don't like your food well done, ain't my fault!" Grabbing a plate with a piece of pie and a fork on it, he got up and limped out of the dining room. He found Sean sitting on the back stoop, scrubbing his face with his hands, "Here, you look like you could use this."

Sean took the plate, looking up at him in wonder, "A pie? Something else I haven't seen in nine months." He dug in, finished the pie quickly, and handed the plate back, "Thank you. Can y'all take care of the kids?"

Old Tom nodded, "And you, too."

Sean shook his head, "Not unless you've got Toprol. I've been having pretty acute chest pains for the past two weeks. I know I ain't got long."

"Nah, I *think* we might still have some aspirin, but that's about it. The drugstore burned the first night. Pretty much everybody that needed meds are already dead and gone. We haven't found any since, not that we've really been looking for it. Not saying we can't look the next salvage trip."

"If I last that long…"

Cherie Crane sat in front of the radio stack, head cocked as she listened to the weekly check-ins, checking organizations and names off the list as people spoke up. Finally, it got quiet, and a plaintive voice asked, "Anyone else, SoCal? Anybody from the Northeast? Bergman? You still out there?"

Scanning quickly down her list, she saw there were at least ten more stations that didn't answer the call-up, all of them in cities or bigger towns. While the reasons could be many, she felt in her heart that they were done and gone. There hadn't been that many Ham operators left anyway, and most of them were getting up in years. They'd been and still were the lifeline for these circuits, considering that there really wasn't any government left, per se.

She listened for a while longer, mostly reports of a few recent outbreaks, but more interestingly, that there seemed to be some mummifications occurring in greater numbers. *Most of the shamblers we saw today were women. He'd said the men would be gone first, something about body fat and survivability. What was it? Two hundred days, or some such, and percentages of die-off around ninety percent? So, what would that be out here? We don't have nearly the population they do in the cities…*

Micah followed the Box H trailer hauling the dead steer as it maneuvered up the on-ramp on I-40. They'd wanted to get it far enough west of the warehouse and a couple of drugstores that might still have some meds in them to give the zombs something to fight over and distract them. Cherie and the scroungers from Box H and Diamond J were an hour behind them with the trailers and Sheriff Coffee, Bruce, and a couple of trucks from Diamond J were up at the Love's Truck stop off 207 trying to siphon more diesel and maybe some gasoline. Bruce thought they'd come up with a rig that would work, and Old Tom had ridden along to run it.

Micah keyed the CB radio, "This should do it, Jake. If we dump the steer here, Amarillo Lake gives us a clear field of fire to the south, and we're okay to the north side too. It's a little over a mile back to the Walgreens and United pharmacies, and who knows what else we might find, right?"

Jake answered, "Yep, let me get turned around and we'll dump the steer. Straight line for the vehicles?"

Micah looked around, mentally gauging where to place the four trucks and Jake's rig with the trailer still attached, "Nah, let's set up on a forty-five across, with you in the middle. That way we can gun front and back, and cover both sides, too. We don't want a protracted battle here, just want to get them riled up and coming, then we bolt back west. Two ahead of you, two behind you."

"K."

Jake jockeyed the truck and trailer around, as the other four trucks backed and filled to get headed back east. After clearing the area quickly, Micah saw one man jump down out of the cab and two more jump down from the box in the bed. One ran and hit the tip release on the trailer, and whirled his arm as Jake jumped on the gas and the steer came rolling out of the trailer.

They quickly latched the trailer back down, and he saw the guy from the cab pull out a big knife and split the steer's belly open, then run for the cab. Once he was back inside, Jake started honking the horn, followed by the other four trucks.

Micah got a whiff of the spilled entrails when the wind gusted, and thought to himself, *If the sound doesn't bring 'em, that smell damn sure is going to!* Glancing over at Tommy and Billy he asked, "You boys know what we're trying to do and why?"

Tommy fingered the safety on his AR, "Uh, well, uh we want to get the zombs away from where we want to be, and we know they react to smell and movement, especially food, right?"

"And?"

"Uh, we don't have a lot of ammo, so no pitched battle. Let them fight among themselves?"

"Yep, that's what we want." Turning to Billy, Micah continued, "We're just trying to lure them away from the warehouse. We can get supplies there that they can't use, so they don't gang up around the place."

Billy nodded, "Okay. So you're kinda feeding them, right?"

Micah replied, "More or less. Now we want to be looking for the fast ones, they just turned. Those we want to take out as soon as we can."

Billy asked tumultuously, "I don't have to shoot, do I?"

Micah said softly, "No, you don't, Billy. Not unless you have to, okay?"

"Okay."

The CB broke the conversation as Jake came on, "Inbound. Looks like some runners up front."

Micah yelled, "Heads up in the back, runners inbound! We're locked and loaded up here!" More quietly he said, "Tommy, make sure you just put the muzzle and nothing else out the window if you have to shoot, okay? But we shouldn't have to shoot, since we're in here, not up in the box." He glanced back to make sure both the boys had eye and ear protection on.

Tommy nodded, "Sure. It's kinda hard to see what is happening from the box, so this is new for me."

Out at the old Loves Truck Stop, Old Tom nodded in satisfaction, "That's going to work! We're drawing fuel now, boys!"

Bruce laughed, "Well, I gotta admit you can cobble some hot shit together, Tom. I'd never have thought of trying that."

"That's why all ranches look like junkyards out in the back forty. Never throw anything away, cause sooner or later, you're going to need it."

Bruce just shook his head and kept swiveling around, checking for zombs as the boys from Diamond J took turns rummaging through the truck stop and standing watch. So far, they hadn't seen a single zomb, but one never knew. Even as far out as the truck stop was, there had been eight or 10 of them around the first time they'd come looking for supplies. They'd popped them and done a quick sweep, but didn't come away with a lot, since most of the stuff was not useful.

Hoppy, the old Diamond J cowboy who had driven the other truck came out of the store and yelled, "Hey, Tom! Guess what I found?"

"What'd you find you old blind fart?"

"Robertson's beef jerky! You still like that shit?"

"Hoppy, you better not be funnin' me!"

"Two whole cases of it!"

"Well, dammit, bring it on out here!"

"If you ask real nice, I'll think about it."

"Hoppy, I'm gonna climb down off here and…"

Bruce interrupted, "Tom, we're about full here. Better shut off the pump and move over to the gas tanks."

Tom nodded, shut the pump down, and eased down to the ground. He disconnected the hose, then started pulling the siphon hose up out of the tank, slowly coiling it back in the rack, cussing as diesel spilled all over him. He finally got all the hose up and racked, then checked to make sure the tank cap was firmly replaced, then looked up at Bruce, "Think you can come down now. We're done. As soon as Hoppy and Ace get ready, we can get out of here and head back for the ranch. I'd like to get their ranch tanks topped off today if we can. Now that we know it works, we can come back later for gasoline."

Bruce looked around then yelled, "Hoppy, let's do it! We're finished. Grab your folks and let's hit the road."

Hoppy waved and started across the parking lot with two boxes, carrying them awkwardly as he juggled them and his rifle, finally dropping one, he kicked it across the lot to the semi, "There ya go, old man. There's your junk food," Hoppy said with a smile.

Tom clapped him on the shoulder, "Thanks for takin' care of me, Hoppy. It's always been us'ns against them."

Hoppy laughed, and turned toward their truck, "Always has been, always will be us cowboys against the managers… I found 'em in the locked storeroom. They hadn't changed the combo since I worked here twenty years ago!"

"Hey, did you check for coffee, or tea, or sugar, any of that stuff?"

"Damn, forgot all about it."

Tom turned to Bruce, "You need to go check, you know that stuff is on every search list. Hoppy and I will stand guard."

Bruce grumbled, "Okay, I'm going…"

Back on the I-40 overpass, Billy whimpered in the back seat of the 3500 as another runner scrabbled at the window, "What do I do?"

Micah glanced over, "Nothing. She can't get in and…" A shot sounded overhead from the bed of the truck and the female zomb fell away, "They are taking care of them from up top." Keying the CB, he asked, "Anybody seeing any more runners?"

A round of "Nope, shamblers only, a couple moving a little fast," was about all.

Micah banged on the top of the cab, "How much longer y'all want to shoot?"

Tammy yelled back, "Down to two mags. Probably time to go. There are shamblers comin', but it'll take them a while to get here."

Micah keyed the CB, "Okay, folks, let's roll out of here. Who's got the Vet?"

"David, from Box H, we've got him. You lead, we'll follow."

"Okay, let's roll. Jake, you okay to go straight to the warehouse? We'll take the other four trucks and hit the pharmacies and meet y'all there."

Jake revved the big diesel, "On the way. I'll bust through them, y'all get on my tail." With that, he let the clutch out and rumbled through the few remaining shamblers in front of him, as the other trucks fell in line behind the trailer.

A quick pass at the Walgreens got almost nothing in the way of any useful drugs, the entire pharmacy counter had been destroyed, and the entire store stank of zombs. They pulled into the United grocery, not hoping for much, but found that the pharmacy counter was still secured. It took a few minutes with bolt cutters, pry bars, and good old-fashioned breaking and entering, but they got in and Darryl, the old veterinarian, grabbed three shopping carts full of medications and various other things like needles and bits and pieces, cackling and laughing the whole time.

Micah and the others fanned out in pairs, searching the aisles for consumables that were always a priority, toilet paper, salt, pepper, spices, tea and coffee, sugar and flour. The store wasn't in terrible shape, and they were able to load up plenty of buggies, but Micah had to call a halt before they overloaded the trucks since they still had to get people in there, too. Billy stayed close to Micah and Tommy, eyes wide as he looked for things he hadn't seen in almost a year. He saw a display of Kool-Aid and asked, "Can we get some? Please? We like Kool-Aid."

Micah sighed, knowing there wasn't enough sugar to do it often, but said, "Go ahead. It's not something we'll be able to have every day, but it will be a once-in-a-while treat, okay?"

Billy nodded enthusiastically, pawing through the display, and filling his pockets with as many packets as he could.

As they headed out the front of the store, Billy and Tommy both saw the candy bars on the aisle cap and looked back at Micah. He rolled his eyes, but said, "You've got to get enough to share with Olivia and Bonnie and the rest of us."

The boys were whispering back and forth until Micah said, "Three, two…"

They grabbed double handfuls of candy and followed Micah out of the store and hopped back into the cab as the rest of the crew loaded the back of the truck with the consumables. David walked over, "Micah, we'll bring Darryl by y'alls place on the way back so he can get a look at the old man and see if the meds will work for him, if that's okay with you."

Micah nodded, "Sounds like a plan. I guess we'd better get down to the warehouse, pull security, and help the working party before they get all irate about us just 'ridin' around up here."

David laughed, "Yep, there is that… I kinda like getting fed."

Micah yelled, "Mount up! Let's head to the warehouse! Working party, ho!"

The trucks rumbled back across the cattle guard, pulled around to the barn, and backed up to start off-loading the supplies they'd picked up. Micah got down and stretched, passing his rifle to Tommy, and told Billy, "Go take Mr. Darryl to your grandpa, okay?"

Billy nodded, "Yes, sir." He trotted over to the veterinarian, tugged at him, and led him toward the house. Dot came out of the house, saw them coming, and turned quickly back into the house, which caught Micah's attention.

"Tommy, let's go stow our rifles first, okay?"

Tommy shrugged, "Okay."

Micah walked quickly across to the house, turned down the hall, and caught up with Dot, "What's going on?"

Dot cocked her head, saying softly, "The old man didn't make it. He asked for a piece of pie at lunch, and I served him one. I went back in the kitchen to finish cleaning up and heard a thump."

"Shit."

"Yeah, shit. He got two bites and had a massive MI. Cherie and I gave him CPR for a while, but…"

"What about the girl, Bonnie?"

"She was hysterical, gave her a big dose of Benadryl, and got her and Olivia in their room. We've been checking on her, but…"

They both turned when they heard a high-pitched scream, "NO, Nooooo…"

Micah shook his head, "I guess Billy just got told." They heard running feet, and a door bang, and Micah turned to Tommy, "Go find him, right now! Stay with him, and carry your gun. Get him back here by dark, understand?"

Tommy's eyes got big at the tone of voice, but he said meekly, "Okay. What do you want me to do?"

"Stay with him. Don't let him do something stupid. You know how you felt when your momma and daddy died, so you can try to talk to him."

"Yes, sir."

"Now go."

Tommy grabbed an AR and went out the door on a run, as Dot leaned into Micah's shoulder, "Where does it end?"

He hugged her, saying quietly, "I don't know Dot, I just don't know…"

Cherie Crane of the Rocking C, Sheriff Coffee, Brad Harmon of the Box H, and Mike James of the Diamond J sat in the kitchen at the Diamond J, drinking coffee as they waited for the Vet Darryl to come in. Everybody had their respective notebooks sitting by their chairs and Cherie was idly drawing a set of curves and doodling numbers on one page when Darryl finally came in. "Sorry, I'm late. Peterson's kids got the flu again. Thankfully, I was able to get some Z-pacs at United, so I'm going to use them while they're still good. I'm not sure how long most of the stuff I've got is good for, but as long as I've got it, I'm going to dispense it."

The sheriff said, "Well, that's some good news. Lemme go over what I've got. As of today, I can account for two hundred thirty-eight people, scattered over a little over thirty-six hundred square miles. That's up two since last week, with the two kids at the Rocking C. There seem to be less shamblers out and about, but I'm not going poking into buildings to see if they're mummifying in there."

Cherie said, "So there is some merit to what the Eaton Rapids guy, Joe, is saying?"

The sheriff shrugged, "I can't put empirical data on it, but yeah, I think so. Most of the shamblers left are females, which matches what he'd predicted. Women need fewer calories per day than men do, assuming the same levels of effort. If we get ninety percent death rates, figuring the total population, less Potter County, is a little over thirty-three thousand, then we're coming up on almost thirty thousand deaths. And that will repeat until there is no one left…"

Brad chimed in, "Well, as few of us as there are…"

Mike replied, "Yeah, two hundred thirty-eight of us against the world. That's not a winning proposition. Stuff is breaking down, we're all tired, all the time."

Darryl said, "Well, we're two hundred thirty-eight *healthy* people. That is a tremendous difference. Granted, we've got a significant age range, what, twelve to? I'm sixty-four and I'm probably the oldest one here. Oh, speaking of that, there will soon be at least one addition to that number."

Everyone looked at Darryl expectantly, "David and Melaina."

Brad asked, "Which David?"

Darryl rolled his eyes, "Your David, and Mike, your Melaina. So I guess y'all are going to be combining spreads."

Cherie coughed to hide a laugh at the expressions on both Brad and Mike's faces. It was obvious they didn't have a clue that their kids had gotten together, much less made a baby. But that led her down the path of Tommy and Olivia, and Billy and Bonnie. They were the four youngest kids, and their prospects weren't really great.

Sheriff Coffee said, "Well, congratulations to them, now back to issues. The roads are going to shit. Bridges are getting washed out, and the dirt roads are degrading way too fast for us to maintain them."

Brad shrugged, "Well, considering how hard it is to get diesel and propane, much less tires and maintaining vehicles, it may not make much difference."

Mike replied, "That's why we've been breeding the horses like we have. We don't have any draft horses, at least not yet, but they're going to be the lifeline moving forward."

Cherie added, "True, but once we lose the propane truck and capability, we're back to cooking with wood, which we don't have in abundant supply.

Matter of fact, we're going to have to start rationing some things, among them coffee and tea, pretty quickly. We've hit a gold mine with the restaurant warehouse in Amarillo, but even with that, supporting all the folks that we are, isn't making me happy for the long term. We've all got gardens in, and doing what we can for food storage, but I'm guessing two, maybe three years and it's going to get really rough. I'm just thankful we've got as big a group as we do, otherwise I don't see how we'd be making it, not with the security issues, having to search for things, and just daily maintenance. We'd be lucky to be doing as well as our great-grands were when they settled this place. I can't imagine what those survivors in the towns and cities are doing!"

Brad laughed, "Well, they aren't eating steak as much as we are, that's for sure."

Everyone laughed at that, but Cherie's point had struck home.

Wesley came charging into the kitchen, "Boss, looks like we got a problem coming."

Brad turned sharply, "What's coming, Wesley?"

"Three trucks, coming from 287, just stopped at the big gate. Coupla guys got out, went around the gate, and walked down a ways. I'm guessing to the top of the hill where they could see the house."

"Armored up?"

Wesley shook his head, "Didn't look like it. I'm guessing some raiders, maybe from down toward Wichita Falls, the way they come from."

Sheriff Coffee stood, "Show me the video. Let's see what we're dealing with."

All of them got up and trooped down to the library come radio room and security station. They saw two Mexicans come back into camera range and ten more people get out of the four trucks. The sheriff said, "Brad, can you deploy some folks right quick in your truck beds? I got a feeling this one is gonna go bad."

Brad nodded and hurried from the room yelling, "Reaction team up! I need nine, *now!*" A clatter of running feet punctuated the call as Brad made for the gun room.

The sheriff turned to Cherie and Mike, "You agree?"

They both nodded, "Not the first time we've been through this shit," Mike replied.

Cherie said sadly, "Why? What do they think they're doing?"

"Dunno, Cherie. Hell, it's been about four months since that last bunch came bombing through here. You took 'em out before we could even get there," Mike replied.

Cherie laughed, "Well, given the LEO response time out here, John…"

"Moi? I was coming as fast as I could!" The sheriff exclaimed.

"Yeah, but you were all the way up by Clarendon. Running balls to the wall, it still took you almost thirty minutes."

Wesley interrupted, "Here they come."

The sheriff turned to Darryl, "You ready to maybe have a little business?"

"I'd rather not, if you don't mind."

The sheriff nodded, saying in a sotto voice, "Neither do I." He led the way out of the library walking quickly toward the front of the house and out onto the porch, grabbing his hat on the way by. He looked at the arrangement of vehicles, then calmly stepped around to put himself clear of the house and in the best position for covering fire from the trucks he hoped Brad had manned up.

The four trucks came charging into the ranch yard, sliding to a stop and the sheriff realized they weren't even armored at all. Just plain three-quarter and one-ton crew cab pickups jacked up, running big tires and wheels. All the tires and wheels looked brand new, which told him these were pure raiders, taking what they wanted, whenever they wanted.

One big, sleazy Mexican with long greasy hair and mustaches climbed out of the driver's seat of the first truck, casually slinging an AR-15 over his shoulder and setting a hand on a pistol at his hip. His other hand rested on what looked like a cheap copy of some big fighting-type of knife, sticking out of a holster on the off hip. The man swaggered over, stopping a couple of feet in front of the sheriff, and smiling.

Cherie noticed that the man overtopped the sheriff by probably five or six inches, but he didn't seem the least bit intimidated by the big man. She eased her rifle around the window frame, staying back behind the curtains so they couldn't see any movement, as she took a sight on the big Mexican's nose. At least she wouldn't have to worry about hitting the sheriff if this went as bad as they thought.

The big Mexican made a hand signal, and the rest of the men climbed down from the rigs, ARs and pistols in their hands, not saying a word, but obviously looking around in wonder. The big Mexican finally said, "So, Sheriffmans. You know there ain't no law no more?"

The sheriff replied, "Round here, I'm still the duly elected law. And I enforce it. What do you want?"

The Mexican laughed, "Anything we want to take, that's what we want! Women, booze, food, we take…"

The sheriff did a speed-rock draw, firing three rounds from his 1911 into the big Mexican's belly, then grabbing and spinning him as a shield, shooting over him and one other that started charging him. Seconds later, all twelve of the men were down and dead, And Cherie realized she'd never even gotten a shot off. Shrugging, she safed her AR and walked slowly out the door as Brad and the others climbed down from the armored truck beds.

Brad asked, "Everybody okay?" There were nods all around, and Darryl came out of the house, medical bag in hand.

"Don't think we need you, unless you want to pronounce them, Darryl."

"I'll do it anyway, need the practice."

The crew was going through the pickups and throwing trash and the contents out on the ground when Riley suddenly yelled, "Holy shit! Brad, Darryl, er… Sheriff, y'all need to—Mrs. Crane. Oh, my God."

That brought everyone on a run to the back of the pickup, where Riley had raised the bedcover. Blinking in the light were three young teen girls, badly beaten and obviously in bad shape.

Cherie didn't even think twice, handing her rifle to the sheriff and climbing into the bed, making soothing sounds as the girls cowered against the front of the bed in the little nest they had. Cherie almost gagged from the stench coming off them, but continued to speak quietly as Brad went and got his wife and two other women.

A half-hour later, Brad and the others were back around the kitchen table, and Mike turned to the sheriff, "John, what set you off? It didn't seem to be… Well, I didn't see anything…"

The sheriff leaned back, rolling the coffee cup between his hands as he looked up at the ceiling, "I was watching his eyes. I saw them dilate and saw him starting to lean in. I knew he was starting to make his move, and I just short-cutted him. I can't tell you how I knew, other than thirty years in law enforcement, but I wasn't going to let him get the upper hand."

Brad nodded, "Glad you did. I didn't relish a shootout, but at least this ended well for us, not so much for them, though."

Cherie thought, *Hard men, hell, all of us are that way, even the kids. John's not really that cold-blooded that he enjoyed killing that guy, but he did what needed to be done as soon as he saw it. Thank God for that. I guess it's a sign of these times that we're sitting here calmly discussing killing twelve functional adults without turning a hair, or a single regret. Maybe it's because of those girls, too.*

As they discussed the plight of the girls, who had been taken from a little town south of Fort Worth after the others in their survivor's group were murdered. The sheriff looked around, "Two-hundred forty-one. Question is, who's got room for them?"

Cherie grimaced, "Well, I guess we can take them, but I'm out of room."

Brad nodded and Mike said, "Well, I've got room, but I've got no teens or single females. At least if you take them, there is somebody near their age." Mike thought about it for a minute, and finally said, "I've got a couple of spare beds in the bunkhouse, I can go get them and bring them over."

Cherie cocked her head. "Bunk beds, by any chance?"

Mike bit his lip. "Um, I *could* do that."

She smiled. "Trade you three singles for three bunk beds, if that works for you."

"Sure." He asked curiously, "How are you going to make that work?"

"I'll move out of the master bedroom, put the bunk beds in there, and I'll take the smaller room. That will give them privacy and a bathroom they don't have to share with any males."

There were nods around the table, and Brad wondered, "Where do we go next? It's been a year now, and I don't know what the future is going to bring."

The sheriff cocked his head, "I'll put the word out about the kids, but I'm betting all their folks are dead, probably killed when they were taken." He rubbed his face ruefully. "Where are we going? The same place we've been going for the last year. Survive, do the best we can with what we've got, and do our damndest to train up the kids. Live or die, they are the future, such as it is…"

The End.

The Tragedy of a Laugh

By William Joseph Roberts

I don't care who you are or where you come from. A dive is a dive on any continent and in any country. The decor may vary and the primary language may be different, but at their heart and soul, they are still one and the same. Know what I mean?

Take this place, for instance. The Rising Moon.

A quaint little roadside tavern off to the side of the A30 on the outskirts of Sherborne England. Out of the way just west of Stonehenge and the Salisbury plains, surrounded by farming and cattle fields. One wouldn't think anything of the joint, other than thick beer, buxom ladies, a welcoming atmosphere, and locals who are barely able to stand the *damned annoying* tourists.

Most major cities had become desolate death traps. And folks with any kind of sense about them avoided the cities unless they had no choice. No one wanted to take the chance of another outbreak of Laughing Jacks. And on the slim odds that the bug had mutated again, the millions of unburied dead within those cities would be the source. The only safe place during the first outbreak and the start of the Hell Years was the back woods, out-of-the-way communities that were more or less isolated from the infecting vectors. Which is what led me here, and every other small town and village I'd passed through since leaving the sandbox. Standing in front of a farm community pub just off from the A30, outside of Sherborne, England, trying to get a drink after a not-so-pleasant job of cleaning out vermin of the asshole kind at the request of a worrisome town counsel a few villages over.

"I hope they have real whiskey," I mumbled as I opened the flaking, red-painted front door of the pub. Patrons filled the common room. What I assumed were farmers and sheep herders, all fell silent and turned to look in my direction as I stepped through and closed the door behind myself.

I smiled, taking in the wide range of patrons around the dark little pub. I sidled my way over to the bar and perched myself on a barstool across from the large, balding barkeep. Setting my ball cap and sunglasses on the bar, I scratched and wiped away the sweat and dust of the road.

"What'll it be lad?" The rotund barkeep, wiping out a heavy glass mug.

"Preferably, whiskey, if you have it."

"Yank, eh?" He frowned down his long, bulbous nose at me.

"Yup," I looked about for trouble, then back to the barkeep. "I'd just like that drink if you wouldn't mind."

"What makes you fink a Yank can walk up into my pub and demand a drink? You blokes most likely caused the shitstorm we're living in now." He motioned at everything with a wave of a rag in one hand and a mug in the other.

"I cannot agree nor disagree with the validity of that statement one way or the other. I do agree that I am openly American, whatever that may mean now that the United States probably no longer exists. But regardless, payment is payment, is it not? What exactly passes for currency around here these days?"

"Gold, jewels, guns," he said coldly, staring at me with a heavy smoldering gaze. "In that respective order of course."

"Well, how about this?" I removed my backpack and reached into it, digging deep into its seemingly never-ending depths. Cautiously, I produced a small pearl-handled revolver and placed it on the bar in front of me.

The barkeep shifted, his gaze locked onto the decorative, but functional .38 caliber, nickel-plated, pearl-handled revolver. I slowly removed my hand and produced half a box of ammunition for the weapon.

"Reckon that's worth a few drinks?"

"Aye, I'd reckon," the big barkeep replied with a nod. "I'd say that's worth half a bottle of our freshest blend." He licked his lips and turned to reach for a half-empty bottle of clear liquid from the cabinet under the rear shelves of the bar.

"Uh, how about no," I said, my hand resting once again on the gaudy-looking weapon. "I want whiskey. And I want top-shelf whiskey, no substitute."

"Top shelf, eh?" The barkeep chewed at his lower lip. "Alright," he agreed slowly. "For that piece, two shots from the top shelf."

"Three," I blurted, interrupting as I slid the revolver closer to my side of the bar.

"Fine, three then," he relented, "but you'll be throwing in all of that ammunition as well." He pointed at the half-full box.

"Deal." I slid the box of ammo to the far side of the bar, but held onto the revolver while he placed a step stool and climbed to reach a dusty bottle of golden brown liquid from the top shelf. Carefully, he climbed down, placed three shot glasses on the bar, and uncorked the bottle. His eyes rolled back into his head as he inhaled deeply. "Heavenly, wouldn't you say?"

He held out the end of the bottle and I sniffed, inhaling the woody charred fragrance as deeply as the barkeep. "Oh, yeah," I drawled. "That will do nicely."

I rested my chin on the bar so that my eyes were level with the shot glasses when he began to pour. The deeply fragrant scent wafted from the glasses as he poured slowly, admiring the glint of candlelight through the golden amber liquid. I slid the pearl-handled revolver across the counter to the barkeep without taking my eyes off of the three glasses of amber bliss.

"Thank you," I said with a longing sigh. I gazed into the amber depths as if they were some mystical scrying stones from an ancient tale of magic and wonder.

The door to the joint suddenly rattled from a swift kick and burst open. I picked up the first of the shots and slammed it back, placing the glass gently back onto the bar as I let the aged whiskey rest on my tongue for a long moment. I swallowed, then turned in my seat to look toward the entrance.

A scrawny, bedraggled skeleton of a man stood proudly in the doorway and slowly looked over the pub's occupants.

"My name is Evan Phillips," he announced and took a heavy booted step into the room. "I come from Nether Compton, just up the road a ways."

I turned back to my drinks and slowly sipped at the next shot. I could feel its tingling amber goodness trickle down into the depths of my stomach where it blossomed into a warming core that began to comfort my sore cold bones.

"Someone, whether hired or by their own greedy intent has seen fit to kill a good many of our workers at the distillery. We had one eyewitness to the event and I mean to chase down the bastard that did this."

"What did he look like," the barkeep piped up.

"He was a wide giant of a man," a new voice announced. I saw another figure appear in the doorway behind the skeletal man through the reflection of the bar mirror. "He had on sunglasses and a gray cap that he wore backward. It had a big blue M embroidered on it, like one of those American sports teams."

The barkeep scowled down his nose at me and examined the dark wrap-around sunglasses and gray ball cap. I slammed the second shot down and quickly picked up the third.

"Is he telling the truth or is this just a bloody inconvenient coincidence," the barkeep quietly asked, keeping his eyes on me.

I shrugged and slammed back the last drink, letting it set on my tongue and wash over every square inch of my mouth. God, it was smooth. I hadn't had such a good shot of whiskey in years.

"You wouldn't happen to have a back door to the place, would you?" I closed up my pack, slung it over my shoulders, and grabbed my hat and glasses as I slid from the barstool. "I wouldn't want to be rude and interrupt or anything."

"Hang on there mate. Hang on. Don't be so hasty, yet." He motioned for me to sit back down then looked over my shoulder toward the doorway. "Is there a reward involved?"

I laughed under my breath at my horribly bad luck.

"Aye," I heard the skeletal man reply. "A cask of our finest brew if it leads to a capture."

The barkeep looked back down his nose at me again. "Did you hear that? That's a full cask, mate," he whispered at me. A tone of greed laced his words.

"Oh, I wouldn't blame you if you gave me away," I whispered back. "I understand that a man's gotta do what a man's gotta do. Especially in this shitty world." I stood and turned to leave, but froze at the distinctive sound of a gun's hammer being cocked. I looked back to see the barkeep and an ancient sawed-off double-barreled shotgun aimed at my chest.

The barkeep shrugged. "Sorry mate. Like you said. A man's gotta do what a man's gotta do."

I unceremoniously caught a good deal of air as two very large and muscular individuals tossed me through the root cellar opening into the basement of an ancient stone church that looked like it had been built centuries ago. The rough stone floor cushioned my fall well enough that I bounced once from my face and a few more times otherwise before rolling to a stop. I suffered minor bumps and scrapes, but otherwise, I'd had a lot worse. The Army had made sure of that.

"We'll deal with you later, you filthy scum." The two men who'd tossed me through the opening spit down into the depths of my dungeon and closed the doors

The sickening wash of senses realigned themselves. I shook my head to clear the dazed sensation and stood as best as I could under the low ceiling. Dust floated about through thin beams of light that penetrated through cracks and missing mortar between the foundation stones of the church.

"Isn't this just a brilliant predicament," I whispered to myself.

Something moved in the back of the darkness that engulfed me. A stifled cough, a sighed breath, all farther back in the dark depths of my prison. The distinctive clank of chains on stone followed another cough.

"Who's there?"

A whispered gasp caught my ear. "He doesn't know, he doesn't know," the voice giggled under its hinted breath.

"What the hell?"

Something seemingly growled from the far depths of the darkness, steel chains clanked and slid across the stone floor.

"Prisoners, such as yourself, though not American," a disembodied voice from the darkness plainly stated in a light Welsh or maybe Irish accent.

Well, no shit Sherlock. You sound like the Lucky Charms Leprechaun.

"Prisoners," I asked, emphasizing the s. "As in plural?"

"Yes, as in plural," the voice calmly replied.

Movement near a beam of light caught my eye. A form stood. I could make out an arm and a filthy side in the dim illumination, but the individual's face was still obscured.

"Each imprisoned for this or that minor infraction to the powers that be in these parts. It isn't any secret that most in these parts blame Americans and their pomposity for the fall of the world. Death may be preferable to what they have in store for you. Why are you here lad," the unseen, now grandfatherly-sounding voice said.

The form stepped forward into the beam of light so that it shone on his face.

"They tossed me in here for doing a job to put food in my belly. They didn't take too kindly to their kinfolk being shot full of holes.

"So just another American cowboy, gone rogue." The voice held a level of disappointed resentment in its intonation.

"Not so much," I replied defensively. "Only passing through and an opportunity presented itself. Nothing more. So I took it. It was a better outlook than hoping that I'd catch a rat for dinner."

"Roasted rat is a fair meal when prepared correctly," the man replied in a jovial tone.

"It isn't when all you could dream about for the last three years is a deep dish Chicago-style pepperoni pizza."

A sobbed cry overshadowed the sound of shaking chain links. I peered into the depths of the darkness. My eyes had begun to get accustomed to the dim light of the church basement.

"What was that," I asked as I pushed past the aged speaker, toward the groan.

"Nothing to concern yourself with, Yank. You're best off to stay as far away as you can, for your safety and for ours."

"He doesn't know, he doesn't know, he doesn't know," the manic voice repeated then broke out into maddened laughter.

"Calm yourself," the man said. It will do you no good to get yourself worked up again. It'll only serve to annoy our jailers."

"Help me," a weak childlike voice whispered from the darkness and broke into heavy sobs. "I'm so very hungry."

"Hello?"

"Please, do not approach her. It is for your own safety." The old man tugged at my arm.

I yanked my arm away. "What the hell is wrong with you people? Who would chain a child in a dungeon? I swear to God you Brits and your kinky...," I barely managed to utter before the back of my skull exploded with a sudden sharp pain followed by blindness and a falling sensation.

When I began my day, eager to do the job I'd been hired to do, I never in my wildest dreams would have guessed that I'd wake up the next morning, trussed up like a Thanksgiving turkey on the cold stone floor of a dank church basement in a backwater nothing of a town of southern England. Why couldn't getting back to the States be a little more forgiving? I mean, what is wrong with wanting to get back home, check on your family after the apocalypse, and hope beyond hope that there is still a place left to get a luscious deep-dish pizza?

What? Dreams and goals are good. Everyone should have them. It gives them a drive, a reason to get up in the morning and push on to the next day. That was a good philosophy before the world turned to shit, and doubly so now. Anything beyond mere survival seemed like extravagance and wasteful, but people needed something.

Most people I'd met since the beginning of the Hell Years, believed that China, North Korea, Russia, or take your pick of other terrorist-friendly countries were responsible for the apocalypse. Almost everywhere I went, people speculated on who started it and why. All I know is that three years ago, while deployed to the hell hole that is Afghanistan, it happened and the world went to shit.

That might as well have been the ancient past because it sure felt like it.

I remembered just how paranoid everyone was back before the world died. For decades, everyone expected nuclear annihilation and mutually assured destruction where the survivors eked out a meager existence in the shadowy remnants of civilization.

We had grasped onto that one scenario like it was a life preserver and for decades, prepared for the end of the world. We had dug everything possible from fallout shelters to elaborate survival bunkers. We hoarded food, ammo, and basic supplies. So much time and effort had been dedicated to the scenario that it permeated our media. Everything from television to movies, video games, and literature were saturated with the worst-case scenario of nuclear war.

Other angles of mankind's demise popped up from time to time. Plague, an asteroid from space, even down to little green men invading and enslaving all of humanity. But none of them stood out as proud and menacing as the great might of the ominous mushroom cloud.

Then, the day that so many had spent their lives preparing for finally came. It happened, but not how anyone had expected it. No, the world did not go out with a bang, but neither did it go out with a whimper. It went out with what most would consider the maniacal laughter of a raving lunatic.

One of the benefits of working for an alphabet agency that was an offshoot branch of the FBI, was that I tended to get information fairly easily and on a regular basis. That's how I found out the truth of the matter. We'd been out in the field for three weeks, talking with locals, digging up any useful intelligence we could come up with as was our usual.

When we left Bagram, everything was situation normal. After that routine intelligence-gathering mission, we returned to Bagram to find the base in total disarray and abandoned. Bodies were scattered here and there, curled up like they were doubled over with pain. Lucky for me, the commander of the 704th Army intelligence detachment had locked himself in the intelligence office and put a bullet through his brainpan before he thought about destroying the intel reports. Things must have gotten really bad at the base while we were gone. He always seemed to be a stable and sane individual. But then, maybe he'd been infected with whatever had killed everyone else on base.

Now, see, this is where things started to get interesting.

The reports stated that two Georgia Tech students, Johnathan Patel and Michael Swanson wanted to get back at several of their more athletic and abusive classmates after years of hazing. So they put their skills to the test and set out to play a simple practical joke. They devised a plan to genetically modify the Bordetella Pertussis bacteria, turning the whooping cough into a laughable prank on their peers by tweaking the genetic code just ever so slightly.

Our dynamic duo had encoded this new strain to cause a short-term laughing attack in its victims that lasted all of twenty minutes in the lab rats they had subjected to rigorous testing. In order to infect all of the bullies at the same time, they modified the virus to be highly contagious, utilizing multiple vectors, but limiting its lifespan to only forty-eight hours.

But unknown to these two outstanding individuals, the bug had a slightly different agenda for humanity. Slightly different as in, it didn't want to stop, and those infected began laughing uncontrollably, unable to do much more than struggle for the slightest of breath.

Initial reports blamed thousands of deaths on what had quickly been dubbed, The Laughing Jacks Virus. Horribly incorrect, but it stuck anyways.

Most of the initial deaths were incidents like car crashes, aircraft plummeting from the sky, and other industrial accidents. By the twenty-four-hour mark, full paralysis of the victim's diaphragm had stopped all breathing and like clockwork, the first official deaths that the prank had been directly responsible for occurred.

It exponentially exploded from there.

The world as we knew it was changed forever when these two nerds struck back against the jocks and released their engineered bioweapon into the frat house of their persecutors, where it spread like wildfire.

And you know what the funniest part of all this is? Of all the days that these two geniuses could have picked, they chose April Fool's Day to destroy the world.

Yeah... Kinda ironic, isn't it?

Not to disappoint the Mutually assured destruction types, I had found out during my travels that a few nukes were *supposedly* detonated in major population centers, but they weren't the big missile-mounted kind. They were rumored to be more like those old Soviet suitcase nukes from back in the 80s that everyone freaked out about at the end of the Cold War.

I know for a fact that London and Paris were both hit with dirty nukes. You can't get within twenty miles of either city without getting sick as a dog. I'd heard that the Vatican, New York, Sydney, and a few other places were hit, but nothing that I'd been able to confirm. When passing through Serbia, I'd heard that Moscow and a number of sites in China had apparently been glassed by American nukes. But without proof, I couldn't take that as any more than just local rumors and speculation.

You know how those things can get out of hand. Ever played the telephone game? You know, when one person whispers to the next person and so on and so forth, and by the end of the line the original message is something totally different and off-topic? Well, grapevine rumors are a lot like that.

And if that wasn't bad enough. In the three years it has taken me to trek from Afghanistan to the backwater nothing of southern England, which in itself had been a small miracle, it got even worse.

The icing on the shitstorm cake so to speak has been the uncontrolled spread of disease. Speculation through the rumor mill figured that millions have died since Laughing Jacks, from exposure to a new strain of the bubonic plague that apparently escaped from some secret facility in Eastern Europe. Needless to say, mass graves and piles of burning bodies had almost become a daily sight for a time.

Every military base I'd stopped at over the last three years had even less info than I started with. Then there were the Army pukes holding down the fort at Rhein-Main Airbase in Germany, who tried to throw me into the brig when I refused to report for duty.

Yeah, no. I don't think so. I was working for special forces, on loan from the KCG. And considering I was pretty sure the United States was more or less gone, I wasn't about to get conscripted for their cause. I wanted to find a way back to the States if at all possible.

Then there was that.

The States.

News from the States had been almost nonexistent. If the States were in the same shape as Europe and the Middle East, then there was little chance I would ever hear anything, or even make it back to those shores. But that was the little niggling of hope that kept me going day in and day out.

In the end, that's also what got me trussed up and locked in this medieval dungeon. Dim tendrils of light streamed into the dark basement space when I opened my eyes, but they seemed to be at a different angle than before. I could make out the steel sheet cellar doors I had been tossed through at the far end of the room. Cold seeped into my chest and chin where I lay against the rough stone floor on my stomach. My wrists and ankles were bound together behind my back. When I fought against my restraints I heard an amused grunt from somewhere behind me.

"Our illustrious American guest has awoken from his nap. I hope that the accommodations were to your liking, ...*sir*," the older man added as a sarcastic afterthought. He shuffled about and sat down on the stone floor just ahead of me

He leaned down, nearly close enough to lick my face. I didn't know how long he'd been stuck down here, but by the smell of his breath, the guy had died two months ago.

"You were warned to leave her alone. She is a mad devil-possessed thing, chained down here by those men for whatever reason it was that they saw fit. That is none of my concern though. For now, I am only concerned with the fact that she is chained and that I am safe. I have every intent to keep this comfortable arrangement, seeing as nothing else at the moment will be comfortable for any reason. The things that she has done since I have been here alone would have her soul condemned to the fiery depths of hell for Lucifer to use as his plaything. She is under the influence of the great beast, and I mean to keep myself free from her grasp at all costs."

He straightened his back and took a deep, soothing breath that he held for a moment before he slowly exhaled.

Now that that is off of my chest, I am Gareth." He smiled from what I could tell in the dim light.

"Ronald Freeman. A pleasure to meet you." I nodded as best as I could. "Well, why exactly were you tossed down here?" I twisted and partially rolled to my side in order to better see my immediate jailer.

"I refused to pay my tithes to those in charge," he laughed.

A commotion of muffled shouts came from outside the basement door. The door suddenly rattled and shook before being flung wide open. Two men carried a third who was trussed up in the same manner as me down into the makeshift dungeon and dropped unceremoniously on the floor.

"You'll think twice before mouthing off to the boss again, won't you," one of the jailers said, then spat upon the bound and gagged man as he exited the basement.

The newest resident to the establishment was a large, bald-headed man. Heavily bearded, and heavily covered in tattoos that decorated most of the exposed skin of his arms and neck. He squirmed and grunted, fighting against his restraints.

"I suppose our captors have spared me the trouble of binding another ungrateful guest," Gareth said.

The new entrant forcefully breathed around a dirty gag. He strained against his bounds, veins bulging across the man's shiny bald head. Single strands at first, then multiple strands of the restraints tore and popped from the man's exertions. Then a loudly audible report of a ripping sound accompanied the man's arms freely separating themselves from the binds.

He groaned with relief, then rolled over onto his back where he calmly breathed, taking a moment to himself before sitting upright. He removed the gag and unbound his legs, then squinted about into the darkness. His thick, bushy black beard parted in a wide smile as his eyes laid upon my helpless form.

"To be sure my luck be a changing. I know you," he grinned wide in my direction. I could hear Gareth slink further away into the darkness and away from the mound of muscle before us. The new addition to our ragtag club stood, having to stoop so as not to strike his head. He reached both arms above his head and gripped the floor joist where he dangled and stretched, flexing his massive and powerful-looking biceps. "It's not good to be on the wrong side of the London Browns. You turned down employment and they are offended. You've a price on your head now, Mate." He strolled over and stooped over my helpless form where he rudely turned out my pockets and otherwise unceremoniously searched every nook and cranny of my person.

"Whoa now, hold on there buddy. Don't you think you should at least buy me a drink first before you get acquainted with my intimate bits?" My ribs suddenly screamed in protest to the invasion of this guy's booted foot invading their personal space.

"Shut your mouth, Yank. No one said you could speak."

The burly bald-headed bloke froze at the sound of a whimpering gasp from the dark nether region of the basement dungeon.

"Well now, what have we here," he said, then straightened, turning his attention to cautiously peer into the darkness behind me.

"Please, for your own sake," Gareth begged. "Ignore her and leave it be at that."

A wide, leering smile crept across his face at the sound of another whimper. He squinted, trying to make out the noise in the dim darkness.

"Please, for all of our sakes," Gareth begged again. "Stay away from her."

"I'd listen to him if I were you," I said. I had no idea why Gareth had said that, but maybe I could use this to my advantage.

His boot responded in the most rudely abrupt manner to my ribs.

"I thought I told you to shut it, Yank," he said with emphasized disdain, then took a willing step forward. "What sort of gentleman would I be if I didn't introduce myself to the young lady?"

"Please, for your own sake leave her in peace. She is a tortured soul."

"Uh hu," the large man said, then proceeded forward.

I could just see Gareth's lunge for the man out of the corner of my eye. Stone in hand, Gareth swung for the back of the man's head, but the large man blocked the strike almost effortlessly.

"Oh, well. Would you look at that, you're bleeding," the large man said.

"What? Where?" Gareth sheepishly asked, looking himself over.

The man punched Gareth square in the face. His now skewed nose gushed forth a heavy stream of blood.

"Right there," the man laughed, then shook his head.

Gareth stumbled backward, falling flat on his ass. He cupped his broken nose and began to wail.

The man proceeded into the darkness. "Well now, isn't this a lovely sight," he said. He hung his weight from a heavy overhead floor beam.

I shifted my position and watched as the smaller figure shrunk away against the cold stone wall at the back of the room. "Leave her alone," I shouted, struggling against my restraints.

"What are you going to do if'n I don't, *Yank*?"

"I said leave her alone."

"Oh yeah? That's it? That's just exactly what I'll do," he laughed then took a step forward. He crouched down in front of the young woman. I could only make out the dingy white of the large man's tank top at the farther edges of darkness.

"Well now, you're just a sweet little thing, aren't you," he crooned.

"It'll be your funeral, mate," Gareth said.

"I said to shut it!" He turned and glared back at Gareth, then slung a rock in his direction. The stone found its target with that solid sort of thud a stone makes against the side of a person's head. He picked up another stone and drew back, prepared to hurl it in my direction.

"Do I need to repeat myself to you too, Yank?"

Something stirred in the darkness behind the giant. A form shifted and slinked just behind him, growing closer.

"No, no. I think I'm good for now."

"You'd better be, ya bloody wanker."

The look of blind surprise that painted his face and was replaced a moment later with the look of abject terror is an image that I won't soon forget.

Now I've seen my fair share of bodies in all stages of decomposition. I've killed men mere feet from me. But those horrific images were easily replaced with the look that washed over the large man's face the moment the chain went taught around his neck, snapping his head backward.

He struggled, fighting for the need to breathe. He dropped to his knees, falling forward, gasping, his face turned shades of purple and blue that I could even make out in the dim light of the underdark.

A young, stout-looking girl came into view in the limited light of the basement prison. As the large man collapsed, she stood on his back, straining to pull the chain tighter until he lay limp and motionless upon the cold earth. Dropping the chains, she sat quietly on top of his motionless form for a moment, then wiped the back of a dirty hand across her grimy forehead and sighed.

She looked exhausted, and I could understand why. Wrestling that behemoth while most likely being semi-starved would do that to a person. She leaned over and picked up the large stone that the man had dropped, fondling it, she rolled the stone about, examining its surface. Careful, she brushed her thumb along a sharp angular edge where it had broken.

I watched in silent, disbelieving horror.

She lifted the stone above her head, bringing the sharp edge downward with all her might against the joint of the man's shoulder.

Over and over again the sharp edge of the stone penetrated through meat and sinew with each sickly wet strike, separating the man's arm from his body. Steam rose from the dark pool that grew, expanding in size before it could soak into the cold earth.

Casually, the girl dropped the stone to one side and picked up the disjointed limb. She brushed away dirt and bits of debris from the stump, then eagerly bit into the still-warm meat.

My stomach wrenched and heaved at the sloppy wet smacking of her lips. She chewed as little as she had to, quick to swallow bite after bite as quickly as she could, as this starved, abused creature fed upon her would-be-attacker. She grunted, breathing deep with each relished bite.

Gareth stirred, a jerk of a leg, then a moan as he rolled over. He stared, blinking in confusion at the young girl sitting atop the large man's back, gnawing on a severed arm like a large turkey leg. He gasped then began to scoot slowly backwards. "I missed something important, didn't I?"

"No, you didn't miss anything at all. She just felt like grabbing a light snack. What the hell is wrong with you people," I shouted in reply.

A growl from the young lady drew my attention from Gareth. She tore away another bite from the stump, then stopped in mid-chew and stared down at her makeshift stone cleaver. She let her meaty treat drop heavily onto the back of the large man's corpse and retrieved the stone. Immediately she struck the stone against the chain, over and over again, letting out a frantic scream with each solid strike at the chain. A maniacal laugh followed as soon as the chain snapped in half.

"Um, hey Gareth," I whispered. "Any chance you might untie me now, please." Before he could respond, she leapt forward, crawling across the distance like some demon-possessed she-devil, stopping nose to nose with me, the blood-stained stone still clutched in her right hand.

"Freedom, is that what you wish?" She chortled. She stared wide-eyed at me, unblinking. A heavy coppery stench tinged her words. "What do you seek, American? Do you not want your freedom? I shall give you freedom," she screamed, then pushed herself upright, her weight pressed down heavily on me as she climbed atop my back. Every muscle in my body clenched, waiting for the killing blow that never came. Instead, she cut at the makeshift chords that bound me, then returned to lay on the ground in front of me once she'd finished, and again stared at me with her wide-eyed gaze.

"You showed me kindness. You attempted to free me. So I have returned the favor."

Chains rattled against the steel door of the basement entrance. She suddenly let out a growled hiss and arched up like some feral cat in a defensive stance.

"Revenge," she growled. Bloody drool trickled from her mouth as she chewed on the word and dripped from the tip of her chin.

She leapt forward, sprinting for the opening as the heavy basement doors opened.

"What in the bloody hell is all this racket," one of our jailers managed to get out before I heard the heavy thud of stone against skull. The sloppy wet strikes that followed told me the ultimate fate of our Jailer. I looked to Gareth, who had yet to move. He looked to the open doorway with slack-jawed wonderment.

I sat up, dusting myself off. "So that's why she was locked down here," I asked.

A gurgled scream from inside the church found us, followed by something akin to a demon-possessed cackle.

"No mate. I don't believe so. I believe that's what they made her. She had already been here for some time when I was tossed down here with her."

"Sounds like they are getting what they deserve then."

"Yes. I'd say so."

We both listened, unable to tear our attention away from the wholesale sounds of slaughter for what seemed like an eternity.

"You said you wanted to get back to the States, did you not," Gareth asked.

"I do. Desperately," I said. "I was in the Middle East when everything went to hell."

"Fuel has long since run out, but if one knew where a wind-driven vessel lay berthed and how to pilot said vessel, one might be capable of escaping the island nation of England."

I turned my attention from the sounds of well-deserved revenge toward Gareth, who now held my full attention. "And I suppose you'd know where a vessel like this might be? "

Gareth busied himself with the dirt under a fingernail. He nervously nodded. "I do."

"Well, that's a step in the right direction." I could already smell it. A piping hot deep dish pizza dripping with grease and sauce. "Can you sail her?"

He looked up at me with a wide smile. "I can."

"This seems entirely too easy. So what's the catch?"

"You see, once upon a time I had a thriving career that involved taking tourists on these little jaunts around the coastline. They paid me well to take them out for a few days, let them sleep on deck in the salty sea air, and point out all of these supposed ancient or important historical sites to them. Gareth's coastal tours," he proudly whispered, motioning to the imaginary words in front of himself as he spoke.

"Tours," Celeste, the rabid crazy lady from the dungeon whispered, then let out a tiny giggle. Somehow she'd managed to track us after we left the church, and her ravenous carnage behind. At least for the moment, we didn't have to worry about her attacking us out of hunger. And I guessed that as long as we didn't make any moves toward her that seemed harmful, she'd be as peaceful as a feral cat. Worst case, if she followed us onto the boat I'd have to figure out what to do then. The thought of weeks on a boat in the middle of the Atlantic with a psychopathic cannibal wasn't my idea of a good time.

We hid in the tall grasses that lined the northern shoreline near Cobb's Quay Marina. The entire area looked to have once been a well-to-do neighborhood at one time, with lush lawns, their own personal marina, and direct water access. Expensive homes now overgrown, in disrepair, burned out, and for the most part abandoned, lined the streets leading up to the marina.

"You see, I had gone inland some months ago to do some trading in Broadstone, just north of here. I'd heard through some other traders that this guy had resin available that I desperately needed for repairs. The old girl was already eighty or so years old. She's that two-masted schooner, just there," he said and pointed in the direction of the only two-masted vessel moored to the dock. She sat moored alongside the old marina repair shop. I could hear several men talking and laughing somewhere off in the distance, but they were nowhere within sight.

"*The Vagabond*," Gareth said in a soft, loving tone. "She's a sixty-five foot long, gaff-rigged, copper-plated hull beauty." He stared at the vessel longingly. "I'd picked her up cheap after a slight incident involving my now ex-wife and the CEO of the company she worked for. Funny how things like that can turn a tight wad of an asshole into one of the most generous souls that you could ever meet." He smiled wide at the memory. "But when I'd returned from my trip to Broadstone, the place was overrun by a group of thugs who'd been pushed out of Southampton by some other more, um…*influential* group.

"And you're sure she can make the trek across the Atlantic?"

Gareth chuckled under his breath. "Without a doubt. She may have a few decades on her bones, but she's as fast and sturdy as the day she first launched."

"Did you get a count of how many men they had?"

Gareth shrugged. "Half dozen, maybe more."

Great…this just had the familiar stench of FUBAR'd from the get-go. But if he could sail the ship and it could make the trip, it could be my ticket home. So, a half dozen enemies is more realistically a dozen or more able fighting men. If they were anything like other groups I'd come across the past couple of years, then you'd have a range of personality types. A mix of hard-core bad-asses mixed in with the worthless lazy shits that only did what they absolutely had to do.

It isn't like I hadn't dealt with similar situations in the past, but during each of those encounters, I at least had a fire team with me. Now, it was just me. Big difference. Those guys camping out at the marina could have anything from baseball bats and broken bottles to fully automatic assault rifles and grenades. You just never know what people have managed to get their hands on, especially since all sense of law or anything resembling rules went out the window. They could even be cannibals, but I hadn't heard any rumors of any cannibal groups in these parts.

I turned to Gareth and asked, "What do you know about these guys? Any idea what kind of hardware they carry or how they operate?" I could just make out the old man's shrug in the dim light.

"A few of them had guns, I think."

"But were they real guns or are we talking about air-soft replicas and BB guns?"

He just shrugged and grunted something that sounded more like a question than an answer.

Great, no intel, no backup, and this might be my only chance off this rock. I wasn't sure that I'd ever been in a worse setup, but I really wanted to get back Stateside. Since she followed us from the church, maybe I could somehow send Celeste in to soften them up? But from the sounds of the light snore a short distance away in the tall grasses, she wasn't going to be of much help at the moment. That might have been for the better, though. If she slept through it all, we could slip away on the boat and leave her to mop up the leftovers.

"Pretend I don't know anything about sailboats. Any leftover fuel has since gone bad unless someone has been processing it. Without a working motor, how do we get that big ass ship out of the harbor?"

Gareth chuckled. "She wasn't originally equipped with a motor, and back in those days, a motorized tug or a team of rowers would hitch up and direct her out of port. Luckily the previous owner installed an electric drive motor just for maneuvering while in port. It's solar-powered. As long as no one messed with the batteries or the solar panels, she should have enough power to get us out to open water."

"Alright, then. Here's what I want you to do, Gareth." The old man turned back to me. I could barely make out his excited smile in the dim moonlight. "We're going to slowly make our way toward the boat. We don't want to rush it or anything. Just get there as quickly and as quietly as we can. As soon as the coast is clear, we'll get aboard and start prepping her to launch."

"Got it. But what about the bad guys?"

"An avoided conflict is the best plan. And I doubt there will be much noise from those electric motors."

"No, they run almost entirely silent," Gareth replied.

"Then there's a pretty good chance we can slip out of port and they'll never even know it. How far do we have to go to reach open water?"

"Mmm…Maybe five hundred meters if I had to guess."

"Five hundred meters, so almost five football fields. That isn't too bad."

"But what if they *do* spot us?"

"Just let me worry about that. You take care of getting the boat out of here."

You'd think that stealing a boat from a more or less abandoned marina would be easy, and for the most part, it is. The problem is the way that sound travels over the water and bounces between the boats still parked and floating in their berths.

From the best that we could tell, the bad guys had set up shop more or less at Cobb's Bar, which sat at the far end of the marina. Gareth had said when he'd been back here before, they had guards at the front gate to the marina, which made sense. With the water acting as a barrier on one side, the rest of the property had been blocked off by either fencing or storage sheds, creating an easy-enough to maintain perimeter.

Scaling the fence was more or less out of the question. They'd systematically tied bottles, cans, pie tins, and anything else that would make a great noise maker along the length of the seven-foot-tall chain link fence that guarded this end of the marina. But, just down the way were several small row boats—probably used for fishing along the foreshore—that had been abandoned near someone's personal dock behind one of the fancy houses of the neighboring subdivision.

So we picked one of the small metal boats, quietly slipped it into the water, and paddled our way along to the end of the dock. Quietly I pulled myself up onto the worn wooden planks then froze at a thought. I turned and looked down at Gareth, who hadn't moved from his seat at the back of the rowboat.

"Do you think anyone is living out here on any of these boats?"

"I suppose it's possible," he said, shrugging. "It has been some time since I'd been here last."

"Then we might want to be extra quiet getting to your boat." I held my hand out, offering to help him up onto the dock.

"Good idea." He took my hand and pulled himself up.

It wasn't far to *The Vagabond* from where we'd climbed up. Just a tiptoe up a metal gangplank the upper dock surrounding the repair building, then a short distance across the pavement to where the boat was moored. She looked like any of the classic sailing yachts you'd seen in old black-and-white movies. We stepped down the short gangplank and Gareth turned to me.

"I have to go below to hook up the batteries to the motors. Release the bowline and stern line if you would please, Mister Freeman."

"Aye Aye, Captain." I snapped to and popped a crisp salute. Gareth laughed and returned the salute before he disappeared below deck. I heard him mumble something about damnable Americans as he made his way into the wheelhouse.

I hurried to the front of the boat and cast off the rope tied there to the mooring cleat, then repeated the process at the rear of the boat. With a good shove, we drifted cockeyed away from the dock. I hurried forward and pushed the nose of the boat away from the dock as well.

We were finally off.

In my moment of triumph, you'd have thought that maybe, just maybe I'd have considered the gangplank we'd walked across to board the boat, but that would be expecting entirely too much for my little pea brain to come up with.

The gangplank slid along with us as we drifted away, then fell into the water with a very loud splash.

"Shit," I said under my breath. Gareth rushed through the wheelhouse door back topside and hurried to unlash the sails.

"What fell into the water?"

"The gangplank," I admitted.

"If we're lucky, no one will think anything of it. Help me to ready the sails. Trim I can control from inside the wheelhouse, but we have to manually hoist the sheets. Unlash them along the booms then release the jib and begin hoisting it with this line by cranking the winch," he said, grabbing hold of a rope that was secured to the forward mast.

"Seems easy enough."

Gareth disappeared back into the wheelhouse and the boat suddenly shifted sideways, then in reverse as the front swung about to the right, turning to aim for the opening of the bay. He wasn't lying about the motors. They were as silent as a kitten's purr.

As quiet as a thief in the night, we slipped along the waterway that ran between the main dock and the outer line of docking slips. I grabbed the hand crank Gareth had pointed out and gave it a good turn. The clattering of the locking mechanism grated on me like nails on a chalkboard. There was nothing quiet about it.

"Gareth," I whispered as loudly as I could. "Gareth." I don't know if he heard me, or just came out of the wheelhouse to see what was taking me so long, but his timing couldn't have been better.

"Why the bloody hell aren't you hoisting the jib?"

"Is there a quieter way to do this? Anyone nearby will know someone is here if I keep cranking this thing."

"Afraid not, mate. That's just the way that winch operates."

"How do you lower it, then?"

"You hold this lever right here," he said, pointing at the mechanism, "and slowly let it down. If it tries to get away from you, just let go of the lever and the locking mechanism will catch."

"That's the ticket," I said, snapping my fingers. I moved the lever, disabling the safety lock and almost silently cranked the winch.

Gareth turned, heading back to the wheelhouse. "The batteries will only last so long before they're drained, then we'll be at Mother Nature's mercy. Get the Jib up as quickly as you can, then get to work on the mainsail." He slapped the main mast and pointed at another hand crank before disappearing below deck.

"Aye aye, Mon Capitan." I continued turning the hand crank until the winch wouldn't go any further, then set the lock. The large triangular sail flapped loosely in the light breeze. It swayed and popped with each little gust that passed by.

"Hey! Someone is stealing a boat!" A voice shouted, from somewhere off in the distance in the direction of the other voices we'd heard earlier.

I really hoped Gareth wasn't lying about knowing how to sail this thing.

I hurried to the main mast, released the straps, and just cranked the winch as fast as I could make it go, not worried about the noise the locking mechanism made. Gareth popped topside again.

"Hey, what's with all the noise?"

"We've been spotted. Got any guns on board?"

"An emergency flare gun down below."

"I'd much rather have my backpack right about now and the M-4 and six magazines of ammo I had tucked down inside of it, but that'll have to do." Gareth hurried below and returned in a moment with the large barreled single-shot pistol. Ahead on our right, several men gathered along the side of the dock, machetes, and baseball bats in hand.

"That isn't promising," Gareth commented.

"You concentrate on getting us out of here. Let me worry about these guys." I tucked the flare gun into my waistband and started searching the deck for anything I could use as a weapon. Mounted to one side of the wheelhouse was an expandable, long-handled gaff hook, used for hooking fish or basically anything floating along that you wanted to grab and bring aboard. It wasn't exactly what I was hoping for, but at least it was something.

It wasn't long before we were rounding a turn along the waterway that brought us close to the dock and several other boats parked there. Several of the men had gathered on one of the boats. Maybe they were planning to chase us down? I really hoped not, because I was going to be useless to Gareth on the sailing side of things.

The closer we got to the bend, the better I could make out what the men were doing. One of them had climbed back up to the top of the docks, with a rope in hand that attached to the top of the nearest boat.

The Vagabond jerked forward, the wind catching and filling the jib sail. The men yelled taunts and jeers at us as we slipped silently by. Then, the one thing I never expected. The man standing at the top of the dock with the rope in hand stepped back, pulling the rope tight, then ran along in an arc, keeping tension on the rope as he swung out, soaring through the air in a long, sweeping arc that Errol Flynn would have been proud of.

Releasing the rope, the man seemed to float across the remaining distance, striking the jib sail that fluttered and engulfed him. He grabbed at the edges and slid down the billowing material. He dropped to the deck with a heavy booted thud in what most nerds would claim to be one hell of a superhero landing.

"The boss don't take kindly to someone stealing from him. I'mma gonna make you fink twice about your life decisions, mate."

The guy was quite a bit smaller than me—both in height and in bulk—but the fire burning behind those eyes told me that this guy was their equivalent of a honey badger, and my shit was about to hurt really bad if I didn't do something about this guy.

The guy didn't waste any time, he drew a very long and wide blade that looked a lot like an expensive kitchen knife from behind his back.

"I'm about to carve up a bit of fresh meat for me and the boys." He lunged forward, blade held underhanded in his right hand, and slashed upward at me.

I easily batted the blade aside with the end of the gaff hook then slammed the butt end into his stomach so hard it lifted him off his feet.

He roared, sprinting forward with the blade held high over his head. I swung the hook end of the gaff toward his knife-wielding hand, and just missed as he ducked, going low. He kicked out, sweeping my legs out from under me. I landed flat on my back with a heavy thud.

The guy was nothing if he wasn't squirrely. He was on top of me in the blink of an eye, blade in hand. Thrusting downward with both hands on the handle of the blade, I shifted to the side just enough that the knife dug into the boat's wooden deck.

Shifting back, I swung a right hook, smashing my fist into the side of the guy's head with as much force as I could muster. He jerked the blade loose and leaned forward for another strike.

Reflexes and training kicked in. I'd grabbed the guy's wrists, blocking his strike before I realized what I had done. He leaned further forward, forcing all his weight down against me, the tip of the blade waivered mere inches from my face.

Excited shouts and screams from the dock caught both of our attention. He chanced a look over and his grip lessened just a hair. I took the opportunity to grab for the flare gun still in my waistband, which I shoved into the guy's mouth as soon as he turned his attention back to me.

He didn't even have time to let out a peep before I pulled back the hammer and squeezed the trigger, firing the flare down his throat. Smoke and white hot flames roiled from his mouth, scorching the back of my hand. He dropped the blade and I let go of the gun when he rolled away, flailing, digging at his own face.

I hurried to my feet and grabbed the guy by his waistband and the back of his shirt, then heaved him over the side. I watched him sink away into the dark waters of the bay, continuing to dig at his throat and chest.

"Kill the bloody witch!!" Someone from the dock shouted. When I turned my attention back to the dock, the man's shout turned into a gasping gurgle. Celeste was perched on the man's shoulders, gnawing at the side of his neck. He frantically grabbed and tugged at her, then tripped and fell to the ground.

"At least she won't be hungry," Gareth said from behind me. He'd managed to sneak back on deck during the commotion without my realization.

"Yeah," I replied and thought for a moment. "That brings up a good question. What are we going to do about supplies?"

"We'll have to put in somewhere else to stock up on fresh water and grab whatever foodstuff that we can before we set out. Fishing along the way is also an option.

A little fishing sounded like just what the doctor ordered. I leaned up against the side of the wheelhouse to catch my breath for a moment. Gareth hurried about, raising several other sails then returned below deck.

The Vagabond continued along the waterway toward the open ocean, silently gliding away into the darkness of a moonlit night.

End

Grenade Blows Up

By Linda Kay Hardie

Grenade popped the top of the can and scooped the contents into four bowls, which she set on the kitchen floor. "Din-din, kitties!" she called. The clowder swarmed around her ankles, four friendly Abyssinian cats, two ruddy and two fawn in color. One of her scavengers had found an entire case of cat food, so it was treat time for her fur babies. A break for her, too, since it was a meal she didn't have to chop and mix and cook for them. Cats, being obligate carnivores, need an all-meat diet. Taurine, an essential nutrient for cats, was hard to come by, except in animal products. Grenade often hunted and scrounged for meat for them.

The lack of electricity was a burden, but not insurmountable. Grenade scrambled eggs for her own breakfast on the propane camp stove out on the back porch. She traded with a neighbor several streets over for eggs and the occasional old chicken or young rooster, a rare treat. She had just finished cleaning up her breakfast dishes and gone back outside, when there was a knock on her backyard gate. Grenade felt for her .32 holstered at the small of her back, then walked over to the gate. Her vision blurred briefly—*damn, it was getting worse*—but after blinking, she could see a shock of ruffled brown hair above the six-foot-tall fence, so she knew who was there.

"Yes?" she said anyway, by way of greeting.

"It's Marmot."

Grenade unlocked the combination lock on the gate and let him in. The teenaged boy carried four canvas bags with old grocery store logos, full of treasures. He'd brought her the case of cat food last night, a special trip since it was a heavy item. Marmot set the grocery bags on her wooden picnic table and sat down. Grenade sat down opposite him.

Marmot reached into one bag and pulled out a stack of paperback books. James Patterson, Laura Lippman, Susan Palwick. He scratched his chin where a scraggly beard grew. "These two are best sellers," he said. "I'm not familiar with the third one, and I have no idea what a 'necessary beggar' is, but the cover is intriguing."

He handed over the trade paperback showing dark hands clinging to a chain-link fence. Grenade smiled. Palwick was a local Reno author. Not a best-selling author, but a very good one. The Patterson and Lippman were new books, published just before the End. Grenade hadn't read them. The Palwick was a classic, and she already had a copy, but she didn't mind having a spare. Few other people bought books from Marmot, and he was the only scavenger who bothered with books.

"I'll give you three hard-boiled eggs," she said.

"Five."

"Four."

"Deal." Marmot stuck out his hand.

He also had tools, but none was anything Grenade needed. Finally, he pulled out his prize, a brick of .22 cartridges that would fit her rifle. They haggled, and in the end, Grenade paid him 20 strips of rabbit jerky.

That's when Houdini appeared on Marmot's shoulders. Dini, a ruddy cat, rubbed his cheek against the boy's. For Dini, there were no strangers, only friends he hadn't met yet. Marmot reached up to skritch the cat's ears. Grenade picked up the cat and settled him on her own shoulders. She had no idea how he'd gotten out of the house, but that's why he had that name.

Marmot left with his food and tools, and Grenade locked the gate. She took Dini back into the house, then put away her new purchases and cleaned up the cat bowls. She was glad the water still ran because it was a hard necessity. Grenade sat down with her spiral-bound notebook and began to write. She used to keep a journal on the computer, but now she used notebooks and pencils. She liked to write down what she'd been up to, what she thought about it, what her wishes and dreams were. In the morning she would write what she planned to do that day and what her hopes were; in the evening she would write what she'd accomplished, what she thought about it, and how she planned to do better the next day. Between journaling and the cats, she didn't get lonely living by herself.

Today was a typical day in the wild west, year one PW. Post war. It wasn't much of a war. The asshole-in-chief hit the red button after feeling emasculated by Estonia's female head of state, nuking Tallinn, which was awfully close to St. Petersburg. Europe endlessly discussed economic sanctions, but before they made any decisions, Putin nuked Washington D.C., solving one problem. Civil war broke out in America, and the union fell apart, each state declaring its own martial law. The rest of the world stepped aside and said fuck it, cutting off contact, and went about its business.

Locally, Reno emptied out as people fled back to where they'd originally come from. It wasn't entirely lawless, but it had reverted to the wild west. Grenade was lucky, having learned to shoot years ago when her best friend, Jack, taught her how to protect herself after her divorce. He helped her recover her essential self, too. Jack had died in the early chaotic days, and she missed him terribly. He was the one who'd resurrected her childhood nickname. Her father had called her Grenade because of her red hair and fiery temper when provoked beyond reason. There was a lot of gray in that hair now, and menopause had softened her temper, but it was a good name for the post-war world.

The manufactured housing community where she lived had emptied out to only about 10 percent occupancy, with people simply abandoning their homes. Even the corporation that owned the land pulled out. Reno still had running water, but no electricity. The homes still looked okay, with a distinct lack of weeds, thanks to chemicals sprayed before the End.

Grenade had a .38 revolver and a .32 semi-automatic in addition to her .22 rifle. They all came in handy during the bad times and the End times. The .38 was a good, solid gun. The .32 was a little small, but useful enough since she was a good shot. The .22 rifle she used for hunting. She still lived in her small three-bedroom home that she'd bought with her divorce settlement, cooking and doing laundry in the backyard. Grenade was glad she'd bought this home with a decent-sized yard since many of them in the community had no yard at all. Most lots in mobile home communities were barely larger than the houses, but this lot backed up to a flood run-off arroyo, so there was more room than most people had.

Today was Grenade's day of rest, partly thanks to the case of canned cat food. She had enough food for herself on hand for a few days, and she was caught up on laundry, wood-chopping, and other post-war household chores. She sat down with the new Lippman book, but she was interrupted in the first chapter by a knock on the front door.

The Banshee, a fawn Abyssinian, ran to the door and stretched up toward the doorknob. *"How!"* She howled. Her tail switched.

Marmot had already come by, and Grenade wasn't expecting any other scavengers today. She picked up the .32 from the coffee table and stood to the side of the door. "Who's there?" she called out.

She heard a mumble through the door. No, it couldn't be. Not Tweedledum. Gun in hand, she opened the door.

"Hello, Roger," she said to her ex-husband. She was surprised at how calm she felt, but the lack of any longing for him or their old relationship was a welcome feeling.

"Long time no see, Renee," he said to her with a grin.

"Not goddamned long enough. What are you doing here?"

Roger's grin disappeared when he noticed the gun in her hand. "Whoa, what's that?" He took a step back.

"This is my friend, Beretta," Grenade said. "Why are you here?"

She stepped out onto the front doorstep, closing the door behind her so the cats wouldn't escape. She didn't want Roger in her house.

"I came to see you," he said. "Look, I brought gifts."

He lifted his hands to show a slightly-swollen can of peaches and a half-empty jar of peanut butter.

"Not interested," she snapped.

"What are you doing with a gun?" he asked.

"Maybe you didn't notice, but the world has changed a lot recently," she said, holding the gun steady, fighting against a slight tremor in her hand. Her vision blurred a bit again, too, but squinting helped with that, and it made her look angrier, she figured. Damn these symptoms though. But she certainly couldn't let Roger know of her condition, because he would exploit it, just as he had every other weakness of hers.

Grenade and Roger had been divorced for 16 years after 20 years of marriage and a year of contested divorce. He had asked for the divorce, but he expected her to do the paperwork to get an easy Nevada divorce without giving her any of the equity in their large home, so when she hired an attorney, he had done the same and fought the divorce every step. She got her share of the property. He had married again the moment the divorce was final.

"Look, honey, I just wanted to say I never should have left you," Roger said. "I miss you."

"Uh-huh," Grenade muttered. "Where's your wife?"

Roger's glance flickered down, then back up to look Grenade in the eyes again. "Connie left me."

Liar. Grenade didn't remember him being so easy to read. He must have a big secret he was afraid she'd find out, or else he wouldn't be so obvious. Or maybe Jack had taught her even more than she'd realized.

"And you thought I'd take you back?" Grenade barked out a laugh. "Fat chance, Tweedledum. But you did stay married longer than I expected. I thought you would divorce again when you hit 50 a decade ago."

Roger's glance turned away again. But before he could answer, there was a crack and zing sound. Grenade reflexively pushed him to the ground and ducked behind a bush. She looked around but didn't see the shooter. There was a new chip in the concrete doorstep.

"All right, come in," she said. She grabbed Tweedledum's elbow and pulled him into her house, locking the door behind them. Dammit. She didn't want him in her house, but damned if she'd let him die before finding out what was going on. She loved a good story.

"What was that sound? What's going on?"

"Someone shot at you. Who's after you?"

Roger didn't reply. Grenade scowled at him.

"I don't know," he finally said, not meeting her gaze.

"I'm tired of you lying to me. You can go back out there and face the shooter by yourself."

His plump, pale face got whiter. He'd gained weight since she last saw him at their divorce hearing. Back then he was trying to look attractive to prospective girlfriends. He wore his hair the same, looking like he used a bowl on his head as a guide for his haircuts. A good wind could blow his bangs back off his forehead and expose his rapidly receding hairline.

Grenade swallowed a few expletives. She was going to have to help him, at least until she figured out what was going on. Nearly every word out of his mouth so far had been a lie, and she had no idea what it would take to get the truth out of him.

Maybe she should kick him to the curb, but she could always choose to do that at a later time. And she was also curious as to why the sniper hadn't fired again. Or stormed the house to fire through the windows. Courteous sniper, this one.

She turned around to see Dini, Aidan, the Banshee, and Fiona watching from the kitchen door. They were just as suspicious of Roger as she was.

Of course, Tweedledum didn't have any luggage. He didn't have any food—besides the spoiled peaches and almost-gone peanut butter—or tools, or anything useful. He still professed not to know who was shooting at him, and Grenade still didn't believe him. But she said he could stay until dark.

Tweedledum claimed to have walked from his home in south Reno—formerly their home—but Grenade knew even without his tell that it was a lie. It was nine or 10 miles. With gasoline expensive and in short supply, a lot of people walked or rode bicycles these days, and Roger used to hike back when they lived in Fresno, California, but that was more than 20 years ago. What was his game?

It wasn't the lying that bothered her because he'd been a world-class gaslighter back when they were married. She'd gone from being an independent woman to an emotionally-abused wallflower. When he had his mid-life crisis 17 years ago and told her he wanted a divorce, it was the best gift he'd ever given her, because after she'd gotten away from his influence, she realized that when she thought she married for love, she'd really married out of fear of being alone. The irony was she was alone now and much happier.

And Grenade was angry that Tweedledum had ruined her day off. She was angry that she had to deal with him at all instead of sitting and reading one of her new books with a cat or two on her lap and a glass of cool sun tea on the coffee table. Goddess, but she missed ice.

The cats were still avoiding Roger, even though he crouched down and made kissy noises at them, trying to look friendly and attractive. Grenade wished she could ignore him, too, but she had to deal with him to get him out of her home. Her hands started to shake, and she clenched her fists to hide the disease's tremors.

"Renee! Do you have something to drink?"

"This isn't a social call. Tell me what's going on and why I should care, or I'll shove you back outside for the sniper."

His face crumpled, and his eyes glistened. But he looked her in the eyes.

"Connie's trying to kill me," he said.

"Your wife? What did you do to her?"

"Nothing." He didn't meet her gaze this time. Finally, he continued. "She wanted to move back to Ohio, and I didn't. That's why we split up. But she wanted me to find a way to pay her for the equity in our house, and she didn't listen when I said there's not really any equity anymore since few people use money and nobody's buying houses in Reno."

While the real estate facts were correct, it still sounded fishy to Grenade, but she'd never met Connie, so maybe Connie was crazy as a bedbug, to mix metaphors. She'd married Tweedledum after all. Then again, so had Grenade.

"Where's your ham radio? I would think you'd be busy helping people communicate these days," she said.

Roger looked down. "Connie wouldn't let me take any radios when she kicked me out."

"You show up with no food, no tools, no radios, nothing helpful, you keep lying through your teeth, and you have the nerve to ask for a huge favor from me. Why should I help you?"

Roger shrugged. Grenade scowled.

Against her better judgment, Grenade finally agreed to let Roger stay the night. The sniper was still out there, and Grenade hadn't gotten to the bottom of Roger's story yet. But she let him share her dinner of cool sun tea, rabbit jerky, and dried apple slices. She let him use her sleeping bag in the spare bedroom, and she locked her bedroom door.

The Banshee woke Grenade. *"How! How! Now!"* the small cat howled.

She jumped out of bed, grabbed her gun, and staggered into the living room. Her legs feeling all pins and needles, where Roger had his hand on the front door knob. Grenade leveled her gun at Tweedledum.

"Hold it right there, asshole," she said. "What are you doing?"

His glance flickered down again as it had so often the previous afternoon.

"Don't lie to me. I've had my fill of that. Look, there's a round chambered. If I pull this trigger, you're dead."

He dropped his hand from the doorknob. "You can't shoot me. You'll wake the neighbors. Someone will hear and wonder what's going on."

"Did anyone rush to help you when the sniper fired? And remember that popping noise we heard on and off all afternoon? That was gunfire from people hunting. And I don't have any neighbors on this cul-de-sac. No one cares, especially about you. Why are you sneaking out in the middle of the night?"

"When did you learn how to shoot? I thought you hated guns."

"Don't change the subject. Jack taught me for self-defense after our divorce. And don't get any ideas. Jack called me Annie Oakley because I'm a crack shot. Talk."

The Banshee howled again. "Now!"

"What's with that cat? Since when do abys talk so much? I would have gotten clean away if she hadn't woke you."

"That's the point. If you don't talk soon, Aidan's likely to come spray you. Or maybe Fiona will scratch her claws up your leg. Or I'll put a round through your skull. What did you steal from me?"

Roger's shoulders slumped. He rammed his hand deep in his pocket and brought it out in a fist. He had several gold rings and a white gold pendant, all of which belonged to Grenade. He dumped them onto the end table.

"I thought I bought you more jewelry than this, Renee," he said.

"Most of it was costume jewelry. I only kept the real pieces, because the price of gold has been too low for them to be worth enough," Grenade said. "At least I thought so until now. Did you steal Connie's jewelry, too?"

There was a knock at the door. Tweedledum jumped about six inches, forgetting Grenade's gun pointed at him.

"Who is it?" Grenade shouted.

"Connie Martin," said a woman's voice.

Grenade motioned with the gun for Roger to move away from the door, and she unlocked the deadbolt and opened the door. A blond woman, a few years younger than Grenade and Roger, stood on the doorstep. She had a .45 gun.

"Wow. You don't mess around, do you?" Grenade said, nodding at the gun.

"What were you planning to do with that pea shooter?" Connie said with a laugh.

"When I hit them right between the eyes, they don't usually get up again," Grenade replied.

"Fair enough."

Roger looked back and forth at the women, then started to sidle off.

"Wow!" howled the Banshee.

"Stop, Tweedledum," said Grenade.

He stopped.

Grenade pointed her gun at him again.

"We were just talking about how he's been stealing from us," she said to Connie. "Is that why you're after him? He spent all afternoon lying to me, then he made the mistake of trying to sneak out in the middle of the night with my jewelry."

"I knew he'd taken my jewelry, both the stuff he bought me and stuff my first husband gave me," Connie said. "But what really lit my fuse was when he killed my dog."

"*Yow!*" howled the Banshee. Fiona squinted her eyes and twitched her tail. Aidan and Dini watched from the bedroom door.

"You said it, sister," Grenade said. "I never would have figured he had the balls to kill anyone or anything."

"He didn't kill Cadbury himself," Connie said. "He took my senior chocolate lab to a vet that didn't know him and lied, saying my sweet boy bit some children and needed to be put down. Then he told me Caddie had bolted out of the backyard when a car backfired. But he was stupid enough to keep the vet receipt, which I found. That's when I bought a gun and took lessons on how to shoot it."

"Maybe I should let you shoot him," Grenade said.

"If you shoot me, you'll never find Connie's jewelry. I don't have it on me. It's in my car," Roger said.

"I knew you didn't walk, Tweedledum," Grenade said.

"Stop calling me that!" Roger shouted.

Grenade and Connie smiled. While they were distracted, Roger reared back and kicked the Banshee across the room. She landed with a thud but without a peep.

"Banshee!" Grenade cried. She dropped her gun and ran to the cat.

Roger grabbed the .32 and darted out the door. Connie took off after him with her .45. Grenade heard a shot. She ran into the bedroom and got her .38 and ran out the door.

Connie was lying in the road, bleeding. Roger had stopped, apparently in shock that he'd hit her. He still held Grenade's .32 that he'd taken. Grenade, without thinking, stopped, took aim, and put a bullet right through his heart. He crumpled to the ground.

Grenade turned back to Connie, who was sitting up. She'd been hit in the upper arm, but it was just a flesh wound. Grenade helped her stand up.

"Are you okay?" she asked.

Connie nodded. "What about Tweedledum?" she asked.

"I think he's dead. I aimed for the heart." Grenade walked over to him and kicked his side. He didn't move. She felt for his pulse. "Yeah. He's gone."

"What about your cat? Is she all right?"

"Yeah, she'll be okay."

Together they dragged their ex back to Grenade's home and into the backyard and put a tarp over him until they could decide what to do with him. They went back and searched for his SUV, finding it parked in a driveway one street over. They found Connie's jewelry, as well as more jewelry that neither of them recognized. He had his ham radios in the back of the SUV and plenty of tools and canned food—none of it rotten, like the peaches he tried to palm off on her. It took three trips, but they hauled it all back to Grenade's house, then left the keys in the vehicle.

"It'll be gone by dawn," Grenade said. "Speaking of 'gone,' we need to hide the body. If we drag it to the arroyo behind my yard, the coyotes and crows will clean up the mess for us."

Back at the house, Grenade bandaged the wound and found some aquarium antibiotics for Connie to take to avoid infection. The cats checked her out, sniffing her hands and legs, and rubbing their faces against her, marking their territory with cheek gland hormones. Grenade made up the bed in the spare room and let Connie sleep there. Dini and Aidan slept with her. The Banshee—looking much better—and Fiona slept with Grenade.

In the morning, the two women had scrambled eggs in the backyard after feeding more canned food to the cats.

"You seem too strong and independent to ever have been married to Roger," Connie said. "What's your secret?"

"My best friend, Jack. I got suckered into the marriage originally by my own feelings of abandonment, of being afraid to age alone. I'm an Air Force brat, and I never had a stable home. I was attracted to Roger partly because he'd spent his whole life in Fresno. After the divorce, Jack helped me find myself again."

"Where's he now?"

"He died during the bad times when a sniper targeted an elementary school near Jack's apartment. Jack managed to kill the sniper, saving the kids, but not before the sniper shot him. Jack died of his wounds. I miss him so much."

Connie reached across the picnic table to pat Grenade's hand. "I'm so sorry, Renee," she said.

Grenade blinked back tears. "I go by Grenade now, ever since the bad times. Jack revived my nickname then. My dad used to call me that." She cleared her throat. "You need a nickname. Something befitting your personality, post-war and post-Tweedledum."

Connie smiled. "Do you have any ideas?"

"My nickname comes from my red hair and fiery temper, but also because it sounds a lot like Renee. Because of the way you stormed into my house yesterday with that big gun, ready to righteously shoot down Tweedledum, I'd like to call you Combat."

Connie smiled. "I like that. You're good with names. How'd you come up with Tweedledum?"

"I never liked calling him 'my ex-husband,' because it made him mine, connected us in a way I didn't like, and I didn't want anything to do with him. I tried calling him 'that person I used to be married to,' but that was too awkward. Remember Tweedledee and Tweedledum from the Alice in Wonderland books? Fat men, shit-eating grins, with bowl haircuts? Tweedledum suited him."

The two women cleaned up the cat bowls and their own dishes, then looked at their bounty in the third bedroom. A box of canned goods, a box of basic tools—always handy—and five different radios, as well as a repeater.

"Nice batch of treasure," Grenade said. "Did you pick up any ham radio skills living with him?"

"Oh, yes. You?'

"Yep. Of course, without a tower and antenna, we can't do as much, but this will help us communicate pretty well."

The women walked back outside to drink cool tea in the fresh air. A light knock on the gate signaled Quail, who arrived with goods and gossip. She looked suspiciously at Combat until Grenade introduced them.

"Quail, this is my good friend, Combat. She'll be living here with me now. She knows how to handle herself. Combat, this is Quail, one of the best scavengers around."

Combat shook hands with the young woman. Quail sat down at the picnic table and opened up her large canvas messenger bag. "Here's what I've got for you today," she said, and began to pull treasures out of her bag.

Quail's most valuable merchandise was always her gossip. Grenade served her cool tea and homemade fudge in payment for that. Today she had a story about a lucky scavenger who at dawn found an SUV that didn't seem to belong to anyone in the area. No one recognized it. There was nothing in it, but it had a full tank of gas and was in good working order. Very valuable.

Grenade felt a twinge of regret at letting that go, but she didn't need a car. And she didn't want anyone to connect the car with her and Combat. Besides, she had a good life as it was. And now with Combat to help her out with chores, food, and more, Grenade wouldn't have to worry about the signs of multiple sclerosis that she'd been noticing: the tremors, the blurred vision, the pins, and needles feelings. There was now someone around to make sure the cats would always be taken care of as they deserved.

END

Our City of Ouroboros

By Michael Craig

Rain fell in sheets on Boise, overflowing the gutters and depositing filth on the streets. It was how I'd felt when I stepped back onto home soil for the first time in years. Like the filth left behind after the war had bankrupted the country and they'd disbanded my unit.

I was working at Barbie's Brews and Cues as a bartender and bouncer when Becca took my measure and playfully elbowed me in the ribs. A smirk touched her lips as she loaded her tray with the drinks I'd set up, "What's got your goat? That old Harley break down? Or did you miss your workout?"

Oddly, she was wearing makeup and her inexperience showed, as a hint of a bruise peaked through.

"My Harley's fine," I smiled, "and don't miss workouts very often. How else can I keep you safe from those creeps?"

In the corner, a group of drunks erupted in cheers.

She turned so that her ass was the center of my attention. "Reactive micro-thistle skirt." She grinned.

Looking closer at the soft gray skirt, I watched the fine needles stand up, almost as if sensing my proximity.

"Envenomated?"

Shrugging, she gave me a vacant-eyed look. "I don't know what that means, sir. But if touching without permission makes them piss razor blades for a few days, I'd say it's cosmic intervention."

I cut my laughter short as glass smashed into a wall near the dartboard. "Stop breaking the glasses, please," I commanded, though the word please had undertones of "or else."

The meathead flipped me off and turned to laugh with his friends.

Becca was younger than me by at least fifteen years. She was blond and beautiful and not impressed by me at all. "Is that all you'll do?" she scoffed.

I chuckled a little, "They're blowing off steam. No need for hero shit."

Becca's glare lanced me with disappointment, "I'd have thought a soldier would take this more seriously."

"Coordinating hospital evacs. That's serious. Putting down insurgencies is serious, and what did we get for it?" The tension was too tight in my voice, so I huffed as if amused.

"I was booted to the curb. Now I'm building up some cash and heading for the Oregon Coast."

Pointing at me with her chin, she said, "You're gonna stand there while they bust up the place, Jax?" a look of disgust passed over her.

I was born Jackson Crandell Shank, and I didn't like nicknames, but for her, I allowed Jax.

"The fact that the army shit on you isn't an excuse to give up on everything," she scoffed.

"They broke a glass or two," I said, dodging her comment. "I'll pick up more from the dollar store. I won't let them get out of hand."

It was another half hour and two more trips to their table before a loud crash demanded my attention. I hadn't seen what had happened, but Becca was on the floor with broken glasses and bottles shattered everywhere. Behind her, the meathead was standing a few feet back, pumping his hips as he pretended to take her from behind.

"What the fuck?" I shouted.

But Becca was already getting to her feet, despite the cuts on her knee and hand from the broken glass.

"It's nothing, Jax. I tripped," her voice quivered with fear and humiliation.

"Yeah, ya stupid goon. She tripped!" the meathead bellowed. He was about my height, though he had twenty pounds on me, and kept looking to his friends for affirmation.

I took Becca's hand and examined it, "I can fix these with some Dermal Mend if—"

"You think that fucking skirt could stop me if I wanted you? You think that ape could?" the meathead slurred.

I waved him off as insignificant.

"We're trained to get past obstacles like that," he laughed sadistically.

"Hell, we could just run you both out to the electronics dump and leave you there."

Anger flared instantly in me, but Becca raised her hands to stop me from doing anything. "They're blowing off steam. No hero shit, remember," she said.

It kicked me in the guts to hear my words repeated back to me.

"I understand the swarms still devour people out there," he taunted.

"Go easy, Marv," said a man in an IXSC hat.

IX Security Consulting, AKA the Niners, were little more than a shakedown organization, but they were as close to cops as we had. I didn't need the trouble. I pushed him away. "You're drunk. Go home."

"The swarm only sees filthy viruses that need sterilizing, not a person. The nasty bastards inject you with custom cytotoxins."

"You know what that is, boy? It breaks down your tissues, then blood seeps from your orifices until you're nothing but loose skin. And"—he looked leeringly at Becca's chest— "cosmetic additions."

They all howled. "Fake ones look like lumps in the rug when they're done!"

My hand shot out and slapped the jerk on the cheek like a grandmother popping profanity from a kid's lips.

He glared at me and touched his bleeding lip, "you touched me?"

His eyes swept over his friends, "do you know who I am?"

A threat was sure to follow that statement, but I wasn't in the mood for it. These idiots didn't intimidate me.

He drew his gun faster than I would have thought a drunk capable of and pressed it to my scalp. I raised my hands in surrender. Okay, I was a little intimidated by the gun.

"Not so fucking tough now, asshole," he leaned in close enough for me to feel his spit pepper my face.

Pivoting my hips, I slammed my hands into both sides of his wrist and forearm and sent the gun flying. Then I continued through the motion and brought my elbow around, slamming it hard into the man's temple. The blow sent him to the ground, and his friends leaped to their feet in shock.

With a glance, I could tell Becca didn't believe me.

"Hey, assholes, pick up your friend and his gun and get the fuck out. We're closed." I commanded. I marched toward them as they all quickly exited.

I tossed Becca a cleaning towel for her bloody hand and went to flip the closed sign over. I glanced out the window and locked the door.

"Let's get you fixed up," I offered, "it wouldn't be worth the tips to stay open after 2300 hours on a Tuesday anyway."

Outside, the streets were too busy. Vansteaders, nomads, often wandered through to places like The Tombs, a city that had popped up in the old military bunkers near Umatilla, or crossed the wastelands down to Slab City in California.

The term came from the 20s when a bunch of hippies started loading up their lives in adventure vans and traveling in search of better prices and peace of mind.

"It's the Ouroboros," Becca breathed next to my ear.

"What kind of neo-tribal society is popping up now?" I muttered, then wondered if a band was raging and I was just too old to know the reference. It didn't matter. None of them were coming in for drinks.

"They heard about the central district food warehouses and the excess food the Big-Agra people are hoarding," Becca said as if reading my mind.

"They pass through in the fall, when the harvest crops fall off trucks, then head back to the warmer climates. It's a survival strategy."

Turning a touch, I could see that she was leaning close to peer out my window. Her soft green eyes reflected something akin to sympathy, or maybe commiseration. I'd seen it in a thousand soldier's faces. The shared understanding of suffering.

"A lot of them camped at the sports complex, but that didn't last long," she murmured, then stepped back as I let go of the curtain.

"The Niners?" I asked.

"No, the Niners showed up, but the camp vanished. Maybe they moved to Camel's Back Park or something?" she shrugged again. "I think they communicate through the FM."

The Dermal Mend was in the office, but she could hear me easily enough. Better yet, I could hear her.

"The farmer's market. I thought that was mostly just the co-op forum," I called as I started reaching into the safe for the magnetic lockbox to stash my evening's take. It wasn't as good as a bank, but at least it meant the banks weren't charging me to hold my money while they used it for their own purposes. With the high-carbon nanotube cable anchoring it to the safe, it wasn't going anywhere, and only I had the code. I know it sounds paranoid, but banks lost their federal insurance when the economy crashed, decimating the major metropolises.

"It is. More or less. People pick up freelance work, odd jobs, and stuff. They can even find dates," Becca replied.

Inside the lockbox was my nest egg, which was just enough to cash out and split town. I paused for a moment to look at the single silver challenge coin from my old unit. Call it a lucky charm, but I'd always kept it close, even after we'd disbanded. It had been nice to matter once.

"Find dates? Is that how you got the shiner?" I said as I slipped back into the main bar just in time to see Becca looking at me with her fingers near her bruised eye. I laughed.

"A date? From the Market?" she scoffed.

"No, I was freelancing a job off the Market. I knew it was dangerous," she said flippantly. "The contact told me it would be, but the money was great." She hopped up on the bar and rested her leg on a stool.

I found a chair, grabbed an ice bucket and some bar towels, and started cleaning the cuts on her knees, "what did you have to do for that much cash?"

I laughed as she swatted my shoulder, then hissed as I dislodged some glass.

"It wasn't a big deal. I got the number from a friend. The jobs are all contracted out by a word-of-mouth thing. Anyway, the job was to sneak out to the abandoned subdivisions and squat in a house for as long as I could," she hissed again as I sprayed it with disinfectant.

"I was there one night. The second night, the Niners caught up to me and escorted me out. I was just glad they only roughed me up and didn't rape me," she motioned to her skirt and smiled warmly.

"So that's how those jerks knew about your skirt?" I asked as I sprayed some Dermal Mend on her cuts, watching as the edges sealed and the wounds became invisible.

"It wasn't those Niners, but you know how boys talk."

Reluctantly, I let go of her leg and reached for her cut hand. "It doesn't sound worth it," I muttered with just a hint more judgment in my voice.

"It was worth it," Becca argued. "They paid my legal bills. I was even at work on time. Sure, I got a black eye, but I also got almost enough cash to head to Santa Rosa."

Her hand was worse than the knee, so I broke out the Dermal Weld gun. It was small, like a tattoo gun mixed with a sewing machine, and the tiny needle-like tip could more precisely line up and seal the edges. "What's in Santa Rosa? Micky Craig and his old dog, Ted?" I said, but I could see at once she didn't get the song reference.

"Well, I have family there, but mostly because it's a smaller city, like Boise, and I know my way around. Besides, I understand there might be a project starting there soon, and I like getting set up and ready for a fresh job."

"What, waiting tables?" I kept my hands steady as I worked, the process moving slowly as I lined everything up.

She had wide, high cheekbones, a Greek nose, and a jawline that reminded me of a young Jennifer Aniston, but unlike the famous actress, her lips were a full kissable bowtie. As you can guess, she was a popular waitress.

"No, I wasn't always a waitress," she swatted me again.

"I used to help coordinate and recruit for Amazon-Microsoft. I just know talent when I see it, but I worked remotely out of Seattle, and with it gone, the job went too."

With a sigh, I sat back and started packing my stuff. "Yeah, it's hard to find decent work," I muttered, taking my kit back to the office.

Becca slid off the bar, the motion lifting her skirt high enough to make me do a double take, then regret it as a blush touched her cheeks, "It doesn't have to be," she called, and I heard her coming toward me.

"Well, I have this gig," I said with a light laugh, but we both knew our jobs sucked.

"These people I was freelancing for, they paid well, and they offered me another job, but…" her head tilted a little as she tried to figure out how to say what she was thinking.

"I'll admit it. Those Niners got to me. I mean, their buddies know where I work," a flush flowered on her cheeks, and she quickly turned away.

"Anyway, it might be enough to help you get out of town," she said.

Suddenly, she was pushing a piece of paper into my hand and leaning in close enough to make me a little dizzy, or maybe it was the late hour and the smell of her perfume. "Just think about the job. If you're interested, call them. Tell them I gave you the number."

I looked around at the mess. "Yeah, well, I'll clean up and think about it."

"Oh, no," she snickered and pushed me toward the door.

"You stay out at the veteran barracks. I live upstairs, so I'll clean up. If you take the job, great. If not, that's cool. You can tell me tomorrow."

I headed back to Barbie's early, kind of hoping to catch up with Becca and see where things led. I wasn't happy to see a closed sign on the door when I arrived. Jessica from the day shift was standing there, trying to peer inside.

"Hey, Jessica. What's up?" I called.

She slowly stepped back, scowling, "It's empty."

"What? Henry didn't make it?" I asked.

Jessica turned around and gave me a withering glare. "I don't know. Henry was opening, and I agreed to come in for the early shift, but no one is here, and it looks like the bar's cleared out," she pouted and stomped her foot in a way that was almost comical until the reality of what she'd said set in.

"Wait. Both Becca and Henry are gone?"

"And the booze. Are you getting it, smart guy? We are officially out of work."

My stomach sank. It didn't take a genius to realize I was screwed. "Oh, hell no. They couldn't have cleared it out in one night." I unlocked the door and raced back to the empty office. Everything of value was gone except the phone, which was hard-wired to the wall. Below it, open on the floor, was my empty lockbox.

"FUCK!" I screamed and drove my fist into the wall. "I'm such an idiot!" I turned my back to the wall and slid down it. No wonder Becca had rushed me out. Why take a dangerous job when she could just take my money? She must have seen me looking at my challenge coin. One thing was clear. I was screwed. Again.

"Hey, I'm out of work too. I have obligations, so don't give me your sob story. Save it for someone who cares," Jessica growled and stormed off, leaving me sitting there with nothing.

Nothing except the phone number Becca had given me. "It has to be fake," I grumbled, but something pushed me toward the phone. Desperation, maybe. Or perhaps I wanted to confirm that I'd been played perfectly. Regardless, I made the call.

"Two-fifty upfront and a thousand sterling dollars payable upon completion of the job. There will be a full contract emailed to you to review, and you may cancel or complete the job at any point in the next twenty-four hours. Does that sound agreeable, Mr. Shank?" the feminine voice on the other end of the phone said in a steady no-nonsense tone that left me seeing dollar signs. This wasn't a job. It was a mission, and it was right up my alley.

"All I have to do is sneak into the old electronics factory area, remove a transmitter, and replace it with an updated model? What's the catch?" I already knew what the catch was, but I wanted her to say it. I wanted nothing ambiguous.

The line was quiet as I looked down at my notes. They'd supply me with surveillance drones and transport me out to the deserted factory, but I had to deal with the drones and cops. Great.

"Avoid the Niners, Mr. Shank. And avoid the Xenowasp swarm. Your references and experience assure me you can handle this job, and our payment should ensure you keep our confidence."

Xenowasps. I'd seen the damn things in action in Africa. A Chinese research company had made cyborg wasps programmed to hunt down rogue viruses and eliminate them. Put a few million Xenowasps into the air in a city and you could inoculate a population in days.

Of course, the government had weaponized the technology almost at once. All they had to do was get the Xenowasps to target the virus antibodies and anyone who carried them. Once a Xenowasp found a target, it would signal the swarm, and each sting pumped cytotoxins into the host until there was enough to turn the host into soup.

"I'm a man of my word," I said absently.

The woman's tone grabbed my attention. "Good! Mr. Shank, we only have so much assurance we can give, and our excellent reputation is vital. For my organization, it means everything."

Our conversation hadn't been long, but there was an odd zeal to the way this woman spoke that sounded unpleasantly familiar. She was too sure of herself, confident to the point of boastful, but for no apparent reason. Maybe that should have been a red flag.

"Don't worry about the swarm. I can use an EMP device to take them down. It's how we did it in Africa," I said.

"NO!" she shouted. The intensity nearly caused me to drop the phone.

She cleared her throat, "sorry. We count on those swarms as a deterrent. Do not destroy the swarm. If you do, you get nothing."

I dropped the equipment in less than an hour, and my ride showed up shortly after.

"Zane," a man called, unfolding himself from the electric cart he was driving and extending a massive hand, "I'm your ride, but don't expect me to get closer than a mile to that place."

I shook his hand, and despite being a big guy myself, I felt dwarfed. Zane was large in every way possible. Even his hair flared out like a lion's mane, an effect made more pronounced by his honey-colored eyes.

"Jackson," I responded as I climbed into the right side of his cart.

"Sorry for the ride," said the big man sheepishly admitted, " I borrowed this from a friend."

Glancing around, I saw they had decorated the cart with pink cartoon kittens, but the big guy didn't seem to mind.

The rest of the ride, he went on and on about the food famine. As large as he was, I understood why he worried.

"Big Agra has all the pollinator patents. I never thought Idaho would be this bad. Did you know they have a commission for growing potatoes? I guess they've had it for decades," he blathered on until he pulled to a stop.

I could tell he was passionate, but I was fed up. I didn't care about his cause or what the hell the people from the FM post were up to. I just needed to get paid. A grand was enough to get me out of Boise, but that would be about it.

The desert southeast of the old computer factory, just off the remains of I-84, smelled like burnt building materials, wild sage, and stale dust.

I had come in from the southwest after catching a lift to Eisenman Road and Freight Street. I knew I could cross the old freeway and drop into a construction yard. The yard was a mess of old building machines, from loaders and tankers to road grinders and pavers. They all stank of grease and dust, but they had enough irregular angles and cast enough shadows to make for good concealment.

The factory had shut down long ago. I could see where it had been stripped of copper wire and anything useful. Now it was just a mile or two of wasteland and empty shells.

I scanned my surroundings, seeing nothing, but something in the back of my head pushed its way forward. "There must be more to all of this than replacing a transmitter."

The Nano-Fab I was headed for, Photronics, was a shell of what it once had been. The industry had taken a colossal hit after the Xenowasps had done so much damage during the war. Riots had staggered entire cities like Portland and Seattle, then laid them to waste with disease and swarms. After that, the fear drove the villagers into the streets, literally destroying businesses like Photronics.

Why is this urgent? I wondered.

I remembered the brief.

"We have a transmitter that urgently needs replacing. You will recover the first and set the second. We believe the response time will be approximately twelve minutes if the Niners come. If you are caught, stash the equipment for later recovery."

I didn't much like working on so little information, but they paid well enough so far. "What choice do I have?" I muttered and used my phone to activate the GPS app.

The signal shown on the map overlay was large enough to take up the space between buildings. In real life, I knew the transmitter was about the size of my fist and located up out of sight. All the clutter and destruction would limit the chances of anyone spotting it, and putting it up higher would limit them even more. Here, they'd put it on the remains of a water tower.

I didn't want to walk right to it. While it didn't feel like a trap, it also made little sense. Any punk off the street could do this gig for pennies.

Why pay someone like me? I wondered.

These people had my account information, so it wasn't like they were unaware of my history. But even so, the price they were paying was high. Why was it so urgent, and why did it require a heavy like me to pull it off?

"Seems like as good of a time as any," I dropped my pack long enough to pull out one drone. Within seconds, it was airborne, and I guided it toward the site. I'd have only a few minutes to scout. Then I'd have to shut it down or risk the automated police scanners pinpointing it. There were ways to bounce signals through surrogate cells, but if I worked it right, the thing would be down in less than a minute.

The screen showed more detritus but nothing of concern. A small patch of greenery in a depression drew my attention for a second. Something about it seemed off, but I didn't have time to investigate. I shut the system down and grimaced as I watched the drone fall from the sky. "I can pick it up on the way out," I told myself as I hurried toward the transmitting site.

Anxiety frayed my nerves like a cut rope under pressure, but I didn't understand why. I felt like too many things were in motion and out of my control. That's how you die; you lose control and play the enemy's game.

Rushing through the open area, I made it to the ladder and climbed. Scrutinizing the landscape, I became aware of what had my senses screaming. The Niners were headed my way.

They were still a kilometer and a half away, so I had enough time to drag the little transmitter out and set it up. Then I ripped the other one off its perch, tearing wires and tin clamps away from rusted metal before allowing myself to drop a story to the unlevel ground below.

I landed with a thump, and my momentum carried me to one knee and drove something sharp and hard through my pants and into the flesh. There was no time for pain. I wasn't sure if they knew where I was, but there was nowhere to hide. I would get caught. The only question was, what would they find me with?

"The bushes," I whispered. I ran for it, scooping up my fallen drone.

The bushes were a bramble of twisted vines with small white flowers and green clusters, but it was fine. I just needed to hide the old transmitter and my pack of illicit drones.

I dashed past the spot and dropped my pack, the drone, and the transmitter into the depression. I smiled as I saw them disappear into the throngs. My leg didn't feel steady as I moved. Blood was seeping down, making my path obvious to anyone looking to find it.

I picked up the low-droning buzz. I'd heard it in Africa and Panama, the drone of flying insects flowing toward me like a wave of hostility. I ran.

The swarm was close, but it hadn't become frenzied yet, and I remembered the law of the jungle: when faced with insects, run. Pick a direction and run deliberately and with determination, but get away.

Something tagged me on the back of the neck. Then a searing pain slammed into my triceps as another one drove its stinger deep into my skin. I made it to the open desert before they took me down. I fled from the swarm but also from the whirring of the electric engine of the Niner's intent to subdue me.

I guessed that they'd hit me with a stunner because the world flooded with light, and before it faded, I saw everything in my field of vision, despite being paralyzed.

Booted feet moved toward me, their heavy steps kicking up fine dust that drifted back the way I'd come. "You can run, but no matter how fast you are, you can't outrun modern surveillance and comms," an electronically modulated voice said.

Two others grabbed me and hauled me to shoulder level. They were dressed in anti-swarm vac suits and glared at me from inside their helmets.

"I hate chasing vagrants. It pisses me off," one of them said.

I couldn't raise my head to see the face of the man who'd slugged me, but as I hit the ground once more, I expected a kick would follow it. I wasn't surprised when the impact sent me rolling. What did surprise me was something else. Just ahead of me, emaciated corpses lay in a shallow ditch surrounded by more vines and flowers. I'd seen this before. Xenowasp swarms had done it, though not recently.

"We could leave him here for the swarm. He's that asshole from Barbie's. He deserves it," one of the men said.

The thought sent a chill through me, even as the fire hit me from several new stings.

"No, the last one walked out. We can't risk it," a deeper voice responded.

"I say we beat him till he can't walk. I want this guy to suffer!" the meathead whined.

"You can beat him, but we're taking him in, Marv. Tell the chief he fell down."

They both laughed.

For a second, just before the blows fell, right in front of my eyes was a Xenowasp, crawling back toward the water tower. It was small with an overlay of conductive material and a Photonics logo on its back. As it took flight, I could see a soft yellow hue on its legs. Then someone kicked me in the head.

I woke to the sound of access cards clattering off each other. Before me, a sinewy man, perhaps five years younger than myself, leaned against the bars and peered in, then considered his datapad. "Jackson Shank, retired army, Special Operations Group. I bet you never expected to see the inside of one of these cells." He looked me up and down, then back at the picture. "You've held up okay. Aside from the ass-kicking you got from Marv." He glanced up, amused.

"I stay out of trouble, eat well, exercise, and swipe left on FM girls. Some are just insistent, like Marv," I said in return.

The cop grinned. "Marv said he thought you were stung a few times." His glance traveled over my arms and exposed skin. "I don't see any necrotic flesh."

I'd wondered about that as well. The spots should have been gray and pus-filled, but nothing. It was as if they had lost their venom. "I guess they didn't like how I tasted," I said.

"I hear you're old friends?" he replied without mirth.

"So, you run this place?" I responded without answering.

"I run this district, yes. I guess I'm lucky you were just trespassing. Unless you're part of whatever the hell's going on in the streets?"

"Chief …" I let it hang, thinking he would fill in a name; he didn't. My guess was ex-military, Africa, or the Mongolian campaigns. Retired after a ten-year deployment and being a Niner was his idea of a peaceful life. A man too mil-spec for civilian work and too burned out to stay in. Sounded familiar. "Anyway," I continued, "I'm just trying to earn a buck, and I can't earn a living working as a bouncer at Barbie's." I shrugged, hands out as if indicating the obvious.

"I know that for the last week or so, we've had Vansteaders drifting in from the north," he said.

"I know that they've been leaving odd marks around town, and somehow, that crowd keeps their camps a step ahead of us. We're constantly finding people like you where you don't belong, doing ridiculous things, like cutting branches off old fruit trees or scavenging old, worthless PVC pipe. There's been something every night, but my gut tells me there's more."

"I don't know—" I interjected, but the cop raised his hand, urging me to wait.

With a deep breath, he gave me an even stare, "I get it. You were doing a job. But it seems too convenient. All around a mob is growing, and right before me is a man who knows how to run an insurgency."

"Chief Abebe. A lawyer paid his fine," a voice called. Another approached with those clacking access cards.

"I'll cut him loose, Boss, and drop him off downtown," said Marv, the meathead, with a vicious grin.

"You'll go back to the front desk and stay there! You're on desk duty until you learn to cool it," Abebe told him with ice in his voice.

"That's bullshit," he complained, "I can't earn a share if I'm on desk duty!"

"You're free to go, Captain Shank," Abebe said.

At that moment, a youthful woman with bobbed platinum hair and round glasses strode down the hallway. She held a briefcase under her arms and a paperwork wad in her pale hands. In minutes, she was directing me. "Sign here. Initial there. Don't forget to date. That's for the other lawyer."

It was dizzying, but I did as she said and was soon walking out of the station with a small clear bag filled with my possessions.

"Thank you for the assistance, Mr. Shank, but your services are no longer required. As agreed, we paid your legal fees and fines."

I took the girl in and watched as she carefully organized every document and stored it away with librarian-like efficiency. She was blond and pretty but too big for her clothes; it looked like she hadn't worn them in a while. I suspected she'd recently gotten fit, rather than scrawny, that she was someone who had made a major change in her life.

Quickly, I checked my bank account and frowned when I saw that the completion fee hadn't been deposited. "Hey, wait up. I didn't get the rest of my money."

"Read your contract, Mr. Shank. In the event of your arrest, you forfeit any remaining payments to cover your legal expenses."

I ran after her, still yelling, "What contract? We had a verbal agreement."

"It's in your email, as stated in the phone call."

"No, fuck that! I need that money," I sprinted to catch up with her.

"The contract was emailed, as we stated on the initial phone call," she called over her shoulder, not even a little bit concerned about me catching her.

"I thought you people kept your word!" I bellowed.

She kept putting distance between us, "Read your contract, Mr. Shank. Everything you need is in the fine print."

Her tone was mocking me as she slipped away.

Panting, I came to a stop and rested my hands on my knees. I was furious, frustrated, and determined. I was sick of being played. "Fuck this! You want to play it that way?" I yelled, "I can play it that way!"

After I stopped panting, I walked back to the Niner station. A strategy was what I needed, but before I could compose a plan, I knew I needed to compose myself.

I was halfway through my walk when my head cleared. A chuckle dripped from my lips. I couldn't rightfully get that mad; I was the one who'd gotten lazy. I was the one who knew better than to get involved in other people's lives, and yet, I'd leeched onto Becca like an old fool. I couldn't figure out how the rest of it had played out. The cop had been right; it was too much of a coincidence. There had to be more going on. I needed to find that lawyer.

I sucked it up and got a ride to the Niner station, the money be damned. I was furious at being played, but I focused on finding the lawyer. I knew someone had to have the lawyer's information, and if I could find the lawyer, I'd get some answers. By dinnertime, I was pounding on the fence and yelling at a camera, knowing someone would eventually respond.

It didn't take long before Chief Abebe marched toward the fence and paused a few feet away, his arms crossed. "Shank, you'd better have a damn good reason for interrupting my dinner, or I'll let Marv and his friends come out here and stomp a mudhole in—"

"Who was the lawyer?" I demanded.

"The cute blond who got you out?" Abebe shot me a leering smile.

"What's her name? Where do I find her?"

"I don't think Vansteaders have offices, but she was under license Aster Harris. What are you after, Shank?"

I moved closer to the fence, close enough for him to tag me with his stunner if he wanted to. "I don't know what's going on here, and I don't think you do either."

Abebe shot a furtive glance down the street. "I'll tell you the truth, Shank. I was in Africa. I know when there's calm before a storm. I just don't know if I'm facing a spring shower or a hurricane."

"No soldier wants war," I said with a note of familiarity, "we've both been there."

He nodded, and I knew I had him.

"I'll tell you what. Give me the lawyer, and I'll find out what this is all about, fill you in, and we're squared," I offered.

Abebe smiled, and his posture eased, "If you're playing with me, I'll be the first to break your arms and feed you to the Xenowasps."

Striding forward, he offered a wolfish grin and a sincere handshake.

The Fort Boise Military Cemetery was one of the first things built in Idaho. Perhaps one percent of the population knew it existed. It was where they'd buried the soldiers when the white man had first settled this part of the world, and it was where those soldiers had soon been forgotten. It only mattered to me because it was where I would find my answers.

Reserve Street wasn't easy to make my way up. Below me, a food riot had broken out somewhere near the old co-op, and around me, they'd narrowed the road with barriers on both sides, making the houses accessible only by foot. Someone wanted access control and had it.

Near Mountain Cove, a large gathering of bikers and street punks had laid claim to the parking lots and skate park in a makeshift nomad camp. Three of the biggest, leanest pipe-hitting badasses I had ever seen were manning a roadblock; among them, was Zane.

"You shouldn't be here, Shank," Zane said in a firm but apologetic tone.

"I need to talk to my lawyer. Her name is Aster Harris," I said with overtones of bar-buddy familiarity. "Is she in?"

"Get lost, asshole!" the reincarnation of stone-cold Steve Austin barked.

I pressed my point.

Making enough noise to get someone's attention, was my specialty, even if it got my ass kicked.

"Mr. Shank," a female voice called out, and I knew it was Aster, "so, you learned my name and tracked me down. Well done."

She slow-clapped as she walked toward me, "Kesey, Zane, let him through."

"Yeah, back off," I said menacingly.

"No one knows me by that name here, and I would be pleased if you refrained from using it." She'd lost the scared mousey appearance and now reminded me of a fang-and-claw kind of predator. A revolutionary, just like I'd seen in Africa.

"What should I call you?" I asked. "The Lawyer seems a little stiff with hints of evil genius in some kind of awful TV drama."

"Everyone here calls me Amanda."

I moved closer, and everyone was instantly on guard. I felt like I was facing a religious cult whose leader had been affronted. They moved in sync, no jostling, no effort wasted until they were around us with only Amanda, a group of women in robes, and some thin children huddled close to them.

Amanda looked up at the goons, then focused on one and smiled. "Don't worry. Mr. Shank isn't here to cause us harm. We hoped you would show up," she winked, "I'm afraid we've been recruiting you."

"You mean Becca was recruiting me?" I said as the pieces came together.

Amanda gave me an approving nod, "Becca and Harvey set up the bar to recruit people. Not you specifically. That was just good luck."

She took my arm like we were old friends, "I thought the micro-thistle skirt was too expensive for a waitress."

She laughed, "Once she discovered your special operations background, we did a little digging. Mr. Shank, we need a man of your expertise."

"Why would I help you? You ripped me off. Twice. And what makes you think you can afford my expertise?"

"We can afford it. The question is, can you do what we need?" she crossed her arms and examined me like a side of beef.

"You mean the food riots?" I asked incredulously.

"The food riots are important, but they aren't our primary objective. What we need is a diversion. Twenty-four hours where you keep the Niners busy, and we work on our project."

"A riot isn't good enough?" I chuffed in laughter, "Look, I got played, and I want my money back. This isn't my problem."

"It's everyone's problem, Jax," she walked into the crowd, and people parted around her. "These Big Agra corporations own most of the politicians. Hell, they attend the same board meetings! They've made it so we can't produce our own food anymore. They killed the bees, so now we rely on chemical pollination processes copyrighted by Big Agra." She gestured to several thin women and men, most of whom were dressed heavily to hide their emaciation. "While they live on rubbish bins."

Taking a deliberate breath, she forged on, "And housing? The wealthy live on The Bench or north end, while we get pushed into the slums of Garden City, or somewhere so far out that we have to work thirty extra hours a week to pay for travel. Meanwhile, massive tracts of housing sit vacant because no one will pay the taxes, even though someone is paying for security. It's madness," she said with a chill in her voice that shielded the fire of her rage.

"P. A. I. D," I spelled out, "as I said, it's tragic, but this isn't my fight."

"Well, I need to make it your fight. What would you say if I told you I could get you a job working as a police officer in a minor city and a two-bedroom, two-bath house with enough room for a garden?"

I laughed and took a step backward, "this isn't going anywh—"

"We did it with the casino in Pendleton, Washington. We can do it here," she stated in a measured tone that let me know she wasn't kidding.

"You had a part in that casino deal?"

"I assisted in leading the project. But, for security reasons, I won't say what we're doing now."

Amanda leaned closer, her bright blue eyes shining, "We have powerful friends, Mr. Shank. People in government who share our goals. But I need a distraction. Not just food riots. I need it organized."

"What if the project fails? Just because you got away with it in Pendleton doesn't mean you will here," I said, but I was growing cautiously enthusiastic.

"It's like I said on the phone. It's called reputation economics," she said. "It's no different from when Klout scores started being used on resumes or fashion designers started giving discounts to customers with an excellent reputation and wide internet following." She grinned. "With a strong reputation, we can accomplish anything."

"And?"

"And, Mr. Shank, if the project fails, we will pay you the difference. You win either way."

"Pay upfront. If what you say is true, I'll refund it," I grinned, looking around at the goons.

"Half. I still have to feed everyone," she pointed to the skinny kids.

Feeling abashed, I nodded and walked away to make a phone call.

Chief Abebe picked up the phone, but all I heard was yelling. "Make sure that riot gear is prepped!"

"Hey, Chief Abebe. It's Shank. I spoke with the leadership. Can we come to an understanding?"

"I don't see that happening. We agreed to pay you for—"

I cut him off.

"For information, and I have that for you. These Vansteaders are only trying to make a point."

"By tearing apart the north end?" he growled.

"They put in for the permits to protest, and they got turned down."

"No one gets those anymore!" he yelled.

"I know, but they're either a dangerous mob or a controlled protest. I don't see any other options."

Amanda shot me a glare, so I turned away from her as I spoke, "Look, I'll have them pull back tonight," I said, "get things organized. You just tell me what you can handle. I'll keep the protests to something reasonable tomorrow. Then you can run around, grabbing people for easy fines. You and the boys can clean up for a night's work. I'll get paid, and everyone's happy.

"I won't have any protests at night!" Abebe growled.

I grunted without answering yes or no, "a figure of speech. Chief, they want to be heard but not enough to end up with their heads bashed in. If they get too wild, I'll get them off the streets. No one needs to get hurt. We won't even carry any weapons. You have my word."

His voice took a savage tone, "I tell you how many people I can handle, and you overwhelm us? I don't think so. I'm guessing there are a few thousand of them out there."

I groaned like a long-suffering sibling. "You know my history, and you know I could make this hard, but I don't care about a few hippies, and I don't need a target on my back when it's done.

"I've tried working for a cause before. Now I just want the money. I know that if this gets too big, you'll call a para-military company you have on retainer, and then we're both explaining how it got out of hand to higher. How many people can you deal with before you call for reinforcements?"

"You'll be off the streets by sunset?"

"We'll be tucked in for the night," I answered.

"I don't approve of this at all, and you don't have permission. But we wouldn't panic if we saw four hundred people, as long as they aren't violent."

I grinned and looked at Amanda. "I'll have only a hundred and fifty. If I can get that many to show up."

Chief Abebe sighed, and the tension eased, "I won't forget this, Captain Shank," he said.

I felt myself flinch when he used my old rank. He thought of me as a comrade, and hell, I wasn't even playing for the old team anymore. I hung up the phone and saw the discouraged grimaces on their faces.

Kesey paced in a tight circle, fists clenched. "We can't do it with a hundred and fifty people. If he says he can handle four hundred, he can handle five hundred. If we say one-fifty, he thinks we're lowballing, but he can still handle it."

Amanda looked dubious.

"Look," I said. "When I was a kid, we had people who organized seemingly random events called flash mobs. People showing up and suddenly bursting into song or stealing a bunch of stuff. I'm planning several flash protests."

"We show up and smash things? I can get behind that!" Kesey growled.

Amanda held her up hands to silence him.

"You're not far off." I laughed and laid out the plan for them.

They arrested the first protestor at 0700.

I grinned as I put Project Sherwood's Bounty into action.

Watching the video from our car, I mumbled to Zane, "Everyone has things they don't want or need or can't use. Give people a chance to trade, and watch how many show up."

"At the Warm Springs Estates?" Zane asked skeptically.

Around us, confused people gathered. One older lady started by exchanging home-canned pears for dried chickpeas, leaving both recipients grinning at their scores. Elsewhere, a thin boyish man was holding up small cans marked 'Tomato Paste' in black marker. Soon, the market was rolling, and wealthy suburbanites stood gawking at their windows.

"The market is full. It's time to send in the protestors," I grinned as people with signs and bullhorns poured out of vans and alleys, blocking access routes.

It wouldn't take long for the Niners to break things up. Too many people were trying to muscle their way out, and too many were trying to get in. It was complete bedlam. "Move to the second site," I told Zane as he shot me an approving look.

"What has you all smiles and giggles?" I asked, but I kept my eyes on the personnel tracker.

"It's you. You try to come off so unimpressed and like you only care about yourself, but you like this, don't you?"

"I enjoy getting paid."

"You're telling me you're not enjoying this?" he scoffed, looking longingly at a popcorn stand. The city was getting into the mood, and so was I.

"No one said you have to hate your work," I called out at the next flash protest site.

"I'm getting reports of Niners pulling up at the co-op market," a caller, Kesey, reported. "I can't believe it's an actual open-air market, a real co-op market."

The Motorcycle X-Games made up for it. We rolled the ramps into place for old, fat bikers, who had been heroes of the sport in their heyday, so they could prove that they could still pull off some impressive tricks; the crowds went wild.

"The Niners are pushing through at Main and Eighth. I think they're ticked; you're so close to the old capitol building," Zane updated me.

I watched a double backflip, followed by an impressive wipeout.

"Keep them busy, at least until the jousting matches kick off. The crowd will love it, and we can melt off and let them deal with the festivities," I said.

But when I looked, Zane was holding the phone out to me. "Jax, this is Amanda," said the voice on the line, "we have an issue."

"I don't have any issues; it sounds like you have an issue. And when did you start calling me Jax?" I responded.

"Come see what we're doing. Zane knows the way."

I hardly noticed that we were headed to the foothills until we pulled onto a busted-up stretch of road, "where are we going?" I asked.

Zane only laughed. "Up Seaman's Gulch! Hold on. These roads are rough."

After bouncing around for twenty minutes, we arrived at a gated community labeled 'Hidden Springs.' a smaller illuminated sign had been added, reading 'Welcome to Our City, Ouroboros.'

Amanda hopped in our car at the entrance, "This place started out as a series of subdivisions for people with enough money to afford it. Eventually, it grew into nearly a town of its own, complete with a post office and a few little stores and businesses. Nothing larger than perhaps fifteen thousand people, but when the springs ran dry, it became too much of a hassle to deal with."

"Everyone just split?" I asked as we passed the houses.

"Nothing works like that. Everyone wanted to hope the water table would come back or that they could talk the city into piping more water out this way. But eventually, it became too much. Now it's abandoned. Perfectly suitable houses, empty."

But the houses weren't empty. People were everywhere, some raising new buildings or planting gardens and grass.

"There must be thousands here," I whispered.

"We have a hundred and seventy thousand personnel, including trained community planners, landscapers, construction crews, and more," she looked back at me, her green eyes shining like chipped emeralds.

"But the Niners will come in and take it all," I called over the engine noise.

"It's called adverse possession," she tapped on Zane's shoulder, and we came to a stop near a gathering of homeless women and children I'd seen before.

"It's political wrangling," she continued. "It's a legal process that says if we show possession, pay the back taxes on the land, we can own these houses. We establish residency by sending registered mail, and with a provisional government in place, we can establish a town. So that's what we did."

I couldn't deny it appeared to be a town. Even a few cars in need of repair sat on the side of the road. "But you said the spring dried up?" I was trying to wrap my head around it.

"This entire thing started because of that earthquake three years ago. It shifted the groundwater, and we were in business," Amanda explained.

"That doesn't explain the gardens. How—" I started to ask, but the memory of the Xenowasps from the tech dump flashed through my mind. They had yellow dust on their legs.

"Xenowasps are pollinating the gardens," I said, dumbfounded.

"That's where I came in," Zane barked in laughter.

"I helped design the source code. I didn't know they'd be used as weapons. I'd always thought we'd evolve the tech to work with crops," Zane said defensively.

"The transmitter you planted changed their operating orders. Now, instead of toxins, they carry an enzyme that they mix with the pollen they pick up, and we're in business."

That's why my stings didn't turn necrotic, I realized, "But you're a nomad biker."

Amanda bubbled with laughter. "Everyone was something before the fall. You were a soldier. Zane was a computer coder. I was a business administrator—"

"Intern," Zane shot out, earning him a dirty look.

"Anyway," Amanda continued, "we have people and resources, and we understand how to use bureaucratic systems against themselves. What we needed was a commander in the field." She shot a significant glance my way. "We need the rest of the night, Mr. Shank."

I nodded, and Zane handed me a phone.

"What the hell is going on, Shank?" Abebe shouted, his Ethiopian accent thick as he screamed on the phone.

"I just spent three hours clearing the streets of motorcycle fanatics, and now I hear you're at the Idaho Department of Agriculture? Are you sure you want to do this?"

It was a horrible idea, honestly. Putting myself in a corner would mean capture, but it would keep them focused on us, rather than on Amanda's project. I didn't have any other ideas.

"There's nothing for it, Chief. I said I'd have them off the streets by sundown, but they aren't satisfied, so we're crashing here for the night," I said, trying to sound annoyed.

There was a pause. Then, with an icy edge in his voice, he said, "Shank, if we have to come, we're coming in hard. I won't keep the leashes on."

Strategy and tactics. Adverse possession, the Xenowasps, the creation of a city. How long had they been planning this?

"I know. We won't carry weapons," I said, still reeling from the revelations.

"I won't promise the same!" the chief shouted and slammed the phone down.

Before we'd occupied the agricultural building, I'd asked for two hundred thugs, people who could take a beating without losing their heads. To my surprise, a green-eyed blond I knew had been the first to raise her hand. "I'll go, Jax. I owe you that much," Becca had said.

A mixture of rage and relief filled me. "You have a lot to answer for, little girl!" I'd growled, but it had ended in a chuckle of sorts.

Where the hell had she been hiding?

"Zane, get online. Get a local buzz going about more pop-up events. Get all of them down here at the Ag building. People have been trying to get out and see what's happening all day. I want half the city to show up pissed that the Niners are taking away their fun."

The Niners showed up in full riot gear only to find a war with two fronts. Behind them, the crowd pushed and shoved to get in, everyone thinking they were missing a rare free show of whatever musical event or expo took their interest. The Niners pushed to keep them back.

The breaking point was inevitable, and it didn't matter who'd started it. Somewhere, someone threw a bottle, or an officer swung blindly and hit a kid. I'd never know, but I saw everything go to hell.

The crowd surged, batons rose and fell, and water cannons fired. Private journalists flew drones to capture the mayhem, even as they competed for airspace with police drones, which released gas just far enough overhead to make targeting them difficult.

It was 0300. by the time they got the crowd broken up, and by 0330, they had refocused on us with the hunger of an insulted lion. They came at us with battering rams and tear gas.

We repelled their primary assault by bracing the doors and using our body weight to keep things closed, rags covering our faces. We would have to make them fight for every square inch. We threw our bodies and any furniture against doors, and we held them, making the Niners breach each new logger jam at any hard point we could find. They pulled people out and arrested them, then retreated to set up all over again.

We were on the second floor with the door caving in when Becca threw her weight in beside me. Splinters flew around us, "I didn't want your money. I just couldn't let you leave!" she yelled.

"Was I that charming?" I laughed and ordered everyone to break contact with the third floor as a gas canister flew through the window.

She found me again as I wedged a flagpole stand under the door and ran old glory through the handles. "You're the best I've seen. I told you, I know talent when I see it!"

"So, you robbed me and left me pissed off? That's not a great recruiting method."

"You're pissed off, but you're here. It gave Amanda time to work something out," She looked into my eyes, "I knew you were the one we needed."

Again, we retreated, and I lost her in the breach as we scrambled toward the roof, but she caught me again before she stepped out into the glow of the drone-filled sky. "When you thought I was in danger, you couldn't hide behind that impassive facade. Just like you couldn't ignore those half-starved kids."

Behind her, the door buckled, but she grabbed my hand as if needing me to forgive her. "I knew you were a hero," she said as the door crashed down. Then she dove into the Niners, giving me a chance to retreat.

Stunned, I stood there for a moment. I'd never been a hero, just the guy keeping my team alive or a city from falling. "Huh?" I grunted and retreated to the roof.

The remaining people piled everything possible onto the hatch, and I walked to the edge to look down at the scene below. On the lawn, our people were in lines, zip-tied and seated, bloodied and bruised, but on several faces, smiles broke through.

It was dawn when they cuffed the last of us. We sat in a line in the grass as the EMTs administered first aid.

It was all over except for a furious chief, who accepted a check from a green-eyed blond, who had come to bail us all out.

"We completed it in time. The inspectors will arrive at 0800, but the City of Ouroboros is ours. Are you ready to see your office, Police Chief Jackson Shank?"

That was over a year ago, and as I stand looking down on Santa Rosa with Becca holding my hand, I know I'd made the right call.

I didn't need a comfy job like Abebe, or the security found in my daily routine. I needed a team, a tribe, to matter again.

"What is our next project, babe?" I asked.

She smiled deviously and kicked off, racing like mad down the hill on her electric motorcycle.

"Later!" she yelled. Then she added, "I'll race you to the beach."

"I'll be right behind you in the Van," I called, and then for a moment, I watched her ride down into wine country, her blond hair flying as she rode.

I honestly didn't know what the future held.

I've made new friends and found a new team. I had a reason to do it all again, to make a difference, and maybe that was enough. But for the first time, since I'd left the military, I've finally found my way home.

My own rebirth.

The End

The Song of the Aquareens

By David Norling

They've diverted the river again. Last night I was awakened not by the usual rushing water but by its slow ebbing, first to a gentle murmur, then a trickle, then nothing. Lina seemed not to notice and slept on beside me. I got up, pushed through the tent flaps, and made my way down the wooded slope to investigate. Reynal and Smithers were already standing in the damp river bottom.

"We warned them about this," Reynal said.

"We shoulda done more than just warn them," Smithers said, picking up a muddy stone and flinging it up the riverbed. "We shoulda chased them off the mountain. Fucking squids."

"Calm down," Reynal said. "They need more water than we do. But we have to find a fair balance." Then to me, "Evening, Grant. Or morning, or whatever the hell time it is."

"Morning," I said, for a pale glow of dawn was already growing in the east. "They turned off the water again?"

"Looks like it," said Reynal. "We've still got the pond, but we can't drink that. Can't go very long without fresh running water."

"There's a stream just north of here," I suggested.

"I guess," Reynal said with some resignation. "That's a good half mile away. Long way to haul water. Let's go on up and talk to them again once it gets light."

"Let's talk to them with a shotgun," Smithers said. "Maybe that'll get their attention."

Reynal looked at me with weary eyes and shook his head. He'd visibly aged in the last few months, but no one was about to challenge his authority. Certainly not Smithers.

"We'll just go and have a talk with them like last time," Reynal said. "They're harmless enough. They just get desperate when the water runs low. Let's get some breakfast and head on out in an hour." He started toward his tent, then said mostly to himself. "Maybe we can help them figure out some kind of reservoir system."

"Reservoir," said Smithers, shaking his head and walking off as well. "Fucking squids."

Lina appeared to be still asleep when I slipped back into the tent, but as I lay down behind her and snuggled up close to get her warmth. She sighed and asked, "Is it morning?"

"Almost. The Aquareens diverted the river again. I'm going up with Reynal and a few others to talk with them. Go back to sleep."

She rolled over and faced me. "I want to come, too," she said. "I want to see what they look like. They sounded cute."

"Not exactly cute," I said. I'd told her about the Aquareens when we returned the last time. I'd described to her their pale, blubbery bodies, their webbed fingers and toes, their cherub faces, and I'd tried to make them sound adorable so she wouldn't worry. They certainly weren't as bad as some of the others that emerged after the Great Mutation, and as Reynal had said, they were harmless enough. But adorable? No.

"It's a long hard hike up the mountain," I said, hoping she would drop it. The truth was, I wasn't so sure they would be as tractable as they'd been last time.

Lina sat up, yawned, and ran her fingers through her hair. "I'm coming with," she said. "I can keep up with you. In fact, I'm not sure you all can keep up with me."

We all assembled with our rifles in front of the big dining tent. Reynal and his two grown sons, Marlon and Matt, plus Smithers and another older man named Wynn who'd only recently joined our camp. Reynal didn't appear pleased that Lina was coming along, but he didn't say anything. Smithers, I knew, wouldn't object, and would walk behind her, eying her as he always did, but he wouldn't do anything beyond looking.

"I figure it will be easier to walk up the empty riverbed like last time," Reynal said. "As far as we can, anyway. Let's stay together."

It was easygoing at first. The riverbed meandered in a gentle upslope between mixed stands of spruce, jack pine, and tamarack. Occasionally, small clearings opened and the morning sun shone through, bright and warm. Lina held her face up to feel the heat, her light brown hair waving in the breeze.

"It's been ages since I've been this far from camp," she said. "We should get out more often." She smiled and slipped her hand into mine.

I smiled back reassuringly and didn't say anything. We had a fairly secure and defensible perimeter, and I wasn't too concerned close to camp. But there was still a lot of uncertainty. Upriver were the Aquareens and I didn't worry about them too much. Downriver was another camp of people like us, a couple hundred or so who'd also somehow escaped the waves of mutation, and we got on well with them. But there were occasional loners, sometimes small bands of wanderers that crossed the river, and some of their mutations were quite startling: arms or legs oddly jointed, some so broad and muscular and hairy they looked almost Neanderthal, while others were naked pigmies with bulging eyes and hairless, wrinkled faces. Some were without speech, and others when they spoke had unnerving accents or obscure vocabulary, the English passed down to them blunted or muddled by brain or vocal cord mutations. And some were violent, there was no doubt of that. They wore the desiccated skins and whittled bones of their victims, and we kept a wary distance from them. But we had firearms, and we had yet to see any of them armed with anything other than clubs or spears, so there was a comfort in that. Still, it was a more dangerous world than I'd let on to Lina, and I loved her childlike innocence and trust that I couldn't bring myself to tell her of my worries.

A couple hours later the heat began to rise, and when we encountered the first dry waterfall, we had to move onto a path that skirted the river. When we stopped to rest in a shaded glade and drink from our canteens, Smithers asked Wynn if he'd seen Aquareens before.

"I saw a population on the coast a while back," Wynn said. "Adapted to salt water. I heard the freshwater ones are smaller." He picked up a few smooth stones and rolled them deftly in his left hand. I looked at the tight wrinkles at his temples, his inscrutable eyes, and wondered just what had driven him to us. He'd been on the move for a long time judging from his occasional comments, and he had valuable skills for the group—a week back I saw him shoot a rabbit at a hundred yards with a quick lift of his rifle, and then skin it casually while walking—but I still couldn't quite figure him out.

"I heard them, too," Wynn continued. "Just when the sun sets they all begin to sing. An eerie sound. Once you hear it you'll never forget it."

"Singing squids," Smithers said, and spat in disgust. "Well, the ocean's where they belong, I guess. Not here on our mountain if I have anything to say about it."

Around noon we crested the high bluff overlooking the Aquareens' home valley. When they'd diverted the river the last time and we came to visit them, the scene from the edge of the bluff had been breathtaking. The waters of the diverted river had flooded the narrow valley and there were hundreds of Aquareens lolling in the shallows and schooling together in graceful waves across the glittering surface. Some were feasting on trout and salmon, and others making love in small groups in open abandon on the surface, that abandon seeming to account for their exploding population. But now.

"What the hell…" Reynal said.

Lina gasped and pressed a hand to her mouth. We all froze and gazed out across the desolate landscape. The dried-up valley was littered with the corpses of Aquareens. It looked like the aftermath of a terrible battle, and we could smell their bodies beginning to decay in the gathering heat. No one moved for a moment until Smithers started walking, as if in morbid fascination, toward the carnage below. We followed him through the trees and down into the harsh sunlight of the valley until we came to the first dead Aquareens. They lay grotesque and bloated, their ashen faces masks of torture, pores weirdly distended as if their very skin had gasped for breath in their final death agony. Lina wept quietly. I put my arm around her and turned her face into my shoulder so she wouldn't have to see.

"What happened to the water?" Reynal asked, but no one had an answer.

We walked on until we came to a small sheltered eddy of the old river, shielded from the sun by a cluster of boulders and the shade of giant juniper bushes. In a shallow puddle lay a female Aquareen, dead, and two of her small children, one dead but one still barely alive. It blinked and gasped, dipping its tiny webbed hand into the water and then dabbing it on its lips and eyes. Lina quickly squatted down and cupped up some water from the puddle and dribbled it over the Aquareen's face. It closed its eyes and lapped its tongue gratefully at the water.

"We have to help them," she said, her face streaming with tears.

Reynal and his sons looked away while Lina continued to scoop water onto the Aquareen. It was a generous but wasted mercy. There was nothing we could do for it.

"Quiet," Wynn whispered suddenly, and crouched behind the rocks. He pointed to the hills on the other side of the valley. Tiny dark shapes were moving along the ridgeline, at first only two, but then more emerged, five, then a dozen, perhaps more. We all ducked behind the rocks and juniper, and Smithers lifted his rifle to peer through the scope.

"You keep your finger off that trigger," Reynal hissed, then said softly, "Who are they?"

"Or what are they," Smithers said. "I can't tell from this distance. But there's a lot of them. At least twenty, maybe more on the other side. I think they are clothed."

"That's a good sign," I ventured.

"Maybe," Wynn said immediately, then turned to Reynal. "Take them all back down and alert the perimeter watches. I'll circle around to see what we're up against."

"You better come with," Reynal said. "It's too dangerous."

"They'll never see me," Wynn said, and as if to prove this he quickly slipped into a thick stand of tamarack and was gone.

Lina was still dribbling water on the tiny Aquareen. "We can't leave it here to die!" she cried.

"Nothing we can do," Reynal said, beginning to back away cautiously.

"Lina," I said, but already knew it was a lost cause. I dropped my rifle, shrugged off my pack, and emptied its few contents onto the dirt, then pulled a poncho from its case and lined the inside of the pack with it. Lina picked up the baby Aquareen and set it gently inside, then we scooped water from the puddle and poured it into the pack until its tiny body was mostly submerged.

"Let's go," Reynal said again. I shouldered the pack and picked up my rifle, Lina grabbed the few items I'd dumped on the ground, and we all began moving for the cover of the trees. All but Smithers. He knelt there still, sighting through the scope of his rifle, and panic began to rise in me when he slipped his finger onto the trigger.

"No," I whispered.

"Pow, pow, pow," he said. He turned and grinned at me maniacally, then ran past to join the others in retreat.

We arrived back at camp in the late afternoon. The children crowded around the backpack, gazing in wonder at the baby Aquareen.

"What's its name?"

"Can it talk?"

"I want to hold it!"

Finally, Lina set off with the children and a couple of their mothers to release it into the pond. After they had gone, the camp leaders, as well as a dozen men and women who did shifts on the perimeter watch, met in the dining tent to discuss the situation. Reynal described what we had seen to the others who hadn't been with us.

"I'm surprised," he added, "that McGinn hasn't sent some of his folks up here to see what happened to the water." McGinn was the leader of the group somewhat larger than ours, perhaps numbering two hundred or so, camped a couple hours downstream from us.

"Probably figured it was the Aquareens, just like last time," I said.

"I guess," Reynal said. "Well, we need to send word to them about what happened up mountain. Normally, we'd go on down since they are the larger group, but given the threat—if that's what it is—is closer to us. I think McGinn should come up here to discuss the situation."

"Plus Wynn will be coming back here," Marlon said, "once he gets an idea of who, or what we saw up there."

Reynal nodded. "We've all had a long hike, so can I get a couple volunteers to go downriver and invite McGinn up?"

A few from the perimeter watch, who were still armed from their shift, raised their hands.

"Fine," Reynal said. "Why don't you set off? Hopefully, you can get back before it gets too dark."

"I'll go, too," Smithers said. "I ain't tired."

Reynal shook his head. "I'd rather have your gun around here in case we get some visitors."

This pleased Smithers. However irritating he could be, he was the best marksman among us. He had once even saved Marlon Reynal's life by a clean headshot on a bear—or at least something that resembled a bear—at fifty yards. Reynal himself would never forget that, much as Smithers got on his nerves.

We all took a rest, and when I got back to the dining tent the day's cooks had prepared a dinner of trout collected from the empty riverbed. I was about to go down to the pond to call the others back, but just then Lina's sister, Asha, returned to pack some food up and take it back down to them.

"The children are just crazy about the baby Aquareen," she said. "There's no way they'll sit still for dinner here."

"Is it taking to the pond?" I asked.

"Lina's swimming with it. It seems very attached to her already. We're all watching from the bank, so we're going to make a picnic of it."

"Why don't you take a few raw trout down for the baby," I said. "I don't think Aquareens eat anything cooked." I didn't know that, but it sounded true when I said it.

Reynal was sitting across from me, and he didn't appear pleased. Finally, he said, "Smithers, why don't you go with and keep an eye on them? Take your gun. We still don't know what's going on."

Smithers stood, slung the gun strap over his shoulder, then picked up his plate and followed. When they'd gone Reynal gave me a long look.

"Grant," he began, then paused and poked at the fish on his plate with his fork.

"I know," I said. "Wasn't a good idea."

"Lina's heart's in the right place," Reynal said. "I know that. Leaving it there to die, that would have been terrible. But all the others were dead. There is nothing we could do for them."

Reynal was right, of course, and I knew it was a mistake the whole time I was carrying it down the mountain. It wasn't like it was a pet. Aquareens were human, or at least related to us. It would learn to talk, to reason, to feel all the emotions we feel, and in the end, it would learn the crushing agony of being completely and utterly alone.

"Maybe when Wynn gets back we'll learn what happened," I said. "Maybe there are other Aquareens further up the mountain. Or maybe…" I paused. Or maybe what?

"Maybe," Reynal said, and then turned back to his dinner, and we spoke no more of it.

A few minutes later McGinn, his daughter, and a handful of their clan arrived. McGinn was a big man, barrel-chested, with a full black beard and dark, penetrating eyes. It was only when he laughed that you could look past his imposing exterior and see the warm, caring man that he was. His daughter, Meghan, was just the opposite; petite and unassuming on first impression, she had a caustic wit, never laughed, and was always heavily armed. She stood now slightly behind her father, scoped rifle strapped across her back, a knife, and an old Glock holstered on her hip on a bullet belt bristling with ammo.

"We've had our own visitors, is why we didn't come up," McGinn said after Reynal had given him a quick summary of what we'd seen earlier in the day. "Meghan here"—and he turned and nodded approvingly at his daughter—"saw a dozen or so, well, we don't really know what they were, walking along the bluffs south of us. She got some of our best guns together and went to investigate. They were gone by the time they got there, but there was some evidence they'd been there a while. Sheltered fire pit, some food scraps. And prints. They are wearing some kind of footwear. They're not barefoot."

"Maybe the same group we saw," I suggested. "But that's a lot of ground to cover."

"Could be," Reynal said. "Or they're split up. Wynn was the last new one to show up here, and he came alone."

"What's his story, anyway?" asked McGinn. "Has he been out beyond?" By which he meant, I supposed, beyond the central mountains and valleys we'd already explored. We really didn't know much of the world, or what was left of it, beyond that.

"He's been to the coast, he mentioned today," I said. "I have the impression he's looking for something, or someone, but he changes the subject when you ask him anything too personal."

"Mark of a wise man," McGinn said. Then added after a moment, "Sometimes."

Reynal finally waved them all to the table. "Please, have a seat. Have some dinner. The dried-up river coughed up a whole mess of trout. More than we can use."

"We got our share as well," said McGinn, and they all sat and joined us for dinner. Afterwards, we walked out to the empty riverbed and McGinn passed around a canteen of home-stilled whiskey while we discussed what to do next.

"We'll need to get the water turned back on eventually," Reynal said, "or we'll have to move and find some other source. I'm just not comfortable taking too many guns away while we're not sure who these folks are."

"Yeah," McGinn agreed. "Let's hear what this Wynn says when he gets back."

Reynal had another swig at the whiskey. "Might be a good idea to bring along some of this here reinforcement if we do need to go up mountain again," he said, shaking the canteen before handing it back to McGinn.

"That can certainly be arranged," said McGinn, and gave a hearty laugh. His daughter didn't laugh, but reached for the canteen nonetheless.

A little while later I decided to head down to the pond and met Asha and the children on the path coming back. The children were talking excitedly about the Aquareen, giggling, and imitating its flapping hands, I guessed a kind of dog paddle it made in the water. Asha said that Lina would be coming in a minute after she settled the little one down. That's what she called it, "the little one," as if Lina had a new baby she was tucking in for the night.

When I got close to the pond I saw Smithers sitting on a boulder up on the hillside, partially hidden behind the low-hanging branches of a tree. He had his rifle pointing toward the pond and was sighting through the scope. A sudden wave of panic washed over me and I began running toward him. He must have heard the rustling of the bushes as I raced along the path, for he slowly lowered the rifle and turned to look at me. There was a peculiar, irritated look on his face, as if I had interrupted him in some important task. He stood, shouldered his gun, then hopped off the boulder, pushed past me, and headed up the path toward the camp.

After I reached the edge of the pond I understood what Smithers had been looking at. Lina was standing in her underwear in the shallow water, and she was naked from the waist up. She was cradling the baby Aquareen, and it looked almost as if it were nursing at her breast.

"Lina," I said.

She turned and gave me a joyful smile. "She's so adorable," she said. "She won't let me put her down. She just wants me to hold her."

"Why are you undressed?" I asked. "Smithers was…"

"I know," she said. "That creep." But she seemed not to care, so enthralled was she with the Aquareen. And then I noticed the scratches. Lina's neck and chest were covered with little red streaks, some of them with tiny beads of blood, and I saw immediately what it was. The Aquareen's little webbed fingers had sharp nails, and even now they were kneading at her breast in a way that must have been painful to Lina.

"She kept pulling at my bra," Lina said. "She didn't like it. It was like she thought it was attacking me, so I took it off. See, she's calm now."

And I could see she—for apparently, it was a she—was calm, her little grey eyelids blinking, seeming to fight sleep.

"Let's go get you bandaged up," I said. "We have some aloe back in the tent."

"Oh, it's nothing," Lina said in a soft whisper. I saw the Aquareen's eyes close finally and her head loll softly against Lina's arm. Lina waded quietly to the pond bank and laid her tiny charge into the water among a cluster of sheltering rocks. She then dressed quickly and we made our way back to our tent.

Night settled over the camp. Out of the north, a wind kicked up, rustling the canvas of the tent. I stepped outside to pull Lina's clothing off the line where we'd hung it out to dry, then stood for a moment scanning the shadowed edges of our little clearing. I had the eerie feeling of being watched, but by whom or what I had no idea. Above us, dark clouds were moving in, obscuring what seemed to me now in my uneasy state, a nightscape of cold, malevolent stars.

Wynn had not returned.

Nor did Wynn return in the days that followed. We waited, tense and watchful, scanning the surrounding hilltops for movement or smoke, but never again saw those we came to call "our visitors." Finally, Reynal and McGinn decided that we needed to investigate, but carefully, leaving our perimeter watches in place but sending out scouting parties to probe the encircling hills.

I was teamed up with Meghan McGill and two others from her group, men I'd met before but whose names I couldn't recall. From the outset, there was no doubt who would be taking the lead.

"We stay together," she said, sliding a full magazine into her Glock. "No hide and seek, no hunting, no slipping into the bushes to pee."

"You want to watch us pee, Meg?" one of the men said, then shot a grin at the other. Meghan gave him a long, withering look and the grin died on his face.

"Let's move out," she said, and like obedient foot soldiers we shouldered our rifles and followed. We headed south, picking our way through a shallow ravine littered with boulders and the charred and stumped remains of firs burned out in a wildfire the previous summer. The clouds that had drifted in over the last few days, dark and threatening, still refused to release their rain but threw ominous shadows across the hills.

We found nothing unexpected throughout the morning, and when we stopped in a clearing to rest and eat around midday Meghan sat apart from us some distance away on a little knoll with a good view across the valley.

"What's her deal?" I asked the others while we sat and ate.

"Deal?" one of them asked. He had a long face with dark, drooping eyes that made him look like he was about to drop off to sleep.

"I mean, what's she so pissed about all the time?" I asked.

The other one laughed. He had fiery red hair and blotchy complexion, but unlike Droopy seemed to have an unshakeable good cheer about him. He was eating pumpkin seeds, and spit out a few shells before answering.

"She's in a good mood today," he said. "If she gets pissed off you'll know it."

"She's had some misfortune," the other added softly. "Might be like that myself if it'd happened to me." And then he told her story briefly, told how a few years back she'd been picking wild berries with her mother and younger sister one day when they'd been assaulted and taken by a group of what we called Neanders—naked, hairy, speechless beasts that usually prowled in packs but generally avoided us for fear of our guns. They'd held her tied to a tree for three days, and she'd had to watch while they killed and ate her mother and part of her sister before McGinn and his men finally found and freed her and slaughtered the Neanders. "She learned to shoot after that," he concluded, "and right well. I've never seen her unarmed since, and I sure wouldn't want to cross her about anything."

"If you're done talking about me," Meghan called from her knoll, "we can move on out again." I was certain she couldn't have heard us from that distance, but her instincts or intuition seemed honed to a fine degree, and I found that strangely comforting. She was, after all, leading us.

It was several hours later when we heard the gunshots, first a few isolated pops, then several bursts of what sounded like a machine gun. Meghan's hand flew up and we all instinctively crouched down, listening intently. We waited maybe fifteen or twenty seconds, then Meghan straightened up and glanced back at us.

"My father's team has that sector," she said, pointing in the direction the shots had come from.

"They found something, maybe," I suggested.

She shook her head, and I could see her finger tapping at the trigger guard of her rifle. "They don't have any automatics with them," she said. "We have company. Let's go."

She began running toward a knot of trees on the ridgeline and we followed, but fear and adrenaline were rushing through my veins. I guessed the other guys were just as reluctant because they were running in a semi-crouch and began lagging behind. When we caught up with her at the crest she already had binoculars out and was scanning the valley below.

"There," she said, pointing to the far slope of the valley. "I think…yeah…it's my father's team. They're standing out in the clear. They're OK."

"But the automatics…" I said.

"Let's go find out," she said, and we began running in switchbacks down the hillside. It took us a good fifteen minutes to get there, and when we arrived McGinn and his team were standing at the edge of a little gully. They'd clearly seen us from far off and showed no surprise when we ran up.

"Meghan," was all McGinn said, not even turning to look at us. We all gazed down into the gully and saw there seven Neanders, four men, a woman, and two young children, all shot to death in a little makeshift camp littered with the skins and tiny bones of what appeared to be rodents.

"A massacre," said one of McGinn's men.

"Like we've been saying," McGinn said, "we have visitors. I'm sure they saw us coming to investigate the gunshots, and they just left us alone. They went off into the forest there,"—he nodded toward the north—"and with all the firepower they're carrying I'm not inclined to follow them."

"But why are they stalking us?" I asked.

"What I was wondering too," McGinn said, then waved the muzzle of his rifle at the bodies in the gully. "But now I'm beginning to think they just might be protecting us."

When we got back to camp I looked around for Lina and found her, of course, in the pond swimming with the Aquareen. She was at the far end, some thirty yards out, where the pond abutted a dense wall of reeds and bushes, and where lily pads choked the murky surface of the water. I called out to her, and she turned and waved, then dipped underwater with her pale little companion.

"She's hogging him."

I turned and noticed Asha and her two children sitting on a little sloping bed of moss at the water's edge. It was her son who'd spoken, a towheaded boy of five with a splatter of freckles across the bridge of his nose.

"The Aquareen?" I said.

"She won't let us play with it," he said sullenly. "We can't even pet it. It's not fair." He scowled and threw a rock into the water, where it plunked up a tiny splash and sent rings out onto the sunlit surface. His little sister added her protest as well, throwing a clump of moss that didn't quite reach the pond.

"Lina's afraid it might catch something from one of us," Asha said, "because it's so small. She thinks it needs to get accustomed to our, I don't know, our germs or something." She gave me a concerned look, and I could read in her eyes that she didn't buy it, that she thought it was something else. As did I. I was becoming increasingly concerned about Lina, who spent the better part of every day in the pond, and was no longer participating in the life of the camp as she had done before.

Asha stood up. "Well, let's go, kiddos," she said, reaching down and taking the little girl's hand. "Naptime."

"For me too," I said. "I'll have a talk with her later when she gets out." I headed off with them, then branched off to my tent. I was exhausted from the day's hike, the fear, and the adrenaline, and I couldn't clear my head of the image of the slaughtered Neanders and the echo of it I'd heard in Meghan's story.

I was awakened sometime later by Lina slipping under the blanket. Her hair was wet, and her naked body was cold and clammy and smelled of pond water. Because Lina was naturally shy and reticent, and because we slept in a tent within earshot of several others, our lovemaking had always been a restrained, whispered affair. But now she climbed onto me as she'd never done before, breathless, insistent, tearing at my clothes, and finally her hands clawing at me, her nails scratching and digging painfully into my neck and back. "Oh baby, oh baby," I heard her gasping, and it was only when it was too late that I understood, with a rush of panic, that what she was really saying was "a baby, a baby." Afterward, she lay panting beside me, her body still eerily cold and damp, a look of bewilderment on her face, as if she had no idea what had just happened, as if she'd suddenly become a stranger to herself.

It was in the days that followed that I began to notice the changes in her. Almost as if she'd become suddenly pregnant, Lina began to gain weight, to fill out. But no, that wasn't it. Rather, it was as if her flesh began to redistribute itself. Her hands swelled slightly but not her feet, which seemed to thin out and elongate. Her thighs became more muscular and her breasts seemed to flatten themselves against her chest. In a certain light, her pallor turned a peculiar hue, losing its flesh color and becoming greyish and in places almost translucent. It was all so subtle that I thought my eyes were playing tricks on me; one minute it was there and then she would move, or the light would shift, and she seemed once again the same Lina I knew and loved so much. I tried to talk with her about it a few times, told her she didn't look well, but she just brushed it off; "Don't be silly," she said, "it's all the swimming." And then she laughed. "Maybe I'm a little waterlogged. But I feel just wonderful!"

And then one morning I woke up beside her and knew immediately that something was terribly wrong. She was breathing irregularly, a faint, wet, choking sound in her throat, and when I reached over to touch her I realized she was burning with fever. I went to stroke her back and felt there a peculiar ridge of cartilage where the smooth delicate slope of her spine should have been. "Lina," I said and turned her over to face me, then felt myself recoil violently. Her face was barely recognizable, her chin had receded, her cheeks and forehead had puffed out, and her eyes had sunk like cold grey stones into the depths between them. I realized with sudden horror and disbelief that she was becoming more and more like the baby Aquareen she spent all day swimming with in the pond.

I clawed my way backward out of the tent, hyperventilating with fear and disgust, and once outside in the cold, misty dawn I vomited again and again onto the damp ground. Then I staggered to my feet. And ran. And ran. And ran.

An hour later the morning haze had lifted and a warm, fresh sunlight filled the valley. I sat at the base of a tree looking for some thread of sanity, some tiny hope I could pinch and pull to unwind the madness I felt was strangling me. You had to believe your own eyes, didn't you? Seeing is believing; it must be. But if something couldn't possibly be true, well, then it wasn't. I'd had a nightmare, I'd seen something that wasn't there. It was dark in the tent. Shadows play tricks. I was sick, delirious, hallucinating. I'd eaten something, something poisonous. Hadn't I thrown up as soon as I got out of the tent? Even now I felt feverish, and that feeling was oddly comforting, because if I was ill then maybe Lina wasn't, maybe when the fever broke I would look around and the world would be just as it was before.

I stood and began walking again, at first aimlessly, then gradually retracing my tracks, moving almost unconsciously back toward camp. It wasn't a decision really, but once I recognized it, I accepted it. I would go back, sneak back, see if possibly Lina had gotten up, gone to eat breakfast, gone to the pond. I would see her standing there at the water's edge, testing it with her toe, her hair waving in the breeze, her small upturned nose, her bright eyes, and joyful smile…

I stopped at a bend in the stream that had become our new source of fresh water. There was a pool where the water collected before cascading over a small dam of boulders and snagged timber, and I bent down to drink from cupped hands. I washed my face and then on a whim plunged my head into the crisp, clear water and opened my eyes. Swirls of bubbles nearly obscured my vision, but through them, I could see the bottom of the stream and tiny minnows there picking among the pebbles.

Then a shadow fell over me, as if an errant cloud had suddenly obscured the sun. When I pulled my face from the water it resolved itself into the shadow of a man.

"Grant."

I wiped my face, and it took me a moment to clear my vision. And there he stood.

"Wynn," I said.

He was on the other bank of the narrow stream, and there was an odd expression on his face, half smile, and half puzzled concern. He was not alone. There were three men with him, two of them wearing battered, wide-brimmed hats, the third bare-headed, an older man, balding but with tufts of grey hair above his ears, and with kind, but weary-looking eyes. All of them were armed.

"What are you doing with your head in the water?" Wynn asked.

I honestly didn't know, wasn't sure how to answer, where to begin, so I asked instead, "Wynn, where have you been?"

Wynn glanced inquiringly at the older man, who nodded.

"Quarantine," Wynn said. "They saw us up by the dead Aquareens, and they don't take any chances. Not with that."

"Quarantine?" I said. "Against what?" But I understood already, and dread like some evil bile crept up into my throat and suddenly I couldn't breathe.

"Aquareens. It's not a mutation, or not one like the others anyway. It gets passed on."

"It seems to be a kind of contact mutation," the old man added. "The slightest exchange, fluids, blood, the smallest scratch, anyway it finds its way into the bloodstream it just explodes in the body. Infection is obvious within a week, and there's nothing to reverse it."

They were still standing on the opposite bank of the stream, and now I understood why. I also understood why they were looking at me so closely.

"Did any of you touch any Aquareens up there?" the man asked. "Even a dead one?"

"No, of course not, no," I said, the lie coming instinctively. "They were all dead. We…we saw you up on the hills there—that was you, right?—and we didn't know who you were, so we hurried back to alert the camp."

"And no one touched any of them? Are you sure?" The old man held his gaze on me, searching.

"No," I said again, lying now with desperate conviction, lying for my life. "Wynn, you were there. We just…we were frightened. We left right away and went back to camp."

The four of them exchanged glances, and then the old man nodded. "It's up to you, Wynn," he said.

"I'll do it," Wynn said. "Grant, I'm going to come back with you and talk with the group. We'll need to quarantine the camp for a week, and they'll watch from outside until it's certain it's safe."

"Sorry," the old man said. "Necessary precautions. We've had some…incidents, not just with these Aquareens, but some other mutations as well. After the quarantine we'll come in and discuss moving, that is if your group is interested. It is certainly your choice. We have two large settlements up in Old British Columbia. Towns, farms, the beginnings of industry. We've been pushing our way south for a long time now, picking up groups of survivors where we can. It's much safer there than out here in the wilds, but like I said it would be your decision. We just want to talk. Safely."

Wynn walked carefully across the small dam, stepping lightly on the irregular rocks, and joined me on the other side. We set off, walking the path we'd all worn fetching water, and he asked how everyone was at the camp, what had happened while he'd been gone. I answered briefly and evasively. I could barely speak. I felt a crushing weight on my chest, and so I wouldn't have to keep talking. I asked him about his quarantine and our visitors. While he described the group—all men, a platoon of heavily armed soldiers—my mind was reeling. Quarantine. Contagious. Any contact. Blood. My god, Lina was infected! And if Lina was… I had been touching her. Intimately. She had scratched me! Did I feel anything, did I feel different? Right then all I felt was terror, the desperate need to escape. Now. Because if we didn't I was certain we would end up just like the Neanders, shot to death in some gully.

As we approached the camp I began lagging, and when Wynn turned back and looked at me, I said, "Go on to the dining tent. I'm going to go get… Go get Lina. We'll meet you there in a minute."

Wynn gave me a puzzled smile, but turned and went on, while I cut through a stand of firs and, once out of his sight, dashed towards our tent. I threw back the flap and saw immediately that Lina wasn't there. I looked around quickly, grabbed a backpack, blanket, and a little store of nuts and dried fruit we kept for evening snacks. I raced to the pond and looked around desperately. At first, it appeared deserted, but I finally spotted Lina and the baby Aquareen at the far end, huddled together on the surface surrounded by lilies. They were not moving. Afraid to call out, I raced around the pond to the bank nearest them and whispered as loud as I dared, "Lina! Lina!" She turned her head slowly and looked at me with her grey, sunken eyes. The baby Aquareen was lying on Lina's chest, clutching her by the hair.

"We have to go! Now!"

Lina raised herself up and looked at me sleepily.

"Now! They're coming to kill us! All of us!" And when she still didn't move, I added, "They'll kill the baby!"

It was then that she stirred, stood, and I could see the water was only knee-deep there. Lina was naked, but the body I saw emerge from the water was not the body I had so loved. It was bluish grey, the thighs, the hips, the stomach at the same time muscular and blubbery, her breasts now mere dots on her expanded, rippled chest, and her face—that lovely face!—was bulbous with deep sunken eyes, eyes that were awake now, alight with terror.

Lina waded quickly to the shore, but once there she hesitated, looked back, frozen in indecision, clutching the Aquareen tightly.

"Water," was all she said, a single plaintive word.

And I could see it too, immediately. How could we escape when they needed water just to survive? Quickly, I plunged the blanket into the pond, soaking it, then took the Aquareen from Lina, wrapped it in the blanket, and put it in the backpack. It squealed in fright, but we had no time. I grabbed Lina's arm and we fled.

We ran around the back side of the pond, Lina struggling to keep up, her flattened feet and thin calves no longer able to move as they once had. I could see that it wouldn't be long before she couldn't walk at all. We slipped down into a ravine, seeking out the covering trees where we could, trying to put as much distance as possible between us and the camp. I knew our stream, where I'd met Wynn and the others a little while before, meandered west and merged with another stream in a mile or so. If we could make it there, I thought, Lina and the baby could quickly refresh in the water and we could follow it wherever it led. Somewhere far away, somewhere safe.

The ravine flattened out to an open expanse of brush and we had no choice but to cross it. We had just about made the tree line on the opposite side when I heard a shout and a single gunshot. We dashed into the trees, into momentary safety, but I knew now that we were being followed. Lina began to flag and I dragged her along by the wrist, the Aquareen in the pack now ominously silent. We ran another half mile or so until we heard the gentle rustle of running water, then raced toward its source. Just as the stream emerged into view, down a steep embankment littered with rocks and dead timber, another shot rang out, kicking up dirt at our feet. Lina flinched, then tumbled down the slope, and I followed her, losing my footing and sliding with the pack clutched in my arms, both of us landing hard at the edge of the stream. I looked up, and just then, on the opposite bank, a man emerged from the trees holding a rifle with a scope. Smithers.

For a moment none of us moved. Then Smithers slowly raised the rifle and pointed it at us. The baby Aquareen had fallen out of the pack and now lay screeching on the sand. Lina held up a hand as if to shield us from the bullets, a single hand, and I saw there the webbed membrane between the splayed fingers. And so did Smithers. A look of utter incomprehension and disgust came over his features.

"Please," Lina cried, her hand still held up, trembling between us. Smithers' finger slipped onto the trigger. "Please," Lina said again, now almost whispering, and maybe it was the sound of her voice, just her voice, a voice that was still the Lina he had known, that moved him, for he turned suddenly, stepped back through the trees, and was gone.

Lina grabbed the baby Aquareen and jumped into the water where they both disappeared under the shallow surface. I counted the seconds, eight, nine, ten, before they emerged in a sudden rush of water and we ran. The rest of the day we skirted the stream, Lina and the baby taking frequent dips, and finally, when the sun dropped behind the wooded hills, settled to rest in a valley we'd never seen before. Lina and the baby slept in the water of a still, sheltered bend of the stream, and I was beside them on the bank. The following morning we all rode a gentle current miles downstream.

It was on the third day when we first heard the sea birds, a distant yapping and cawing that at once frightened and thrilled us. It was also on that day that I felt the first faint aching in my hands and feet, the first hollow throbbing in my chest, the first mysterious, almost mystical, longing for water. I watched Lina cuddling with the baby in a deep pool of the widening river, saw the gentle, protective smile, and for the first time since this all began I saw the delicate beauty of her new face, her transformed body. But it was not until later, as evening was finally falling and we emerged onto the beach, that a new sense of hope dawned within me. The sun was setting behind a fiery nest of clouds, the surf was crashing against the rocks, the sea birds circling high above, and it was then, far up the coast, that we first heard it. It began with a single voice, then another joined in, then another still, the notes fluttering high above the sound of the surf, then more voices joined in, chorus after joyful chorus, the song of the Aquareens welcoming the stars.

Scorched Earth

By Lorraine Sharma Nelson

"**H**ey, you"'
Gita froze.
Footsteps. Coming up behind her.
Fast.

Move. Move. Move. Her feet finally decided to follow orders. And she took off. Scampering across the scorched hillside.

"Hey? Didn't you hear me? Stop."

Screw you, Asshole. She quickened her steps, churning up ash and dust with each footfall.

But he was fast. She could hear him behind her, pounding the ground with each step, his breathing ragged. She could almost feel his breath on the back of her neck. And shivered. *No way.* No way was he getting a hold of her. It took everything she had to escape from the last psycho who'd overpowered her.

And she wasn't about to let that happen again.

Gita tore down the embankment, thinking at this point that she'd rather run into a stray *Kelon* or two than deal with another desperate man who hadn't seen a woman in weeks, months—however long it'd been since the world was invaded by the warlike aliens.

Their ships had dropped from the sky one beautiful, sunny, Wednesday morning, re-materializing as they descended. One by one. All over the globe.

Mankind hadn't stood a chance. One day, man was fighting man for control over borders, oil, religious freedom, and a myriad of other insane reasons. But the next day? That's when mankind realized too late that they should have focused their warlike tendencies toward the stars, not each other.

Oh, they tried to rally. They at least get points for that. But ultimately, humans were no match for the advanced race of seven-foot, six-fingered, glistening, gun-metal grey beings that wreaked havoc across the globe. Gita didn't know how many people died during the invasion, because, on the fifth day of their arrival, all communications shut down for good.

The *Kelons* had caused a worldwide apocalypse in barely a week, and they did it as easily as a child stomps on a colony of ants.

That's all humans were to them. Ants. Bugs. To be exterminated. And exterminate they did. Those that remained in her tiny corner of the world, scattered, hiding wherever they could. She'd encountered survivors in caves, in basements that were still miraculously intact, in drainage pipes. And had heard stories of those who were lucky enough to find bomb shelters.

The animals? They were still here, except for those that lived too close to human settlements, and perished along with them. The *Kelons* had no interest in the lesser beings.

Most days it was all Gita could do, just to put one foot in front of the other. To forage for food. To keep going. What did it matter anymore? What did anything matter anymore? There was nothing left to live for.

Nothing.

Except *this* was something. Being chased by a psychotic man, who didn't know or care enough to give up. God, how much longer was he going to chase her? She could barely catch her breath. And the thirst, that dull ache at the back of her throat that had been a constant companion since the invasion. It raged now, threatening to consume her. If he didn't give up soon, she was going to collapse. And she'd rather die than do that.

"I…said…stop!"

Startled to hear the voice so close behind her, Gita whipped her head around, just in time to register a large, male body hurtling toward her. She opened her mouth to scream, but instead found herself body-slammed to the ground.

Gita's face smacked against the hard earth. Tiny pebbles, still radiating heat from the blast of the last attack, peppered her cheeks like tiny pellets. She spat ash from her mouth, struggling to throw the man off.

"Stop it. I'm not going to hurt you. Calm down, okay?"

"Get off me, then."

The guy immediately rolled off her, sitting up and raking a hand through his dark hair. Gita spat one last time, then scrambled up into a sitting position too, scooting away from him until there was at least five feet between them.

"Who are you?" She eyed him warily, tense, primed for flight. Her cheeks throbbed, but she ignored the pain. "What do you want?" As soon as the words left her mouth, Gita wanted to retract them. Too loaded a question.

His eyes, a startling green, narrowed as they stared at her. "Not what you're thinking, anyway," he said. "From a distance, it was hard to tell you were a girl, what with that baseball cap jammed down so low, and that oversized hoodie you're wearing." He peered closer, his eyes twinkling. "It's still hard to tell you're female under all that grime."

Gita stiffened. "Then why did you chase me?"

He shrugged, dusting off his shirt sleeves. "Call me crazy, but you're the first person I've seen in weeks. I was just really happy to see that I wasn't the last man…person…standing." He finished dusting off his arms and glared at her. "Why did you run?"

Gita glared back. "Are you serious?"

"Sometimes."

She shook her head. "I'm a lone woman, in a world where there doesn't seem to be too many of us left. Figure it out, Genius."

His eyes widened. "Did … have other men … I mean—"

"They've tried, but I managed to get away each time. And not before making them sorry, either."

"What does that mean?'

Her eyes narrowed. "It means that if you try anything, you'll be mighty sorry you did." Her hand curled around the handle of the bowie knife at her belt.

The guy held his hands up, palms out. "Whoa. Look, I'm not gonna jump you or anything, okay? Chill. Like I said, you're the first person I've seen in weeks and I wasn't going to let you get away."

"And that's it?"

"That's it, okay? I swear." He held up two fingers of his left hand. "Scout's honor."

Gita raised an eyebrow. "Isn't that supposed to be done with your right hand?"

He grinned, revealing surprisingly white teeth in a grubby face streaked with soot. "I wasn't a very good scout, I guess." He cocked his head to the side, scrutinizing her. Gita shifted, wondering if she looked as hideous as she felt.

"What's your name? I'm Royce."

"Why do you want to know?"

"Oh, I don't know. Maybe because our world's been attacked by aliens, and whatever survivors there are should be exceedingly grateful to still be alive and find each other. Band together. Rebuild. All that stuff."

She stared at him. "Rebuild? Are you insane?"

"Pretty sure I'm not, but, considering I've been talking to myself for a really long time, I guess it's debatable." He flashed her another grin.

Gita shook her head, spreading her hands wide. "Look around you. There's nothing left. Nothing. Just blackened, scorched earth as far as the eye can see. Just how do you intend to rebuild?"

The guy glanced around him, his grin fading. "I didn't say it would be easy, but we have to try, don't we?" He glanced back at her, his expression unreadable. "What choice do we have?"

Gita stared at him again. "Who *are* you?"

"I just told you. Royce. Still waiting for your name."

She sighed. "I'm Gita."

"Gita? Pretty name. Glad to meet you."

"Yeah, well. We'll see," she muttered, scrambling to her feet. She turned, heading east toward the river. He fell in step beside her.

"So, where we headed?"

"*I'm* going to find some food," she said, sliding a glance at him. "I don't know about you."

"How do you know where to look? I mean, are you good at setting traps, snaring rabbits? That kind of thing?"

Her eyebrows shot together. "I've had to learn. What about you? If you don't have any useful skills, you can get lost."

"It's so refreshing to meet someone warm and welcoming, after all the assholes I've come across."

Her face burned. "Things are different now. Being friendly only gets you into trouble. Trust me, I know."

He shot her a quizzical gaze. "I believe you. I've had a few run-ins myself."

"Well, then, why expect me to be any different?" She stepped over a fallen log, black and smoking from the last attack. Everywhere she looked, whispers of smoke curled toward the sky.

He shrugged. "I dunno. You have a kind face, I guess."

Whatever she expected him to say, it wasn't that. Flustered, she quickened her pace, but he kept up.

"So, what've you been living on?" Royce asked. "Squirrels? Fluffy little bunnies? The odd dog or cat?"

She shot him a disgusted look, but he ignored it and kept prattling on.

"Me? I had to make do with some cans of spaghetti I found. You know the kind with little o's that you ate as a kid? Way past their 'use by' dates too.

Kinda surprised I haven't kicked the bucket yet. That stuff can't be good for you." He looked at Gita. "So, what's your poison been?"

"Whatever I can get a hold of," she said, wishing he'd just shut up. She wasn't used to being around people anymore. For a long time now it had been just her. And she'd come to prefer it that way. Especially when she'd been waylaid by men who thought they could ditch all the rules of civilized society. Not that there was any society anymore. Civilized or otherwise.

"So, what do you think?" Royce said, smiling down at her.

She frowned. "About what?"

He made an impatient sound. "About what I just said."

"I didn't hear what you said. I was…thinking."

"About what?"

She shot him a sharp glance. "None of your business." *God, didn't he ever shut up? And why was he so Goddamn cheerful? Just what the hell was there to be so happy about?*

"Fair enough. You're suspicious of me. I get it. Although why you wouldn't trust me is beyond my understanding. I mean, look at me. Have you ever seen a more sincere face?"

Gita laughed, the sound surprising her as much as it spooked her. She clamped her mouth shut and quickened her pace.

"*Aha.* So you do have a sense of humor. Good to know. I was beginning to get a little worried."

She groaned, rolling her eyes. "Why are you still here? Can't you go bother someone else?"

"Fine. Point me in the direction of someone else, and I'll leave you to your own devices."

Unable to comply, she lapsed into silence.

They walked quietly for a while, the only sounds were the crunching of charred twigs and brush beneath their feet.

Then she smelled it. That stomach-clenching odor of rotten eggs.

The *Kelons* were somewhere close by.

Without thinking twice, Gita grabbed Royce's arm, pulling him down flat on the baked earth, behind a large charred tree trunk that blocked the path ahead of them. She scooted as close to the tree as possible, pressing her entire side up against it. She glanced at Royce, but he was way ahead of her, his body pressed close to the trunk, his expression somber.

He turned suddenly, meeting her eyes, and winked. And even though Gita was scared senseless of being caught by the *Kelons*, she suddenly felt tons better having him here beside her. Maybe he was right. Maybe there was something to this seeking out other survivors. Unbidden, her grandfather's words, whispered to her when they were hiding out in the bottom of his dried-out well, in those last terrifying days of the invasion, echoed in her head.

"Always remember, *pëtti*, people need people. No matter what happens, don't become a loner. Promise me that if something happens to me, you'll seek out other people. You'll need them to survive. You'll need to belong to a family." He firmly believed that. Indians, regardless of which part of India they hailed from, and regardless of which language they spoke, believed fervently in family. Prior to the invasion, it was not unusual to see families of up to fifty people getting together on a regular basis.

Gita swallowed. He always called her *pëtti*, the word for granddaughter in Tamil. Knowing that she would never again hear him call her which made her heart ache so badly, she wondered if she would ever recover from his death.

When he died, protecting her from some falling bricks that had been jarred loose when the *Kelons* launched yet another attack, Gita had kept her word to him, and sought out other survivors; people as traumatized as she. And for a while, there was some comfort in that. In not being alone. Until, in one of the groups, some of the men started making claims about the women. When Gita had tried to run from the man who'd claimed her—a big, burly man at least twice her age—he'd overpowered her, tying her hands together, and pulling her along behind him as he walked.

Like a dog on a leash.

When she'd finally managed to free herself and escape, before he'd had a chance to do anything to her, she'd left him with a parting gift—a massive headache—courtesy of the rock she'd dropped on his head while he slept. Gita smiled, remembering the satisfaction of—

Royce grabbed her forearm, making her jump, drawing her from her thoughts. She glared at him, eyebrows raised. He shook his head slowly, raising a finger to his lips. She nodded, her heart rate speeding up.

The *Kelons* were approaching.

How many were there? Gita strained to hear their footsteps. Two, maybe three? *Oh crap.* There's no way they could take on that many. One *Kelon* was more than a match for three full-grown human males. They were incredibly, frighteningly, strong. And those six-fingered hands of theirs were unbelievably dexterous, wielding weapons at speeds that would put to shame the best fighters Earth had to offer.

Royce's hand tightened on her arm. She turned her gaze back to him, hoping he couldn't see how terrified she was. His face was close to hers, and she searched it for some indication of his own fear. But he didn't look scared. In fact, he looked downright calm. He was either really brave or really stupid.

A series of clicks caught her attention. The *Kelons* were conversing amongst themselves. Royce placed his hand on top of her head, pushing her further down against the tree trunk. She went still, heart hammering so loud against her ribcage, she was sure the aliens' hypersensitive hearing could pick up the sounds.

The clicks increased in volume, almost as if they were arguing. Then it sounded as if two sets of feet were moving away from them, in different directions. Royce raised his head slightly, but Gita grabbed him by the collar of his tee, pulling him back down.

They waited, holding their collective breath.

Sure enough, a few beats later, they heard the splintering of wood underfoot, and the sound of footsteps moving closer toward them. Gita squeezed her eyes shut. *Oh please please please…*

The footsteps paused on the other side of the log. Gita heard three short intakes of breath. A pause. Another long breath.

It was sniffing them out.

Gita forced her eyes open. And almost passed out. The *Kelon's* skull-like, metal-gray face loomed over them. Its yellow eyes, located deep within their sockets, burned into hers. She opened her mouth, but no words came. Her body froze. Unable to move, unable to breathe, unable to blink, she lay helpless, staring back at the monstrous alien.

Then, everything happened at once. One second Royce was stretched out beside her. The next, he reacted like white lightning, lunging for the alien. Caught off-guard, the *Kelon* toppled over, and Royce was on it in a flash, pummeling it over and over with his fists, his mouth set in a grim, tight line.

But the *Kelon* recovered quickly. Its inhuman, six-fingered hands snaked out, grabbing both of Royce's fists. Gita watched, horrified, as a slow, bone-chilling smile spread across its grotesque face. Razor-sharp teeth gleaming from a terrifying, gaping maw. Beckoning.

It bent Royce's arms behind his back, stretching them further and further, taking its own sweet time. As if it relished the look of agony on Royce's face. Royce clamped his mouth shut, refusing to utter a sound. Even though she barely knew him, Gita felt a rush of pride for him. The emotion warmed her, bringing life back to her limbs.

And she moved.

Yanking her trusty bowie knife out of its makeshift sheath on her belt, Gita pounced on the *Kelon* from behind, snaking her arm around its neck, and sinking the blade into its throat.

Thick, mustardy-yellow blood spurted out from the gash, spattering Royce in the rotten egg stench. Gita reeled back as Royce pushed the prone alien off of him, kicking it away. He lay back, panting, holding his arms splayed out on either side.

"Are you all right?" she whispered, trying not to stare at the thick, sticky, viscous fluid covering his shirt and face, and hair. She swallowed, willing herself not to heave. "You don't have to worry. Their blood isn't harmful to humans. Apart from the gross stench that makes you want to vomit."

"Yeah, I know. Just … just give me a moment."

Gita nodded, then snapped her head up when she heard the faint sounds of twigs and underbrush crackling. She held a hand, smeared with the *Kelon's* blood, out to Royce. "Up. Now. We have to go. The other ones are coming back."

Royce didn't need to be told twice. He was on his feet before the words were out of her mouth. Grabbing her hand, he ran, and she tried her best to keep up with his long strides.

The sun was low in the sky by the time the duo reached Gita's destination. They hunkered down behind some charred remains of a bush, watching the front of the mall. Surprisingly, it wasn't incinerated completely, like most of the buildings in the area. Parts of it were destroyed, with the roof caved in in some places, and large gaping holes in some of the walls, but, for the most part, the building was intact.

"What do you think?" Royce whispered.

"Well, I know there's a GrabMart in there," Gita said. "You know, the kind with the grocery section? There may be nothing left if other people got there first, but it's worth checking out."

"Yeah. Unless it's a trap."

"What do you mean?"

Royce shrugged. "Well, don't you think it's kind of strange that everything else has been reduced to smithereens, except for this convenient mall, which may have a large deposit of food inside?"

Gita chewed on her lower lip as she pondered this new train of thought. "Okay. So, we just have to come up with a plan."

Royce snorted. "Oh, sure. Let's do that."

Gita whirled on him. "What do you suggest? We have to eat. We have to drink. If we don't, we die anyway. If you have an alternative, I'm all ears."

Royce sighed, sitting back on his haunches. He ran a hand through his sticky hair, which stood straight up like a Mohawk, thanks to the alien blood coating practically every strand. "Okay, look. I'll go in first. Try to grab as much food as I can. Providing there's anything in there to grab. If I don't come out in …" —he checked his watch— "… fifteen minutes, leave. Head as far away from here as you can. Got that?"

Speechless, Gita stared at him, then laughed, shaking her head. "No, I don't *got that*. Who died and made you king? Besides, do you honestly think I'd turn tail and run if someone I knew was in possible danger?"

He scowled at her. "Gita—"

"Don't *Gita* me. You're not the boss of me. *You* got that?"

Royce blew out a deep breath. "Look, all I mean is, there's no point in both of us walking into a trap and—"

"First of all, we don't even know if it's a trap. Here's the plan. We wait until nightfall, then go in together. We keep to the shadows. We scope the place out. If we agree it looks safe, we ransack the store, and slip out quietly. Easy peasy."

Royce gaped at her for a second, then burst out laughing. Alarmed, Gita clamped a hand against his mouth.

"Shhh. Quiet, you idiot. Do you want something to hear you?"

But he kept laughing softly against her hand, and when she finally removed it, he shook his head, swiping at the tears running down his face. "You're a hell of a girl, Gita. Did anyone ever tell you that?"

"Yeah. My *tãttã* … granddad. All the time. But he didn't always mean it as a compliment."

Royce's face softened as he looked at her. "You loved him a lot, didn't you?"

Swallowing, Gita nodded. Then, clearing her throat she turned back to the mall, glancing at the setting sun behind it. "Not long now," she said. "We might as well get comfortable, for a little while, anyway."

Royce settled beside her, stretching his long legs out in front of him. "I could do with an ice-cold beer."

"Don't start that," she said, nudging him.

He smiled. "What are you in the mood for? A manicure. Blow-dry?"

She scowled at him. "God, you're a chauvinistic jerk, you know that?"

His smile widened. "Come on. If things were normal again, what would you be in the mood for right now?"

Gita sighed, closing her eyes as she leaned back against the bush. "After an incredibly long, hot shower, I'd go for a double-dip French-vanilla hot-fudge sundae, with extra whipped cream and three cherries, covered with crushed peanuts."

Royce groaned. "I had to ask."

Gita laughed softly, and they lapsed into silence. Her eyelids grew heavy.

"Go ahead and take a nap," Royce said. "I'll keep watch. I promise."

Too tired to protest, Gita sighed, closing her eyes. "Thanks, Royce," she murmured, and was already in the throes of sleep when she heard him murmur something back.

It seemed she'd barely closed her eyes before Royce was shaking her awake. "What?" she mumbled, still groggy with sleep.

"If we're going to go into the mall, we should do it now. Everything seems pretty quiet, but who knows how long that'll last."

At his words, Gita came fully awake, yawning and rubbing her eyes. "I could sleep for a week," she muttered.

"Yeah, I get that. Me too."

Gita glanced up at him, noting the dark shadows under his eyes, amplified by the light of the full moon. "Why didn't you wake me earlier? I'd have kept watch so you could grab some shuteye."

"I'm not that tired," he said, getting to his feet, but keeping to the shadows.

"Liar," Gita whispered, rising to join him. "Next time I'll keep first watch." He smiled at her, and for the first time since their meeting, she found herself smiling back without any apprehensions.

They made their way quickly but silently to the gaping hole in the wall nearest to them, keeping as much to the shadows as they could. Gita silently cursed the full moon, knowing they were still visible to anyone staking out the place as they had.

Once inside the room, they flattened themselves against the wall, peering around, allowing their eyes to adjust to the darkened interior. Here, the roof was intact, but moonlight filtering in through the gash in the wall and the broken windows, lit up bits and pieces of the room.

There were racks everywhere, some empty, some with a few items of clothing still on them, and some on their sides, with clothing strewn all over the floor.

"We're in a department store," Royce whispered.

Gita nodded, not wanting to break the eerie silence. Why did she get the feeling that someone…something…was watching them? She tried to shake it off as nerves and her overactive imagination, which reared its head at the most inopportune of times, but it didn't help.

"Let's get out of here," she whispered back.

"Follow me," Royce said, inching his way along the wall. "I think I see the entrance into the mall." His hand found and closed around hers, warm and comforting, and she was immensely grateful for it. Her *tãttã* was so right. People did need people.

After what felt like an eternity of groping and feeling their way around the perimeter of the store, Royce found the entrance. The glass doors leading into the mall were broken, shattered glass scattered everywhere. They stepped cautiously, careful to keep the noise of crunching glass underfoot to a minimum.

Inside the cavernous belly of the beast, it was dark, with insidious shadows looming everywhere. Luckily it wasn't pitch black. The main portion of the roof was destroyed, and this time, Gita was grateful for the fingers of moonlight spreading across the middle of the enormous atrium.

She squinted, trying to read the signs over the remaining storefronts. "There," she said, pointing to one to the right of them. Over a set of large double doors that were also broken, was the telltale orange 'G' overlaid with the 'M.' She pulled Royce along behind her, eyes darting every which way.

"Slow down," he whispered. "If we rush, we'll get careless."

"I just want to get what we came for and get the hell out of here," Gita said, glancing back at him.

"Watch yourself," he said. "Some of those shards on the doors look pretty nasty."

They made their way into the store, stopping just inside. Royce let out a low groan. "Son of a bitch."

Gita bit her lip to keep from crying out loud. Whatever she expected to find, this wasn't it. Practically every shelf was upended or on its side. Electronics, games, clothes, toys. There was no end to the stuff strewn everywhere.

"I guess we can rule out being the first ones here," Royce muttered, running a hand through his hair.

More dismayed than she cared to admit, Gita nodded, not trusting herself to speak.

"Come on," he said, tugging on her hand. "Let's find the food and get the fu … hell outta here."

It wasn't hard to guess where the groceries were kept. The smell of rotting fruit and vegetables guided them. Soon enough, they came across the aisles where the boxed and canned goods were shelved. Or had been shelved.

"Guess we'll just have to root around the floor. See what we can find," Royce said.

Gita blinked back tears, so hungry and thirsty, she could barely think straight. Royce must feel the same way as she. If they didn't find rations here, what would happen to them? How would they survive another day of gut-gnawing hunger and raging thirst?

"Gita, come on," Royce whispered, already on his hands and knees, crawling around.

She joined him on the floor, crawling over to a pile of goods a few feet away from her. For the next several minutes, the only sounds in the cavernous room were the rustling and clanging of various items as they rooted around for anything edible.

Another few minutes passed before Royce let out a soft whoop that made her jump. She turned toward his voice. "What did you find?"

"A bunch of cans. Can't quite make out the words, but the pictures show fruit on the labels."

Gita's mouth filled with saliva at his words, her stomach rumbling. "Hold on. I'm coming over there." She crawled over to him, and within minutes of her joining the search, they had a small pile of canned goods between them.

"Do you think we have enough?" she whispered, eyeing the seven cans.

"For now," Royce said. "Let's not push our luck. Let's just grab our haul and get out of here."

"I wish we had a bag or a backpack or something," she said, glancing at the chaos around them. "I hate to have our hands full, in case we get ambushed."

Royce laughed softly. "We're in a store, Gita. Pretty sure there are bags around somewhere. Wait here."

Before she could protest, Royce rose to his feet and carefully shuffled his way toward the back of the store.

"Royce," she hissed when his outline melted into the shadows.

He didn't answer.

Taking deep breaths to keep from panicking, reminding herself that before he came along she'd been on her own, surviving quite nicely, thank you, Gita sat quite still, every sense on high alert.

She could hear a faint rustling in the direction Royce had disappeared and took comfort in the sound.

An eternity later—or so it seemed—she heard his soft footfalls. She opened her mouth to say his name, but stopped short. What if it wasn't him? What if it was another survivor, scrounging around for food as they were? Or worse. What if it was a *Kelon?*

"Gita? Where are you?"

"Here." Relief flooding through her, she reached out a hand, closing her fingers tightly around his when they brushed hers. "Did you find anything?"

In the dark, she saw the flash of his white teeth as he grinned at her. He held out something, shaking it so that it made a rustling sound. "Good ol' plastic shopping bags. Let's fill 'em up with whatever we can find and get going."

Two bags later, they stepped out of the store, back into the main atrium. Gita turned to Royce with a smile, holding up the bag she carried. "Honey, you shouldn't have," she said, smiling.

But Royce didn't respond to her joke. Didn't even look at her. He was staring straight ahead, his jaw clenched. Gita followed his gaze.

And bit back a scream.

Standing not ten feet away from them, were two men, one of average height, the other taller and more muscular. Their gazes shifted from Gita to the bags they carried.

"Looky what we got here, Bud," the big one said.

"That one's a chick," Bud responded, leering at her. "Nice rack, Honey."

"I see you've done all the hard work for us," the big one said, gesturing at the bag in her hand. "We'll just lighten your load for you." He glanced at Royce. "And by that, I mean your girl too." He took a step toward Gita, reaching out a hand. "Come on over here, Honey. With that bag." He gestured to his friend. "Get the other one from him."

Royce moved, planting himself in front of her, at the same time that she reached for her knife. Except it wasn't in her belt. The makeshift sheath was empty. Gita's breathing constricted. *Oh crap.* It must have slipped out in the store when she was crawling around in the dark. How did she not notice? She looked at Royce. How the hell was she supposed to help him without her knife?

Her eyes darted over Royce's shoulder to the man staring him down. *Oh God.* He looked deranged enough to tear Royce's head off his shoulders. And he was big enough to do it too.

"Better get outta the way, Hero, or I'll mess up that pretty face of yours so's you'll never get laid again. Know what I mean?"

"Actually, no," Royce said. "No, I don't. Why don't you explain it to me?"

The man looked at his friend, and they both took a step closer. "Give me the fuckin' bags and the girl, and I'll let you go." He smiled, revealing stained, yellowing teeth that made Gita's skin crawl.

Royce didn't move. Gita tightened her grip on the bag. There were four cans in it. If she swung it at their heads it could do serious damage. She just needed one of them to come closer. And for Royce to drop the macho act and get out of the way. Much as she appreciated his chivalry, she didn't want him to die because of her. She didn't need that on her conscience. Having her *tãttã* die saving her weighed so heavily on her conscience, most days she felt she could barely keep going. Having Royce die would tip her over the edge.

Royce finally spoke, his words slow and succinct. As if he were talking to a child. Or a very slow-witted adult. "We can share our haul with you guys if you like. Be happy to." He took a deep breath, released it slowly, and stiffened his spine. "But there is no way in hell that you're taking her."

Gita watched as the big man's face turned purple. This was not good. They were going to kill Royce and take her. She had to do something. She opened her mouth to say something, anything, that would stall them. But, something in the shadows caught her eye.

She turned, just as a *Kelon* stepped into the moonlight, its hideous skull-like face all angles and shadows. Gita reeled back, her stomach clenching. "Royce," she whispered.

Something in her voice must have registered with all three men, for they all turned to look at her. Then slowly followed her gaze.

"A fuckin' clicker. goddamn motherfucker," the big man spat, as he and his friend turned toward the alien, assuming fighting stances. "Whatcha gonna do, Clicker? Take on all of us? It's four against one."

Royce and Gita exchanged glances. He reached for her hand, squeezing briefly. And took a small step back, pulling her with him. The *Kelon* took a step forward, its demeanor confident. Self-assured. Then another step, glass crackling underfoot.

Gita's eyes widened. *No! It couldn't be.* It was dead. She plunged the knife into it herself. Saw it topple over. Beside her, she heard Royce's quick intake of breath. Knew he recognized it too.

At the base of its throat, right where she'd sunk her knife, there was a thick, corded layer of its blood. It looked like a yellow scarf twined around its neck.

The Kelon's long, tapered fingers touched the site, its eyes burning into hers. She saw the mouth split open in a toothless semblance of a grin. An icy finger trailed down her spine. That wound she delivered would have been fatal to any human…or animal…for that matter. But it did nothing more than put the *Kelon* out of commission for a brief period of time.

If a stabbing to the neck couldn't kill them, what chance did humans have? She almost laughed out loud. They didn't, did they? The *Kelons* came from the skies and decimated them. Started and ended a war of the worlds before anyone could figure out how to fight back.

Afterwards, with humanity in tatters, they moved on, leaving behind just enough *Kelons* to keep humans in line. And, as they left, more arrived. Although these *Kelons* were different. The *Settlers*, people called them. Because causing the near-extinction of the Human Race wasn't enough. They now laid claim to the earth, the beautiful blue planet that humans had taken for granted since they could walk on two legs.

The first group she'd joined up with were scientists, who theorized that the *Kelons* were conquerors, going from world to world, annihilating first, before settlers arrived to populate the worlds.

Now, Gita watched as the two men circled the *Kelon*. They were cocky and arrogant. Almost as arrogant as the *Kelon*.

Stop! She wanted to say to them. *Run! You don't stand a chance.* But she didn't. Five minutes ago, they were prepared to hurt Royce, maybe even kill him for their food. And for her. Now, her only concern for them was that they were also human. But that's as far as her concern went.

Beside her, Royce tugged on her hand, pulling her back, back, into the shadows. She glanced at him, wondering where he was going with this. The only way out was behind the alien. And there was no way it was going to let them slip past.

As if reading her mind, Royce lowered his head marginally toward her. "Trust me," he breathed, his lips barely moving. His words a whisper across her cheek. Gita shot him a sidelong glance, nodding imperceptibly. Then turned her attention back to the stage in front of them.

"Well. Come on, Clicker. Come on," the big man was saying. Gita looked at his friend. What was his name? Bud? He danced back and forth, fists raised in front of him, a smug grin on his face, Completely oblivious to the danger he faced.

The big man chose that moment to charge the *Kelon*, barreling into him with a cry that probably alerted every alien in a five-mile radius.

And Royce chose that moment to act.

He turned, grabbing Gita's arm, and pulling her back toward the store. But, the way back was blocked.

By another *Kelon*.

Gita bit back a scream. Where had he come from? Was he with the other alien, or was he alone?

Either way, it didn't matter.

They were trapped.

The *Kelon's* mouth opened, revealing razor-sharp, spiked teeth, skin stretching in a grotesque parody of a smile. A series of clicks emitted from its mouth. What was it saying? That they were done for? As good as dead?

Beside her, Royce breathed slowly, and Gita got the impression he was trying to calm himself down. His hand, still on her arm, tightened, tugging her back with him.

"I can throw the cans at it," he whispered. "Enough to slow it down."

"No. That's our food. Wait." She reached into her shopping bag as they retreated, the alien advancing. It was in no hurry. Enjoying itself. Savoring the moment. She'd seen it before. The equivalent of a cat playing with a cornered mouse.

Her groping fingers brushed against a bag that was split at one end, but still half-filled with salt. If all they needed to do was slow it down, maybe tossing the salt in its eyes would do the trick. With no time to ponder her decision, she flung the bag at the *Kelon's* face, salt crystals spraying into the air, glistening like diamonds in the moonlight, before the bag made contact with its face.

A series of roars burst from the *Kelon*. It clutched its face, bending forward, shaking wildly from side-to-side. Poised to run, Gita hesitated, watching the *Kelon*.

"Come on," Royce hissed, yanking on her arm. "Now's our chance."

"Royce," Gita whispered, eyes widening. "Look."

He followed her gaze to the *Kelon*. Ugly yellow blisters popped out on its face, one after another, the skin smoking as if it were on fire.

"What the hell —?"

"It's the salt," she said, her heart doubling its hammering as the significance of what was happening hit home.

Behind them, another roar. They turned as one to see the first *Kelon* holding up the big man as if he weighed no more than a baby. Bile rose in Gita's throat as she saw that the man's face was missing. Torn off.

"We need to go. Now."

Royce's urgent words penetrated her numbed brain, and, nodding, she took his hand, and together, they raced for the store.

 Once inside, Royce didn't stop. Didn't give either of them a chance to get their bearings. He led her through the piles of goods, stumbling, tripping, but not slowing his stride.

"Royce, where are we going?" she whispered, struggling to keep from falling flat on her face. Only his hand on her arm kept her upright.

"When I went in search of bags, I saw some small windows near the ceiling that were still intact," he said. "It seemed safer to go back the way we came instead of breaking one and raising an alarm, although in retrospect it's what we should have done. Anyway, it's our only way out now."

"They'll hear us," Gita said. "They'll follow."

"They know where we are, anyway," he said.

At the back of the store, Royce threw a stool through the nearest window. After hoisting Gita up, and using another stool to hoist himself up, they scrambled out, making a beeline for the tree cover. They didn't stop running until the first rays of the sun peeked over the treetops.

When Royce finally deemed it safe to stop for a while, Gita sank to her knees and keeled over onto her side. Royce knelt beside her, taking her hand in his.

"Are you all right?"

She nodded, too tired to speak, and shut her eyes. He brushed a few stray wisps of hair back from her face, tucking the sticky strands behind her ear. "We'll stop here for a while. Are you hungry? Thirsty?"

"Both," she murmured.

"Okay. Just lie there for a minute. I'll open up a can of something."

"Royce, we have to talk. The salt —"

"I know. We'll talk about that later. Let's take care of us first."

Gita nodded, shutting her eyes, thinking how nice it was to have someone take care of her for a change. She'd forgotten what it was like. She heard the rustling of a bag. The clinking of cans. The pop of an O-ring. In the next instant, Royce was back beside her. "Here," he said. "Take a sip."

Gita opened her eyes to see a can of peaches held out to her. They were tightly packed in syrup, and staring at them, she thought they were the most beautiful things she'd ever seen. Slowly, she reached out, taking the can from him. She took a sip. The liquid was too thick. Too sweet. Too warm.

It was the most delicious thing she'd ever tasted in her life. She struggled into a sitting position, crossing her legs. And took another, longer sip.

"Try a peach," Royce suggested, watching her with a smile. She dug her fingers into the can, pulling out a long, limp slice. She closed her eyes as she popped it into her mouth. And moaned as the juice from the peach filled her mouth when she bit down. She heard a soft chuckle and opened her eyes to see Royce grinning at her.

"What?" she said, handing him the can.

"Nothing," he said, helping himself to some of the fruit. "Who knew canned peaches would be the way to a woman's heart."

She laughed, helping herself to more. "What makes you think you've won my heart?"

He shrugged. "Oh, I don't know. My dashing good looks. My charming smile. The twinkle in my eyes. Take your pick."

"My, my. Someone has an overinflated opinion of himself."

Royce grinned. "I'm humble too. Don't forget humble."

Gita laughed again. She drank more of the syrup, and, as the sugar hit her bloodstream, felt better than she had in days… weeks. "God, that's good. I could eat all our haul in one sitting."

"I could too, but we can't. We have to conserve as much as we can. Who knows when we'll be able to find a haul like this again." He fit the lid back on the can of peaches. "Let's save the rest for later."

Gita looked at their plastic bags, lying in a small heap near them. "What are we going to do? We can't walk around with all this food. We'll be targets for any other survivors out there."

Royce scratched his chin. "Yeah, I know." He glanced around, his eyebrows knitting together. "Don't worry. We'll think of something. Right now, let's hide them and—"

"We have to talk. What happened back there—"

"I know, but I'm too tired to think right now. I hear water rushing. Must be a stream or something nearby. I'm for getting cleaned up, and grabbing a little shuteye, then we can talk, okay?"

They found a thick, dense bush that was only partially scorched and stashed the bags inside it. Then, holding hands, they ran toward the sound of water gurgling over rocks. Royce whooped as he threw himself into it, fully clothed. Gita followed suit, wincing at the icy-coldness of it, a stark contrast to the heat already making itself known in the early morning hour.

"Man, this beats everything," Royce said, shaking his sodden hair and making Gita shriek.

"Quit it. The water's freezing."

Royce laughed. "It's not so bad once you get used to it."

"Don't get me wrong. I'm so happy to finally get clean, but I prefer my water warm."

"The only way that's gonna happen is if we boil some over a fire."

Gita sighed. "I know. I miss soaking in my *tãttã's* big bathtub until my fingers and toes pruned. God, it's amazing how much we took for granted before the invasion."

Royce didn't respond. She looked up to see him staring at the skies, his expression pensive.

"You okay?"

He didn't answer, instead, he turned to look at her. "I used to love astronomy," he said, his voice soft. "My dad bought me a telescope for my twelfth birthday, and I watched the stars every single night through them, from then on. Once the invasion happened, I can't … I can't bear to watch the night sky anymore, you know?"

"I know," Gita whispered, swallowing hard. "This is the first time you mentioned your dad. Is he—?"

"Yeah. A goddamn *Kelon* shot him with some kind of ray gun. I watched my pa evaporate before my eyes."

Gita sucked in a breath. "I'm so sorry, Royce. I can't even—"

"I'm just glad my mom wasn't there to see it." He looked at Gita, his eyes misting over. "She died when I was a kid. When the world was normal."

Gita nodded. "I lost both my folks too."

"*Kelons?*"

'No. They were doctors, working for Doctors Without Borders in Sierra Leone, a country in West Africa. There was a severe outbreak of Ebola in the village they were working in, and they both contracted it. Papa died first, and Ma a week later."

"I'm so sorry, Gita."

She shrugged, wrapping her arms around her stomach. "It was a long time ago. I barely remember them. I was pretty much raised by my *tãttã.*"

Royce moved over to her, wrapping both arms around her and holding her close. For a long moment, they clung together in their shared grief before Gita pulled away.

"I'm hungry again," she said, needing to change the topic to something safer.

Royce smiled. "I am, too." He turned toward the bank. "First one back gets the first mouthful."

After eating a few more peach slices, they curled up beside the bush, and Royce put an arm around Gita, holding her close. "Lucky you threw some tee shirts and shorts into the bags back at the store," he said. "It's nice having something clean to wear."

Gita smiled. "You wouldn't think we were so lucky if you could see yourself. We look hideous. What is lucky is that the shorts have elastic waists."

Royce laughed softly. "Beggars can't be choosers." She heard him sigh, a sound of actual contentment. "You know," he said, his voice slurring as he drifted into sleep, "it's nice to see that under all the grime, you really are female." His arm tightened marginally around her waist.

Gita didn't quite know at what point their relationship had graduated to this level of intimacy, and she wasn't sure how she felt about it. But, she was too tired to think, and it felt so right to be with someone. To know they had your back as you had theirs. Sighing, she burrowed closer to him, and closed her eyes, but opened them almost immediately.

"Royce?"

"Hmmmm?" His eyes were shut, his face relaxed.

"That *Kelon?* How…how do you think he survived my knife to his throat?"

"Beats me. Maybe you didn't cut him as deeply as you thought."

Gita shook her head. "I drove the knife in. You saw for yourself. There's no way anyone could survive a knife to the jugular like that"'

Royce didn't answer. Gita decided he'd fallen asleep, and closed her own eyes, when he said, so softly, she had to strain to hear him, "Maybe his jugular isn't where ours is."

And just like that, Gita came fully awake. She lay there beside Royce, unmoving, listening to his rhythmic breathing. *Of course.* How could she have forgotten, when the evidence stared her in the face every time she came across one of them? They were *aliens.* Foreign in every conceivable way. Of course, their anatomy was different from humans.

If the remaining survivors had any chance of defeating the *Kelons*, they had to learn everything they could about that race. Find their Achilles Heel. Isn't that what all the humans she'd come across since the invasion had been saying? They could be hurt. They could be killed. The humans had taken out as many as they could during the invasion. But there were too many of them. Their technology too advanced.

Their Achilles heel.

Had she unwittingly found it?

Could it be something as simple and commonplace as salt?

Simple and commonplace to humans, maybe. But, what if that was their weakness? Or one of them? She recalled the *Kelon's* reaction to the bag of salt exploding in its face. The horror on its face, the pustules breaking out, peppering its skin. If that was all it took, they had a chance to turn the tide. All they needed were large salt reserves.

Where would one go about finding those?

Restless now, Gita tried not to squirm, for fear of waking Royce. He needed to sleep. She sighed, willing her eyes to remain open. She'd told him she'd keep the next watch while he slept. And she intended to keep her word.

Gita's brain churned with a million different thoughts as day turned into night. They had to keep moving, that much was obvious. They needed to get as far away from this part of the land as they could. The *Kelon* she'd stabbed might still be after them. And what if it didn't need much sleep? What if its metabolism could keep it going at optimum level for days, maybe weeks? The thought sent a spark of fear shooting through her. She shook her head.

After all, there was always the possibility that Bud somehow managed to injure it. However slight the chance.

And, what of the other *Kelon?* The one she'd disfigured with the salt? Was it still alive? Was it also out for revenge? Was revenge a concept that the aliens understood?

Salt, she thought again. *We have to find some. We have to. It may be our only salvation.* Her eyelids grew heavy, despite her frantic thoughts. Beside her, Royce snored softly. She hated to wake him, but she could no longer stay awake. Before closing her eyes, she shook him awake, and succumbed to slumber before he even opened his.

Someone, something, was shaking her. Roughly. She grunted, shrugging off the annoyance. Turned over and threw an arm over her eyes to block out the light.

"Gita? Wake up!"

In an instant she was fully awake, heart pounding. She turned over to see Royce sitting up, staring at something. *Oh God. Now what?* She sat up slowly, trying to calm her heartbeat.

Then she heard it.

Soft clicks.

In a flash, she and Royce scrambled to their feet, and dove into the bush hiding their bags. Twigs and branches tore at Gita, narrowly missing her eyes at one point, as they burrowed into the center of it. Thank God it was thick and lush. Protected as it was by the giant oak under which they'd slept, it had escaped damage from the *Kelons'* weaponry.

The night offered them an extra layer of protection as they huddled together, Gita gritting her teeth to keep from panting in fear. A leaf-covered branch tickled the space between her shoulder blades, but she didn't dare shift into a more comfortable position. Perspiration beaded her hairline and her upper lip, as she listened to the heavy thuds of the creatures moving closer.

They paused on the other side of the tree, their clicking interspersed with droning sounds that reminded her of a jet engine preparing for take-off. Was that their form of laughter? She'd heard that sound before when they were in a pack. The notion that these hostile creatures engaged in laughter, something she considered uniquely human, surprised her. Then again that could be their way of passing gas, for all she knew.

She heard sounds—rustling, ripping, hissing, then a noxious scent filled the air—and she realized they were preparing food. God, how long would they be? How long would she and Royce be able to remain in this position, on their haunches? Hers were already starting to ache. Her muscles trembling.

An eternity later, with the sky turning a rosy hue, the *Kelons* rose to their feet. She heard more sounds and held her breath. *Please, God, let them be leaving.* She felt a hand on her forearm and looked up at Royce. With his fingers on her arm, he mimicked a walking motion with two fingers.

They *were* leaving.

A moment later, they headed off in the direction from which she and Royce had come the day before. They waited another few minutes, until they couldn't hear their heavy footfalls anymore, then ventured out of their hiding place.

Royce groaned as he straightened, his hands on his lower back. "Christ, I feel like I'm eighty," he muttered. "Everything hurts."

Gita nodded, shaking her legs to bring back some circulation. "I thought they'd never leave."

Royce strode around to where the aliens had been not minutes before. "Gita, take a look at this."

She hurried to join him. He jerked his head toward something lying on the ground. Gita stooped to pick it up, but he held her back. "Don't. We don't know if it's contaminated or anything."

She snorted. "We were covered in their blood, and nothing happened. But, just in case…" She reached for a stick, lifting the item. "It's a glove, Royce. It's part of their uniform. I've seen them wearing this." She frowned, peering closer at it. "Weird fabric." A glimmering, metallic-gray, the glove was covered in ridges.

Royce grinned. "Yeah, almost like it was from another planet or something."

Gita rolled her eyes. "Smartass. I meant it's different from their uniform."

Royce shrugged. "Probably to protect their hands. You saw what the salt did to that *Kelon's* face."

He froze, his gaze widening as they stared at each other.

"Holy shit," Royce whispered. "I didn't dare believe it when I saw it last night, but that's it, isn't it? That's their weakness?"

Gita nodded, her brain on overdrive. "Took you long enough. Listen, the first group I joined up with were some scientists from MIT. You know, Massachusetts Institute of Technology? I'd watched them from a distance for days before approaching them. I figured if they were scientists, they would be safer than the usual mobs, you know?"

"And, were they?"

She shrugged. "For a while, anyway. Until a couple of the men started fighting over me, and the person in charge told me I was too much of a distraction and I should go. I guess when the world is coming to an end, people are just people."

"Well, you are a hot property," Royce said, trying to keep a straight face.

Gita jabbed him in the arm. "Shut up. This is serious. When I was with them, they talked about this constantly: *What if there were some earthly properties that were dangerous to the aliens? What if it were something simple that would enable us to gain the advantage?*" Gita took a deep breath. "I barely listened. Back then I thought it was all over, that these people were in denial. But, what if they were on the right track? If we can find them, maybe they can help us figure out where to—" She stopped, mid-sentence, her mouth forming a silent O.

"What?"

Gita stared at him.

"One of the men, an older one that I liked, told me they were heading west. He said they were working on some theories."

"Oh. Well, *that* narrows it down." Royce spread his arms wide. "Come on, Gita. Be reasonable. *West* covers thousands of miles. Besides, they could be halfway across the country by now."

"Shush, I'm thinking." Gita frowned, pressing her fingers against her temple. "He said they were going someplace in particular. Where was it?" she muttered. "Nevada. No, that wasn't it. Arizona? No." Gita's frown deepened. "Come on. Think." She tapped her forehead.

"Well, I'm hungry," Royce said, turning away, and heading for their bags. "What should we eat for breakfast? We have the rest of the peaches, plus either canned cherries, canned pears, or another can of peaches. We also have baked beans, with salt-pork and—"

"Salt! That's it. That's where they were going."

Royce threw her a glance that clearly said she'd lost her mind. "They're going to Salt? There's a place called Salt out west?"

"No, you twit. Salt Lake City. That's where they're going. To Utah."

"Utah?" Royce stared at Gita as realization dawned on his face. "Salt Lake City. Salt flats. Isn't that where a ton of salt is produced?"

Gita nodded, her breathing accelerating. She felt her cheeks warm, her fingertips tingle. The group of scientists had figured it out months ago. Oh, if only she'd listened. If only she'd paid attention.

She and Royce stared at each other for a long moment as realization dawned.

Slowly, almost as if he were in a daze, Royce's gaze dropped to the glove, then rose to meet hers. "I guess we're going to Utah," he whispered. "But first, breakfast."

END

The Eaters

By Sarina Dorie

I was six when people started to whisper about my unnatural abilities. Not knowing what else to do, Mama brought me to the pastor.

He smiled and greeted us when we knocked on the door of the empty church. Mama looked over her shoulder, like she was afraid someone might have followed us there. She set down the long rake just inside the church door. It was our protection against the "eaters." Not that we'd seen any. I'd used my talent to warn my friends to stay back, mostly so Mama wouldn't hit them with the rake.

The pastor was tall and willowy like a tree. His face looked too young for all the gray hair on his head. My older sisters said the death of his family two years before had turned him old overnight. His children had gotten the sickness like most everyone's children and gone feral, turned into eaters. His wife had committed suicide not long after.

Mama tugged me inside the church. "You know what folk are saying about my daughter. Is there a cure for her?" She spoke with an accent, a touch of Cajun spice my sisters used to say, but she worked hard to hide it.

The bright daylight streamed down from the stained-glass windows, painting the pews in a kaleidoscope of colors. Red, blue, and green danced over Mama's blonde hair and the pastor's silver hair. My skin was darker than both of theirs, and I wanted to dash into the circle of light to see if the rainbow would light up my skin like it did theirs, but Mama gripped my hand so tightly I thought it would fall off.

He escorted us past the rows of empty pews. There were so many seats in the great room it was hard to imagine there'd ever been this many people in our town.

He walked with a cane like an old man, the stick tap-tapping against the wood floor. "Maybe this ability isn't a curse, but a blessing. After all, God has taken from us, this might be a gift he's given us back."

"She calls them to her." Mama's pale cheeks flushed with red. "She could get hurt. Someone else could get hurt." Her blue eyes got all watery, and she looked like she would cry.

The pastor handed her his handkerchief. "Would you be willing to wait in my office? Let me take a walk with Josette and speak with her about this."

We walked outside, but he didn't say much, just asked me if I could read yet and if my sisters read the Bible to me. I suspected that was chit-chat for a religious man. We passed his garden and a peach tree in bloom. Branches of overgrown trees poked through the wrought-iron fence, blocking most of the neighborhood from view. He crouched so that we were eye-level. His gray eyes were warm and friendly. He didn't look at me with fear like our neighbors did.

"Tell me, Josette, why do you call the other children to you?"

"They're lonely and I feel bad for them. They listen to me if I tell them not to eat my sisters."

"Why do you think they listen?"

I shrugged. "Maybe they'd listen to you if you spoke to them real nice."

"Could you show me how you do it?" he asked.

I bit my lip. "Mama don't like it when I call them to me."

"What if I told you I had one of them locked up in the cellar? He's in a cage. There's no chance of him biting either of us."

I wasn't that concerned about one of them biting me, but I supposed the cage would make Mama feel better.

The cellar smelled of urine and old meat. The little boy was my age. He dropped the bone he was gnawing and attacked the metal cage as soon as he saw us. He was in a dog kennel, like we had for Spot. The child growled.

"There, there," I said. "Don't be afraid. We ain't going to hurt you."

He immediately quieted.

"Amazing," said the pastor.

"Does he have a name?" I asked.

Pastor John swallowed. "Clyde."

The boy pressed his dirty face up against the cage. His hair might have been blond or brown, but it was hard to see with all the dirt in it. I giggled when I saw Clyde was only wearing a tattered shirt, and he didn't have no pants.

"Where's his clothes?" I asked.

"He took them off, I suppose," said Pastor John. His cheeks flushed. "I'm sorry, I would have dressed him if I'd known you were coming. I clean out the cage when he's sleeping. Sometimes I can even get him washed up."

There were leather gloves on a hook on the wall and a thick leather apron next to it. He was a man of God, and I supposed that meant he was supposed to be charitable, but I was surprised he tried so hard.

"Most folk don't like the eaters," I said.

He nodded. "There are hospitals for the children up north. Places to take care of them. Some of the children recover, but doctors haven't been able to figure out how to produce consistent results. I can't stand the idea of hurting these poor lambs who need a shepherd more than ever. Can you understand that?"

I shrugged and poked a finger into the cage.

"No!" The pastor lunged forward.

Before he could pull me back, I stroked Clyde's forehead. The boy tilted his head to the side. His eyes didn't look as vacant, and his face twitched. Half his mouth lifted into a smile.

"Oh, he didn't bite you!" Pastor John said.

"If you open the door, real slow like, I can talk to him, so he won't bite you neither. If you have any other clothes for him, I reckon he'll let you dress him."

I showed the pastor how to talk slow and calm like one would with a wild animal. Pastor John imitated me. Tears filled his eyes as he reached out for the boy. Clyde bared his teeth and growled.

"That's not nice," I said. "Come here." I snapped my fingers at him. He half-crawled, half-scampered to my side.

Pastor John tried to help me dress Clyde, but each time the older man reached out, the boy moved away. I didn't know why talking gentle wasn't working for Pastor John. It worked for me.

I took the pants from the pastor. "Let me do this." Even though Clyde was an icky little boy, and I didn't want to help dress him, I knew it was the right thing to do.

I scratched Clyde behind the ears and told him he was a good boy after I was done. I looked up when I heard Mama calling me.

Pastor John straightened. "Perhaps that's enough for one day. Would you be willing to come back and teach me to talk to him like you do another time?"

"Sure, but you'd better not tell Mama."

I didn't pay much attention to Pastor John's sermons on account of them being so boring. On the following Sunday, I sat with Mama on one side of me and my two older sisters on my other side. No one else sat in the row with us but another family sat a few pews ahead and there were others peppered here or there around us.

A few words from the service made it past my ears and into my head. Probably it was cuz Pastor John made eye contact with me when he talked about God's little helpers. He kept talking about love and not giving up on our children, even if the Lord might test us. He said we didn't know they didn't have no souls. Even though I was six, I knew it was more than the hard wooden pews that made people shift uncomfortably.

Pastor John started talking about how the radio said the sickness didn't last in all children, and some actually got better and were cured. A man and woman walked out on him as he mentioned this.

"Maybe if we just pray hard enough, everything will be better," my older sister, Sidonie muttered in a snotty tone. Mama reached across Aurelie and me and swatted Sidonie.

Over the next week, I tried to help the pastor reach Clyde's soul, but I was the only one Clyde listened to. Still, I think my lessons must have done some good because he didn't try to bite the pastor so much. Then one day after Mama delivered me to speak with Pastor John, he told me that Clyde had escaped. Clyde had squeezed through the bars of the garden fence and kept on going. For once, he didn't try to bite no one.

The pastor's gray eyes looked so sad as he told me how Clyde had chewed through the kennel's wire.

"I can get you a different child to put in your cage to look after," I said. I could always feel their presence. The neighborhood was crawling with them.

Pastor John shook his head. "No. I just want my son back."

With those words, I understood the pastor's sorrow. He'd lost a son to the disease. I'd lost a father and a brother—neither of which I'd met, but their deaths still hung thick in the air at my house. I took his hand. Neither of us said nothing. We just stood there feeling sad.

It didn't surprise me when Clyde showed up a few days later in our yard. He whined under my window and didn't let me sleep none. The sky was bright with the edge of dawn when I went out to see who it was. He'd crawled under the crisscrossed wire of the fence and cut himself up. I cleaned the backs of his hands and wrapped him up in bandages. He let me lead him back through the field and down the old dirt road to the church.

I found the pastor gardening in the early morning air. He dropped the hoe and rushed toward us. Clyde's snarl stopped him.

"Clyde, no! Sit," I commanded. Clyde spun around three times like he was chasing an invisible tail and then plopped himself down in the dirt.

"Where is your mother, Josette?" Pastor John's gaze flitted back to Clyde.

"She's at home. I just wanted to bring you Clyde so you wouldn't worry no more. Hey, I want to show you a new trick I taught Clyde."

Pastor John cleared his throat. "A trick? Clyde isn't a dog."

"Just watch." I sang patty-cake and Clyde clapped his hands in imitation of me. His gestures were jerky and his movements lagged behind, but he did it all the same.

Pastor John leaned on his cane. "Remarkable. How do you do it?" He reached out to touch the boy's head.

"Don't bite," I said firmly.

Clyde snapped at the pastor anyway. If he had wanted to bite, he would have. It was only a warning. The older man withdrew his hand and shook his head. "Perhaps my son would be better off with you."

On most streets, there were only one or two families who remained. My playmates were my older sisters and when I could sneak it, the eaters. Children couldn't play outside, except in their own yards if they had fences like we did. We only got to see the other families at church and the community meeting afterward, and when you did go outside your own property, you had to bring stones to throw at the infected children to drive them off or big sticks. I wasn't supposed to leave our street, but sometimes when Mama was busy with my oldest sisters making preserves, or taking a nap after she had one of her headaches, Sidonie and I would sneak out.

Sidonie was sixteen when I was eleven. She was pretty with her long blonde hair and large blue eyes. Out of all of my sisters, she was the one who looked the most like Mama with her delicate features, long eyelashes, and fair complexion. I think all the blonde hair must have been used up on Sidonie and Aurelie, cuz by the time it came to me, I got black hair. It wasn't straight and easy to brush neither. People at church whispered Sidonie was the most beautiful girl in all our town, but I suspected it was only true when she smiled. She had a way of convincing people when she smiled. Most people anyway.

Being her sister, I was immune to her charm.

Sidonie sat back from weeding in the garden and wiped sweat from her forehead. She drank from a cup of water and held it out to me. "Thirsty?"

I took it, wondering why she was being nice to me for no reason. I set my hoe down against the fence, careful not to let it touch Bastian's grave. I didn't want no ghost of my brother accusing me of being disrespectful. I couldn't tell where Papa's grave was anymore, the wooden cross having rotted away last winter.

"You've been working hard out here for two hours," Sidonie said. "What do you say to a break?"

I glanced over my shoulder at the house. "We could go inside."

"It's too bad we can't go to the Washburnes' house," she said. "You could play with Jasmine and Lily's toys."

I rolled my eyes. "I'm not stupid. I know the reason you want to go there is cuz of some boy."

She crossed her arms. "So are you saying you won't take me?"

A mischievous smile curled to my lips. "I didn't say that." It gave me a little thrill to know what power I had. Sidonie was five years older, but I was the one who had to protect her.

"I'll take you, but only if we get to take Clyde with us," I said.

Sidonie made a face and shook her head.

"Fine, then. Another time," I flicked a pigtail over my shoulder and turned away, a gesture I often saw from my older sisters. I picked up a hand trowel to dig up dandelion roots. Aurelie, had asked me to save them for her to make some medicine.

I stopped when a flash caught my eye. Someone stood out in the field behind our chain-linked fence. He was nearly hidden in the head-high grass.

Sunlight shined off a metal button on his jacket. From his unkempt appearance, I thought he might have been one of the eaters.

I didn't have to speak loud. The eaters heard me thirty yards away. I whispered, "Go hide with the others so you won't be alone."

There was nothing more dangerous for an infected child than to be out alone with no pack. Except, of course, being out alone during the day where he could easily be seen. Then again, when they were hungry enough, they lost all sense, and they might do anything for food. Our community usually let them be on account of them driving off folk from the gangs, but there were a few who would just as soon kill the eaters for sport.

The figure in the field stepped closer.

I narrowed my eyes and concentrated. I pushed my will into my breath. "Join your pack."

He was close enough I could see his leather jacket was relatively clean, and no blood covered his face. Plus, he had a beard and most of the eaters were too young for that. He wasn't anyone I recognized, eater or otherwise.

That most likely meant he was a raider from out of town. A jolt of fear shot through me. There was nothing worse than a stranger. I called my friends to scare him off.

The high grass beyond the fence shifted. A moan erupted into the air. The man turned his head, looking over his shoulder and jumped. Two females and a male shambled closer. They were all older teenagers. They wouldn't last much longer. Any of them that made it into their twenties got too sick and weak. They got older just like other kids did, but they didn't age too good. They became easy prey for child hunters and raiders who came into the town.

One eater swung her head side to side, sniffing the air. They lunged forward and stumbled after the man.

Sidonie gasped. She stared after them as their speed increased and their slow, teetering gait turned feral and ferocious. They were just as uncoordinated though. One of them tripped and toppled into the biggest girl who fell over. The last one almost reached the stranger, but the man ran out of the field, hopped on a motorbike, and sped off.

Who needed a guard dog when one had guard eaters to protect you?

"Oh, gawd!" Sidonie leaned closer to me. "If Mama knew we'd just seen an outsider, she'd make us stay inside the rest of the day! Promise you won't say nothing to her."

I shrugged. "It don't matter since we aren't going nowhere anyway. Not without Clyde."

Sidonie cleared her throat. "Fine, we can bring your pet zombie. I'll go fetch the leash." She dashed off.

He wasn't really a zombie—none of them were. He would have rotted if he was a dead body. Just as I had grown and gotten older, he had too. I didn't know if that meant he had a soul or not, but he minded me and made a good guard dog.

He smelled just as bad as a dog and had fleas too. His tattered clothes were always caked with mud, and you couldn't tell what he actually looked like with all the dirt in his hair and on his face. I'd tried to show him how to work the gate so he didn't get all scraped up and dirty, but he didn't have the coordination for it. If I didn't let him in, he crawled under the fence and sat outside our kitchen window like a lost puppy.

"Clyde, here boy," I called. I didn't have to shout his name anymore. I just said it softly and he came. Sometimes he was slow if he wasn't near our yard and out running with the pack of feral children.

By the time Sidonie snuck the leash out of the house, Clyde shuffled up to the front gate. My sister had put on her good Sunday dress that Mama had made, and a hand-me-down sweater Mrs. Johnson had given us last fall. My sister smelled like old lady perfume, and her hair was brushed.

I patted Clyde's head. "Good boy. Now stay still, and let me put on your leash." He didn't need a leash, but it always made everyone else feel better when I used it.

It was only five blocks to the Washburnes and then across a wide highway that hardly anyone ever used. We couldn't walk fast with Clyde, but I always felt safer with one of my pets near. Sidonie walked ahead of us, pretending she didn't know me, which was silly considering everyone who lived in the houses we passed knew we were sisters.

You could tell the houses that were lived in because of the fences. The trees were pruned and the yards kept up in those lots. Roofing material had been appropriated from vacant houses. Shattered windows and doors falling off hinges marked the homes that had been ransacked, not by eaters, but by people. Some of them folk in our neighborhood, some of them raiders who came from other towns, only to be driven off by our pack of feral children.

We'd made it three blocks when Clyde paused and lifted his nose. The air reeked of musty decay and urine. I looked over my shoulder. The street was empty. When I turned back, I saw a dozen eaters scrambling out of the bushes of one of the run-down houses. They started toward us.

My sister shrieked and ran back to my side, making a wide arc around Clyde. She acted like he would bite her, but I'd already told him not to, and he ignored her. He wasn't like Spot, our old Rottweiler, always biting anyone at random. Spot had given Mama a nasty bite that had gotten infected, which is why I'd let Spot out of the house when Clyde had been hungry.

The pack of children shuffled closer.

I held up a hand. "Stay where you are and leave us be." I doubted they would attack Sidonie with me so close, but I said the words anyway, just in case.

Clyde snapped at them and strutted back and forth. He growled deep in his throat and warned them off like a good guard dog. The children backed away, but they didn't take their eyes off us.

As soon as they were gone, Sidonie rounded on me. "You did that on purpose, didn't you?"

"Did what on purpose?"

"You made them jump out and scare me to be mean."

"No, I didn't."

"Yes, you did."

"Shut up!"

"You shut up!"

A bicycle chimed behind us. Riley Washburne rode up, three of his friends following on their bikes.

"Hi, Sidonie!" Riley said. He stopped his bike alongside us. He lifted the bat from his handlebars and glanced at Clyde.

Clyde's eyes narrowed. I knew he wanted to lunge forward, but I put up a hand to stop him.

"Stay," I whispered.

"So, um, you going to my house?" Riley asked.

"Duh," Sidonie said.

Dalton rode his bike closer. "No way. I thought you were coming over to see me."

Sidonie smiled and made goo-goo eyes at Riley and Dalton. I wasn't sure which boy was her latest boyfriend.

The skinny boy with freckles on a Frankensteined bicycle poked Clyde with a stick.

"Jake Fuller, you knock it off," I said. "Or else I'll let him bite you."

They backed off. I tugged on Clyde's leash. He crouched by my side. I patted his head and his tongue wagged out of his mouth like a dog's. Sidonie rolled her eyes and looked disgusted.

Something must have been said while my attention had been diverted because Sidonie sat herself on the handlebars of Riley's bike, and they sped off. The others rode off after them.

"See you in an hour or two!" Sidonie said.

"Hey!" I shouted after her. There were eaters out there, and she wasn't safe. Worse yet, there was a strange man out there, and he might be part of a raider gang. But she ignored me in the way stupid older sisters do.

"Fine, you deserve what you get!" I yelled. But I didn't really mean it. What if something bad happened to my sister? Mama would be so mad at me for not taking care of her.

I knew what I had to do. I closed my eyes and whispered. My scalp prickled and a rush of adrenalin shot through me. I called my friends closer and made them stay together. They emerged from inside run-down houses and from behind sheds. I kept them a few house lengths back, where I could see them. There were about twenty in all.

A scruffy man I didn't recognize poked his head out of a shed as we walked toward the Washburnes' house. I pushed breath deep into my lungs and exhaled in a whisper. "Join us."

He remained where he was. Maybe he wasn't an eater, just a man covered in filth. Sometimes it was hard to tell the difference between human scavengers and the infected. He slammed the shed door closed.

That's when I noticed a rusty red van parked past the bushes. I'd never seen it before. At the next house over, Mr. Smith's had two motorcycles parked out front. I didn't like that at all. I hurried past, tugging on Clyde to make him walk faster. With my mob of feral children, no one was likely to follow me, but I worried about Sidonie more than ever.

It was only a few more houses to the Washburnes and across a wide street. Mama said the street had once been a small highway with horrible traffic, but there were no cars coming in either direction now. The Washburnes had taken up residence in a colonial-style mansion next to the golf course after the previous tenants had been eaten by their own children. The Washburnes probably liked being next to the flat, grassy expanse where they could see anyone and anything coming for a mile.

Plus, the house had a generator. Sometimes they charged stuff for us. I should have thought about bringing our reusable batteries and now could have kicked myself. I bade the eaters to stay on this side of the highway and keep out of sight behind someone's house. All except for Clyde. He could come with me.

I skipped across the road and knocked at the door. Jasmine peeked out. "Mom and Dad aren't home. Do you want to come in?"

I smiled. "Sure."

"You have to leave your mutt outside."

"Sorry, Clyde." I tied him to a tree. "Sit. Stay."

It was no big surprise Mr. and Mrs. Washburne weren't home, considering they scavenged old houses for tools, chemicals, soap, old packages of Twinkies, or whatever else might not have gone bad in the last five years since the attacks had started. They were the ones who always supplied my mom with wax and canning jars. She gave them grape jelly and apple preserves in return.

Lily, Jasmine, and I played with dolls. Every so often I went to the window to peek outside to be sure no biker gangs had snuck up on us. I jumped up once hearing a motorcycle, but it raced by on the highway. Soon I was having so much fun watching a movie, I forgot all about any danger. It was a treat to be able to watch a DVD. Sometimes the Washburnes let us recharge Mama's old laptop, and we watched videos of things she had recorded back when Papa had been alive.

Halfway through _Beauty and the Beast,_ a yowl from outside made me nearly jump out of my skin. I recognized Clyde's cry immediately. I leapt to my feet and ran out the door, afraid he'd bitten someone.

Outside I found Riley's friends beating Clyde.

None of the adults approved of Clyde. Sure, they tolerated him because Mama said I had him trained, and people talked about him being the minister's son before becoming my pet, but they complained about Clyde all the same. But when he'd got caught in Mrs. Roberson's barbed wire fence, she'd sent her son on over to tell us to get him out. So, it wasn't like everyone hated him.

Beating him with a baseball bat was just plain mean.

I rushed out the door of the Washburne's house and screamed at those stupid boys to stop.

"Leave him be!" I said. "He wasn't hurting no one."

Clyde was crumpled up on the ground, whimpering.

I rushed forward to put myself between them and Clyde, but Dalton Hallet, the biggest boy, grabbed me by the pigtail and yanked me back. Clyde lifted his head, spittle flying out of his mouth like a rabid dog. In a jerky lunge, he shot forward, but his leash kept him from going any farther. His loyalty to me earned him a swift kick to the face from Jake.

"Let me go." I punched Dalton in the stomach as hard as I could.

He laughed. "You punch like a zombie. Maybe you are a zombie."

Clyde howled, sounding as wild as a wolf. Lily and Jasmine screamed behind me, from the safety of the doorway.

"Help!" I screamed. "Sidonie!"

But Sidonie was somewhere far away, probably off smooching Riley. I had to save myself. I knew I wasn't supposed to call eaters to me, but I didn't see no other choice.

"Come to me," I whispered. "Help us."

"Whatcho doing? Your creole black magic?" Dalton asked.

"I'm warning you, Dalton, if you don't let go of me, they'll come get you," I said.

He laughed. "You're a freak! You love zombies so much, we should just throw you to them."

"Is that supposed to scare me?" I asked.

Jake and Tanner suddenly stopped laughing.

A moan came from behind me. A chorus of whimpering cries and groans rose from the highway. A pack of twenty children and teens shuffled closer. A few fell into the ditch that separated the road from the yard and struggled to get back up. The others kept on closing in. Dalton released me, and I dove for Clyde. I pushed him down and kept him behind me where he couldn't get hurt worse.

Clyde's nose bled and one side of his face was swollen. His hand hung limp from his wrist. His gray eyes were empty and his expression blank as he gazed up at me. It was hard to tell how badly hurt he was because he didn't react like a normal child.

"Just scare them. Teach them a lesson. But don't eat them," I whispered to the eaters.

Dalton swung out with his bat at the nearest eater. The boy was stiff and uncoordinated. He couldn't dodge like a person. He simply fell over in an attempt to get out of the way. Dalton chuckled victoriously.

"Those eaters are stupid. They're slow and ain't very strong."

Now it was my turn to laugh. They were only weak when they hadn't eaten. And the smell of fresh meat always made them stronger. Dalton was the stupid one.

He smacked a little girl in the head with his bat. The sound of the wet thump made bile rise up in my throat.

Two more closed in on him. They grabbed each of his arms. He couldn't swing the bat no more. More circled Tanner and Jake. Drool dribbled down their chins. Their eyes were hungry.

"Don't eat them," I said louder. Even if they deserved it.

They batted at Dalton with their fists and pommeled him to the ground, but they didn't claw at him. One opened her mouth and leaned forward.

I repeated myself again. "Do not eat him." It probably would have helped if I had meant it. Likely they sensed my loathing, and it riled them up.

Over the moans and cries came my sister's voice. "What's going on here?" Sidonie's hair was all mussed, and there was grass stuck to her dress.

The shock of seeing her so disheveled alarmed me. Had she been attacked by stray eaters? Raiders? Then I saw Riley tagging behind her, grass in his hair and his shirt unbuttoned, and realized the attacking had all been between them two. Gross.

She elbowed two eaters out of the way and rushed over to me. "You okay? What happened?"

"They were beating Clyde, and he wouldn't let me go." I pointed to Dalton where he cowered on the ground.

"Tell your pets to back off," Sidonie said.

I shook my head. A door slammed behind me. Riley and his little sisters stared out the window from inside.

Sidonie said through clenched teeth. "Do it now. Or else I'm telling Mama."

An emaciated young woman with clumps of hair missing from her head and open sores on her face licked Jake's cheek. He whimpered.

I sighed. I waved my friends back toward the street. "Get on back over there."

Slowly, they withdrew.

My sister plastered a smile on her face and smoothed out her hair. "Now, is everyone okay?"

Jake sniffled but didn't say anything.

"They hurt Clyde," I said.

"I'm asking about everyone else," Sidonie said.

No one said anything. They just kept staring at her like she'd gone crazy.

Sidonie batted her eyelashes. "Now it sounds like you boys were riling up my sister's pet. That isn't very nice, is it?"

"Well, she shouldn't have brought him here."

My sister shook her head and tsked. "What would your parents say to you beating up someone's dog or cat? If I's to tell them what you did, picking on a ten-year-old and her mutt, what do you think they'll do? I'll tell you what they'll do—beat the living tar out of you!" She wagged a finger at them.

I crossed my arms. I wasn't ten.

Jake swallowed. "You won't tell on none of us, will you, Sid?"

I felt my eyes widen. I was the one who would get in trouble if anyone told what I'd done. It was bad enough that people whispered I was a witch and a voodoo princess on account of my parents being from Louisiana, but now they would have a first-hand account to prove it. Despite all this, my sister had somehow twisted these boys all around so they thought they'd be the ones in trouble.

Sidonie smiled, all fake sweetness again. "Well, I just don't rightly know. It weren't very nice of you to pick on my little sister. Just what do you think Pastor John will say when he hears how you've been treating his boy?"

"Yeah!" I said.

Sidonie silenced me with one of her glares. I didn't want to break her spell on the boys, so I shut my mouth.

"We didn't mean nothing by it. We were just playing around," Dalton said.

"I'm sorry. I really am," Tanner said. "Don't say nothing to my dad."

"I suppose I could do that, on account of all of us being such good friends." Sidonie winked and giggled in a way that made me want to barf. "Now, if I were you, I'd go home and keep quiet about all this. Hmm?"

The boys nodded and grabbed their bikes out of the driveway and left. I couldn't believe my luck. Sidonie had saved me! I didn't know how she charmed them. It had to be magic.

Sidonie turned to the house and knocked on the door. No one opened it for her.

She knocked louder. "Excuse me, I would like my sweater back."

The door jerked open. Riley handed her the sweater, along with a package about the size of the Bible, wrapped in brown paper. "You'd better get out of here before my parents come home," he said.

Lily and Jasmine clutched each other, sobbing behind him. Lily looked up and horror crossed her pinched, little face. She shrank back and hid her face behind her older sister. My stomach cramped.

They'd seen me call the eaters. There would be no ignoring what I could do now, what a danger I was. Everyone would know and hate me.

And then there was Clyde. They'd know he wasn't trained and take him away from me.

Clyde only made it a few steps before collapsing. Something was wrong with his leg. We had to borrow the little red wagon from the Washburnes' yard to get him home. Sidonie pulled and I pushed.

"You enjoy this, don't you? Using your little friends to ruin my life," she said.

"I was protecting myself," I said. "I had to do it."

Clyde reached out for the package under Sidonie's arm, but she swatted at him.

"No, this is mine," she said firmly.

He kept on reaching until I told him to stop. After that he just stared in her direction, his eyes vacant and his jaw slack.

Mama met us at the end of our street. She held a baseball bat in her hands. I didn't like to think she would hit one of my pets with it, but I also didn't like the idea of her being eaten.

She scowled at us. "What's gotten into you two? Sneaking off like that without telling anyone where you went off to!"

Sidonie blurted out, "That's nothing compared to what trouble Josette's gotten herself into. She sicced her zombie friends on some boys for no good reason."

"That ain't how it happened, and you know it!" I said. "Those boys attacked us!"

"I hope you're happy!" Sidonie said. "This is what you get for bringing your pets everywhere." She threw the package at me, square in the chest.

Clyde reached for it again, but I picked it up, hugging the solid mass.

"What's that?" Mama asked, eyeing the brown paper.

"Probably the last bit of squirrel meat you'll be having for a while." Sidonie stomped off.

Mama looked to me. "What'd she mean? Where'd she get it?"

I had this sick feeling in the pit of my stomach. The last time Sidonie had brought stew meat home she'd said she'd traded beets and onions for it. But anyone could grow vegetables, and I had suspected she'd stolen it from the Washburnes' kitchen at the time. Before that, she'd said Dalton had given pigeon meat to her. Not everyone had a store of BB gun pellets that their parents had scavenged from vacant houses, so that meat had been precious to us.

I reckoned I knew why Sidonie always had so many boyfriends. It made me sick thinking about those disgusting boys and what she might have actually had to trade for a morsel of raccoon for the stewpot.

I called after Sidonie. "I can go hunting with Clyde. We can get squirrel meat for dinner."

"What? And get his zombie drool all over it? Ha!" She shouted over her shoulder.

Mama pointed a finger at me. "I will deal with you later."

She tore the package out of my hands and followed Sidonie. I pulled Clyde uphill the rest of the way on my own and tucked him into the dog kennel in the backyard. I crouched inside and used a rag to wash up his face so there wasn't so much blood and dirt. His eyes were dark and sunken, his skin sallow. He rested his head on my knee and whimpered. He looked like a sick little boy more than a monster.

I went and fetched Aurelie since she was the one good at herbs and healing and if anyone could fix up Clyde's wrist and leg it was her.

Her pretty face scrunched up as she looked Clyde up and down. She didn't look like Mama or Sidonie. Her skin was dark like mine, like Papa's. Her hair a muddy in-between like it couldn't make up its mind who it wanted to look like. She was born between Sidonie and me, and I expect the blue eyes hadn't gotten all used up yet, which was why she got them and there was none left by the time Mama had me.

Aurelie shook her head. "Why bother with this one? He'll just kill me in my sleep later if I do."

"Shut up! You know he won't. He's never tried to get inside the house."

She put on a pair of gardening gloves and made me turn his face away so he wouldn't be tempted to bite her. He didn't even cry out as she popped his ankle into place and set his arm.

"I probably have fleas now," she grumbled.

I stayed outside with Clyde, stroking his hair. I fed him insects since that was the closest to meat we had and let him chew on bones that had been boiled in yesterday's stew. He was a good boy. It broke my heart that anyone would want to hurt him. If any of the boys complained to their parents, they might blame Clyde, even though he'd been provoked.

Aurelie fetched me when the sun sank behind the horizon. "You'd best be indoors when they come, so you won't be in anyone's way."

"Whose way? Who's coming?"

She grabbed me by the arm and shoved me inside. "Dalton Hallet's father and the Washburnes. They'll be coming for Clyde."

My insides twisted at her words. I'd been afraid of that, but I didn't like hearing it out loud. I glanced at his cage but he remained on his side, staring off into the distance.

The kitchen was a mess of jars and sticky stains around the wood stove from a day of making preserves. Mama was nowhere in sight, so I expected she had to be upstairs with Sidonie. I could hear Sidonie blubbering and crying about how I had ruined her life. Aurelie grabbed a rag from the drawer in the kitchen.

I tried to twist out of Aurelie's grip as she scrubbed at my face. "It wasn't Clyde's fault," I said. "You know that, right? It was all my fault."

"Mabel rode up on her motorcycle an hour ago. She said your pet bit one of those boys. They aren't likely to let the boy live after that. Maybe if I see to the bite and Dalton doesn't take ill, but that's a stretch."

"But Clyde didn't bite no one. It must have been one of the other ones. The feral ones I called to help us. And if Clyde did bite him, he deserved it. They hit him with a bat. I should have let the eaters eat all of them."

Aurelie shook her head. "No, you shouldn't! And don't you let anyone hear you say that. Don't you understand the mess you've started? Folk will say you're dangerous. They ain't going to trust you after this."

Tears welled up in my eyes. I hung my head in shame. "I'm sorry."

"You'll be lucky if they stop at Clyde."

"What do you mean?"

"They'll probably hunt the pack of them down. No one is going to care about using the eaters to keep away raiders no more."

I shook my head. "No, no, they can't! They're my friends." They were people's children. Some of them might come back to us from their illness like the pastor said.

"Well, they ain't no one else's friends. Don't you get it? They eat people."

"So do wild animals like wolves and bears, but you don't see people killing them for the sport of it."

Aurelie shook her head at me. "Yes, you do. Or you did in the past. Only, you're too young to know what the world was like before eaters existed."

Not half an hour had passed before they came for us.

At dusk, Mr. Washburne kicked in our door. Mama held up her hands in a placating gesture, but he pushed her out of the way and headed for me. The Sullivans rushed in after Mr. and Mrs. Washburne, knocking over the glass jars on the kitchen counter. Dalton's mother slapped Mama and knocked her down.

Seeing the rage in Mr. Washburne's eyes, I tried to dodge out of the way, but he grabbed me by the arm. "You is a voodoo witch. We don't need your kind around here," Mr. Washburne shouted, but I could barely hear him with people stomping around and Mama sobbing.

Dalton's father grabbed Aurelie and shook her. "You's coming with me. My son needs healing. I don't care if you use your witch magic or medicine but you're gonna fix him up."

Her voice was high and tremulous, sounding so young even though she was older than me. "Yes, sir. Of course. Anything I can do to help."

Sidonie took hold of Mr. Washburne as he dragged me toward the door.

"Please," Sidonie begged. "Don't let anyone hurt my sister. We'll control her better next time."

"Don't let that one bewitch you with her words," Mrs. Washburne said. "She's as vile as the younger one."

"My sister isn't—" I started, but someone backhanded me in the mouth. I tasted blood and choked.

"It's unnatural, those girls. None of them got diseased. It's devil magic," someone said.

Mama cried, "You can't take my babies away from me! Not after all I've been through. Not after eaters killed my husband and my son became one of them. Don't do this to me."

They taped our mouths shut and then our ankles and wrists. I couldn't call for the eaters to help us and Sidonie couldn't sweet talk her way out of this. I felt bad for Sidonie. She'd never be able to get the gray tape out of her pretty hair that she'd been growing out.

The Washburnes threw us in the back of a pickup truck. My shoulder hit the side of the bed, and it hurt something fierce. They drove off and I rolled into my sister.

Sidonie said something to me, but her words were muffled by the tape and the roar of the engine. It sounded like, "Hate you."

She fought against the tape and shook her head like an animal and then sank beside me in exhaustion. She breathed heavily through her nose and then started making faces and shaking her head again. I was as scared as she was, but I was frozen and still. This was all my fault. I had to get us out of this, but I couldn't use my special talent with my mouth taped up.

At least, I didn't think I could. I closed my eyes and felt for the presence of my friends. I tried calling them to me, forming the words inside my sealed mouth and whispering out my nose. I didn't know if it worked. I didn't know if I could save Sidonie and me.

And it wasn't just me who was in trouble. I didn't know what they did with Aurelie or Mama. I didn't know what they did to Clyde. My eyes burned and vision blurred.

I was relieved when the truck stopped a minute later at the church. Pastor John wouldn't let him do nothing to us.

Mr. Sullivan threw me over his shoulder. "You and your witch sisters are going to pay for this."

Loads of people were already inside the church, people who didn't even come to church like the Bryants and the McAndrews. Voices erupted in argument. Mrs. Roberson wagged her finger at a man with a gun. "They're just children. There's no such thing as witchcraft."

"I tell you, they're the devil."

I heard the pastor's voice. "Everyone needs to calm down. We can get this sorted out without violence."

They dropped us into a corner past the altar. I squirmed my way into the shadows.

Mrs. Washburne's voice rose above the rest. "They aren't natural, that family. It's time we put an end to their witchcraft and voodoo. You hear how that mother talks. She's not from around these parts."

"People like them are probably the reason those zombies exist in the first place."

"Yeah, they're a regular coven of necromancers."

I shook my head.

Sidonie's latest boyfriend was there. Riley stood in the corner with his hands in his pockets. He didn't look at either of us.

Sidonie had worked part of her tape loose around her mouth. She leaned her head closer to mine. I thought she said, "Hate you," again but then I realized after a couple more times she said, "Bite through."

That's when I realized all those faces she'd been making like she was possessed were to work her skin loose from the tape. I started doing the same now. I was pretty distracted by working the tape and the shouting. I didn't think much about the roar of the motorcycle engines outside.

The doors burst open and a voice louder than all the rest roared, "Where is the girl? We know you have her."

As he stepped into the light, I saw it was the man we'd seen earlier. The one with the scruffy beard and the leather jacket. He stood with Mr. Smith. It didn't completely surprise me after seeing outsiders at his house, only now I wish I'd had the sense at the time to mention it to someone. A group of men were with them and the strangers pointed their rifles at the crowd. People backed away.

"Where is your zombie whisperer?" the scruffy man demanded.

Zombie whisperer? Is that what I was? What would he want with me? I looked to Sidonie. Was this stranger our savior?

Pastor John stepped in front of us. He put up his hands in a placating gesture. "Now let's be reasonable about this. We're all good Christians. There's no need for violence."

The scruffy man leveled the rifle at Pastor John and shot him in the chest. The thunder of sound vibrated through me. Blood splattered across Sidonie's face. The pastor dropped to the floor. His gray eyes stared at the ceiling.

Bile rose up in my throat. I shook my head, and tears filled my eyes. What kind of monster would kill a pastor?

Sidonie screamed, her voice muffled by the tape. Mr. Smith shouted at the scruffy man, but he was the next to be shot. Chaos broke loose all around us. People screamed and tried to run away. The back door was locked and people pounded on it to break it. The newcomers blocked the other exit. The windows were too high to get out. A few of my neighbors who had guns with them shot at the intruders. The newcomers were quick. They fired at anyone who drew guns—and a few who didn't.

The bearded man hauled Sidonie to her feet. He tore off the tape from Sidonie's face.

"Call the zombies, girl."

She shook her head. "I can't."

"Call them here and make them attack these 'good Christians' who were about to kill you. Don't you want justice?" His smile was cruel as he stared out at the people huddled against the walls. Mrs. Roberson lay unconscious on the ground. Was she dead too? My vision blurred with tears. The world I'd known was shattering all around me.

I closed my eyes and reached out to every presence I sensed in the neighborhood of the church. I whispered in my head. "Come to me."

I could feel my friends coming closer.

Sidonie sobbed. "I can't call them. I don't have that skill."

"You little liar. I saw you do it earlier." He smacked her across the face, hard enough to whip her head back.

"Try the other girl," one of the men behind him said.

The leader's gaze fell on me. He dropped my sister and swooped in for me.

He grabbed my arm, the one with the hurting shoulder, of course. Someone screamed outside, and he hesitated.

Before he managed to do anything more, the back doors crashed open. The odor of decay and musty dirt washed over me. The biggest pack of infected children I'd ever seen flooded into the room like a wave.

Even without words, I had done it! I had called them.

Men fired shots, but eaters kept dragging themselves forward. Some toppled over, knocking over the men closest to them. Another tide of them came in. They crawled over the children feasting on the adults nearest to the door and kept coming toward us.

Sidonie squirmed back toward me. Her eyes were wild. "Bite through the tape. They'll eat us all if you don't."

I kept trying, but it wasn't working. She leaned forward and sank her teeth under the tape next to my cheek and pulled. My head bonked into hers, and she fell back. A shadow loomed over us. I looked up to find a girl in a tattered blue dress leering at us. She tilted her head to the side, her red hair shifting out of her face as she looked from one of us to the other.

I knew this one. She was one of our neighborhood eaters. "Raggedy Ann," I tried to say, but the tape distorted my words and my voice was muffled. "Leave us be," I said but it came out, "Reeeb mmooofff hmee."

I made eye contact with her. I centered myself and took a deep breath, intending to breathe my intention through my nose.

Before I could do so, she lunged.

Just as she was about to claw my eyes out, a figure smashed into her side and knocked her down. The two of them rolled away. It was Clyde!

Two more feral children scrambled toward us. Clyde pushed Raggedy Ann away and limped toward us. He half-growled, half-moaned. The nearest eaters paused in their approach.

Something sharp jabbed me in the cheek. It was Sidonie, attempting to bite through the tape again. She loosened it and tugged at it again with her teeth. I tried to concentrate on the words in my head, but there was so much going on. She bonked her head into mine again. I peeked at what was going on in the church.

A child had climbed up onto the back of the scruffy man and bit down into his neck. He howled and tried to throw the child off. A teenage boy dragging himself across the floor grabbed onto the man's ankle and yanked him off his feet. Clyde pushed another girl away from Sidonie and me.

The closest children stopped their feeding frenzy and turned to Clyde. He roared again, sounding like a beast challenging a pack. Blood covered their mouths. They turned away from their current meals and trudged toward us.

Maybe his challenge hadn't been such a bright idea.

Sidonie dug her teeth into my cheek and yanked the tape downward.

My mouth was at last free. I shouted. "Leave us be. Go to your homes. You can return another day."

Faces turned to the bloody mess on the floor and back to me.

"Go, now!"

Sluggish now that there was no meal in store for them, they shambled toward the door.

Clyde looked from me to the door.

"You can stay, Clyde," I said.

He dropped to his knees and let me pet his head with my bound hands. "Clyde, what a good boy! You saved us!" I said.

Once Sidonie and I bit through our tape, we still couldn't leave as easily as that. My knee was in bad shape, and I had to lean on Clyde and my sister to make my way out. I tried not to look at the carnage. It was hard not to stare at the crimson blossoms spreading from the bullet holes in Mrs. Washburne's chest. I looked past the bite marks and scarlet smears across Mr. Roberson's arms and neck. He and his wife had always been so kind to my family. Now they were gone.

The scruffy stranger lay face up, his face half chewed off. There were so many others, and we had to climb over them.

Sidonie squeezed me to her side. Her expression was blank, her eyes looking, but not seeing. She resembled one of the eaters with the way she stared vacantly.

Clyde stopped before the pastor. He stared at the gaping hole in the man's chest. Pastor John's gray eyes stared vacantly at the heavens.

Clyde left my side and kneeled beside the older man. Tears spilled from his gray eyes. Eyes that were so much like our pastor's. Clyde turned, taking in the bloody bodies as if noticing death for the first time. His eyes weren't empty like they usually were. They were sad. He turned back to the pastor.

A sob erupted from him. "Daddy?"

My breath hitched in my chest. I whispered Clyde's name, but he didn't hear me. He wasn't mine anymore.

"Come on, Clyde," Sidonie called softly.

Reluctantly, he returned to my side. He didn't snap at my sister when she petted his head. He took my hand. His lips twitched into a melancholy smile as his eyes met mine.

I had just lost my pet but gained a friend.

Pastor John had been right about Clyde. He did have a soul. Or maybe it had taken this tragedy to get it back. Only, I wished the pastor had been able to see it himself.

The Palace at Midnight

By Robert Silverberg

The foreign minister of the Empire of San Francisco was trying to sleep late. Last night had been a long one, a wild if not particularly gratifying party at the baths, too much to drink, too much to smoke, and he had seen the dawn come up like thunder out of Oakland 'crost the bay. Now the telephone was ringing. He integrated the first couple of rings nicely into his dream, but the next one began to undermine his slumber, and the one after that woke him up. He groped for the receiver and, eyes still closed, managed to croak, "Christensen here."

"Tom, are you awake? You don't sound awake. It's Morty."

The undersecretary for external affairs. Christensen sat up, rubbed his eyes, and ran his tongue around his lips. Daylight was streaming into the room. His cats were glaring at him from the doorway. The little Siamese pawed daintily at her empty bowl and looked up expectantly.

"Tom?"

"I'm up, I'm up! What is it, Morty?"

"I didn't mean to wake you. How was I supposed to know, one in the afternoon—"

"What is it, Morty?"

"We got a call from Monterey. There's an ambassador on the way up and you've got to meet with her."

The foreign minister worked hard at clearing the fog from his brain. He was thirty-nine years old and all-night parties took more out of him than they once had.

"You do it, Morty."

"You know I would, Tom. But I can't. You've got to handle this one yourself. It's prime."

"Prime? What kind of prime? Like a great dope deal? Or are they declaring war on us?"

"How would I know the details? The call came in and they said it was prime, Ms. Sawyer must confer with Mr. Christensen. It wouldn't involve dope, Tom. And it can't be war, either. Shit, why would Monterey want to make war on us? They've only got but ten soldiers, I bet, unless they're drafting the Chicanos out of the Salinas *calabozo,* and—"

"All right." Christensen's head was buzzing. "Go easy on the chatter, okay? Where am I supposed to meet her?"

"Berkeley."

"You're kidding."

"She won't come into the city. She thinks it's too dangerous over here."

"What do we do, kill ambassadors and barbecue them? She'll be safe here and she knows it."

"I talked to her. She thinks the city's too crazy. She'll go as far as Berkeley, but that's it."

"Tell her to go to hell."

"Tom, Tom—"

Christensen sighed. "Where in Berkeley will she be?"

"The Claremont, at half past four."

"Jesus," Christensen said. "How did you get me into this? All the way across to the East Bay to meet a lousy ambassador from Monterey! Let her come to San Francisco. This is the Empire, isn't it? They're only a stinking republic. Am I supposed to swim over to Oakland every time an envoy shows up and wiggles a finger? Some bozo from Fresno says boo and I have to haul my ass out to the valley, eh? Where does it stop? What kind of clout do I have, anyway?"

"Tom—"

"I'm sorry, Morty. I don't feel like a goddamned diplomat this morning."

"It isn't morning any more, Tom. But I'd do it for you if I could."

"All right. All right. I didn't mean to yell at you. You make the ferry arrangements?"

"Ferry leaves at three-thirty. A chauffeur will pick you up at your place at three, okay?"

"Okay," Christensen said. "See if you can find out any more about all this and have somebody call me back in an hour with a briefing, will you?"

He fed the cats, showered, shaved, took a couple of pills, and brewed some coffee. At half past two the ministry called. Nobody had any idea what the ambassador might want. Relations between San Francisco and the Republic of Monterey were cordial just now. Ms. Sawyer lived in Pacific Grove and was a member of the Monterey Senate and that was all that was known about her. *Some briefing,* Christensen thought. He went downstairs to wait for his chauffeur. It was a late autumn day, bright and clear and cool. The rains hadn't begun yet and the streets looked dusty. The foreign minister lived on Frederick Street just off Cole, in an old white Victorian with a small front porch. He settled in on the steps, feeling wide awake but surly, and a few minutes before three his car came putt-putting up, a venerable gray Chevrolet with the arms of imperial San Francisco on its doors. The driver was Vietnamese or maybe Thai. Christensen got in without a word, and off they went at an imperial velocity through the practically empty streets, down to Haight, eastward for a while, then onto Oak, up Van Ness past the palace, where at this moment the Emperor, Norton VII was probably taking his imperial nap, and along Geary through downtown to the ferry slip. The stump of the Bay Bridge glittered magically against the sharp blue sky. A small power cruiser was waiting for him. Christensen was silent during the slow dull voyage. A chill wind cut through the Golden Gate and made him huddle into himself. He stared broodingly at the low rounded East Bay hills, dry and brown from a long summer of drought, and thought about the permutations of fate that had transformed an adequate architect into the barely competent foreign minister of this barely competent little nation. The Empire of San Francisco, one of the early emperors had said, is the only country in history that was decadent from the day it was founded.

At the Berkeley marina, Christensen told the ferry skipper, "I don't know what time I'll be coming back, so no sense waiting. I'll phone in when I'm ready to go."

Another imperial car took him up the hillside to the sprawling nineteenth-century splendor of the Hotel Claremont, that vast antiquated survivor of all the cataclysms. It was seedy now, the grounds a jungle, ivy almost to the tops of the palm trees, and yet it still looked fit to be a palace, hundreds of rooms, magnificent banquet halls. Christensen wondered how often it had guests. There wasn't much tourism these days.

In the parking plaza outside the entrance was a single car, a black-and-white California Highway Patrol job, that had been decorated with the insignia of the Republic of Monterey, a contorted cypress tree, and a sea otter. A uniformed driver lounged against it. "I'm Christensen," he told the man.

"You the foreign minister?"

"I'm not the Emperor Norton."

"Come on. She's waiting in the bar."

Ms. Sawyer stood up as he entered—a slender dark-haired woman of about thirty, with cool green eyes—and he flashed her a quick, professionally cordial smile, which she returned just as professionally. He did not feel at all cordial.

"Senator Sawyer," he said. "I'm Tom Christensen."

"Glad to know you." She pivoted and gestured toward the huge picture window that ran the length of the bar. "I just got here. I've been admiring the view. It's been years since I've been in the Bay Area."

He nodded. From the cocktail lounge, one could see the slopes of Berkeley, the bay, the ruined bridges, the still-imposing San Francisco skyline. Very nice. They took seats by the window and he beckoned to a waiter, who brought them drinks.

"How was your drive up?" Christensen asked.

"No problems. We got stopped for speeding in San Jose, but I got out of it. They could see it was an official car and they stopped us anyway."

"The bastards. They love to look important."

"Things haven't been good between Monterey and San Jose all year. They're spoiling for trouble."

"I hadn't heard," Christensen said.

"We think they want to annex Santa Cruz. Naturally, we can't put up with that. Santa Cruz is our buffer."

He said sharply, "Is that what you came here for, to ask our help against San Jose?"

She stared at him in surprise. "Are you in a hurry, Mr. Christensen?"

"Not particularly."

"You sound awfully impatient. We're still making preliminary conversation, having a drink, two diplomats playing the diplomatic game. Isn't that so?"

"Well?"

"I was telling you what happened to me on the way north. In response to your question. Then I was filling you in on current political developments. I didn't expect you to snap at me like that."

"Did I snap?"

"It sounded like snapping to me," she said.

Christensen took a deep pull of his bourbon and water and gave her a long steady look. She met his gaze imperturbed. She looked annoyed, amused, and very, very tough. After a time, when some of the red haze of irrational anger and fatigue had cleared from his mind, he said quietly, "I had about four hours sleep last night and I wasn't expecting an envoy from Monterey today. I'm tired and edgy, and if I sounded impatient or harsh or snappish, I'm sorry."

"It's all right. I understand."

"Another bourbon or two and I'll be properly unwound." He held his empty glass toward the hovering waiter. "A refill for you, too?" he asked her.

"Yes. Please." In a formal tone, she said, "Is the Emperor in good health?"

"Not bad. He hasn't really been well for a couple of years, but he's holding his own. And President Morgan?"

"Fine," she said. "Hunting wild boar in Big Sur this week."

"A nice life it must be, President of Monterey. I've always liked Monterey. So much quieter and cleaner and more sensible down there than in San Francisco."

"Too quiet sometimes. I envy you the excitement here."

"Yes. The rapes, the muggings, the arson, the mass meetings, the race wars, the—"

"Please," she said gently.

He realized he had begun to rant. There was a throbbing behind his eyes. He worked to gain control of himself.

"Did my voice get too loud?"

"You must be terribly tired. Look, we can confer in the morning if you'd prefer. It isn't *that* urgent. Suppose we have dinner and not talk politics at all and get rooms here, and tomorrow after breakfast we can—"

"No," Christensen said. "My nerves are a little ragged, that's all. But I'll try to be more civil. And I'd rather not wait until tomorrow to find out what this is all about. Suppose you give me a précis of it now, and if it sounds too complicated, I'll sleep on it and we can discuss it in detail tomorrow. Yes?"

"All right." She put her drink down and sat quite still, as if arranging her thoughts. At length, she said, "The Republic of Monterey maintains close ties with the Free State of Mendocino. I understand that Mendocino and the Empire broke off relations a little while back."

"A fishing dispute; nothing major."

"But you have no direct contact with them right now. Therefore this should come as news to you. The Mendocino people have learned, and have communicated to our representative there, that an invasion of San Francisco is imminent."

Christensen blinked twice. "By whom?"

"The Realm of Wicca," she said.

"Flying down from Oregon on their broomsticks?"

"Please. I'm being serious."

"Unless things have changed up there," Christensen said, "the Realm of Wicca is nonviolent, like all the Neopagan states. As I understand it, they tend their farms and practice their little pagan rituals and do a lot of dancing around the maypole and chanting and screwing, and that's it. You expect me to believe that a bunch of gentle goofy witches is going to make war on the Empire?"

She said, "Not war. But definitely an invasion."

"Explain."

"One of their high priests has proclaimed San Francisco a holy place and has instructed them to come down here and build a Stonehenge in Golden Gate Park in time for a proper celebration of the winter solstice. There are at least a quarter of a million neopagans in the Willamette Valley and more than half of them are expected to take part. According to our Mendocino man, the migration has already begun, and thousands of Wiccans are spread out between Mount Shasta and Ukiah right now. The solstice is only seven weeks away. The Wiccans may be gentle, but you're going to have a hundred fifty thousand of them in San Francisco by the end of the month, pitching tents all over town."

"Holy Jesus," Christensen muttered, and closed his eyes.

"Can you feed that many strangers? Can you find room for them? Are the people of San Francisco going to meet them with open arms? Is it going to be a festival of love?"

"It'll be a fucking massacre," Christensen said tonelessly.

"Yes. And the witches may be nonviolent but they know how to practice self-defense. Once they're attacked, there'll be rivers of blood in the city, and it won't all be Wiccan blood."

Christensen's head was pounding again. She was absolutely right—chaos, strife, bloodshed. And a Merry Christmas to all. He rubbed his aching forehead, turned away from her, and stared out at the deepening twilight and the sparkling lights of the city on the other side of the bay. A bleak bitter depression was taking hold of his spirit. He signaled for another round of drinks. Then he said slowly, "They can't be allowed to enter the city. We'll need to close the imperial frontier and turn them back before they get as far as Santa Rosa. Let them build their goddamned Stonehenge in Sacramento if they like." His eyes flickered. He started to assemble ideas. "The Empire might just have enough troops to contain the Wiccans by itself, but I think this is best handled as a regional problem. We'll call in forces from our allies as far out as Petaluma and Napa and Palo Alto. I don't imagine we can expect much help from the Free State or from San Jose. And of course, Monterey isn't much of a military power, but still—"

"We are willing to help you," Ms. Sawyer said.

"To what extent?"

"We aren't set up for much actual warfare, no, but we have access to our own alliances from Salinas down to Paso Robles, and we could call up, say, five thousand troops all told."

"That would be very helpful," said Christensen.

"It shouldn't be necessary for there to be any combat. With the imperial border sealed and troops posted along the line from Guerneville to Sacramento, the Wiccans won't force the issue. They'll revise their revelation and celebrate the solstice somewhere else."

"Yes," he said. "I think you're right." He leaned toward her and said, "Why is Monterey willing to help us?"

"We have problems of our own brewing—with San Jose. If we are seen making a conspicuous gesture of solidarity with the Empire, it might discourage San Jose from proceeding with its notion of annexing Santa Cruz, don't you think? That amounts to an act of war against us. Surely San Jose isn't interested in making any moves that will bring the Empire down on its back."

"I see," said Christensen. She wasn't subtle, but she was effective. Quid pro quo, we help you keep the witches out, you help us keep San Jose in line, and all remains well without a shot being fired. These goddamned little nations, he thought, these absurd jerkwater sovereignties, with their wars and alliances and shifting confederations—it was like a game, it was like playground politics. Except that it was real. What had fallen apart was not going to be put back together, not for a long while, and this miniaturized *weltpolitik* was the realest reality there was just now. At least things were saner in Northern California than they were down south where Los Angeles was gobbling everything, but there were rumors that Pasadena had the bomb. Nobody had to contend with that up here. Christensen said, "I'll have to propose all this to the defense ministry, of course. And get the Emperor's approval. But basically, I'm in agreement with your thinking."

"I'm so pleased."

"And I'm very glad that you took the trouble to travel up from Monterey to make these matters clear to us."

"Enlightened self-interest," Ms. Sawyer said.

"Mmm. Yes." He found himself studying the sharp planes of her cheekbones, the delicate arch of her eyebrows. Not only was she cool and competent, Christensen thought, but now that the business part of their meeting was over, he was coming to notice that she was a very attractive woman and that he was not as tired as he had thought he was. Did international politics allow room for a little recreational hanky-panky? Metternich hadn't jumped into bed with Talleyrand, nor Kissinger with Indira Gandhi, but times had changed, after all, and—no. *No.* He choked off that entire line of thought. In these shabby days, they might all be children playing at being grownups, but nevertheless, international politics still had its code, and this was a meeting of diplomats, not a blind date or a singles-bar pickup. You will sleep in your own bed tonight, he told himself, and you will sleep alone.

All the same, he said, "It's past six o'clock. Shall we have dinner together before I go back to the city?"

"I'd love to."

"I don't know much about Berkeley restaurants. We're probably better off eating right here."

"I think that's best," she said.

They were the only ones in the hotel's enormous dining room. A staff of three waited on them as though they were the most important people who had ever dined there. And dinner turned out to be quite decent, he thought—seafood, calamari and abalone and sand dabs, and grilled thresher shark, washed down by a dazzling bottle of Napa chardonnay. Even though the world had ended, it remained possible to eat very well in the Bay Area, and the breakdown of society not only reduced maritime pollution but also made local seafood much more readily available for local consumption. There wasn't much of an export trade possible with eleven national boundaries and eleven sets of customs barriers between San Francisco and Los Angeles.

Dinner conversation was light, relaxed—diplomatic chitchat, gossip about events in remote territories, reports about the Voodoo principality expanding out of New Orleans and the Sioux conquests in Wyoming, and the Prohibition War now going on in what used to be Kentucky. There was a bison herd again on the Great Plains, she said, close to a million head. He told her what he had heard about the Suicide People who ruled between San Diego and Tijuana and about King Barnum & Bailey III who governed in northern Florida with the aid of a court of circus freaks. She smiled and said,

"How can they tell the freaks from the ordinary people? The whole world's a circus now, isn't it?" He shook his head and replied, "No, a zoo," and beckoned the waiter for more wine. He did not ask her about internal matters in Monterey, and she tactfully stayed away from the domestic problems of the Empire of San Francisco. He was feeling easy, buoyant, a little drunk, more than a little drunk; to have to answer questions now about the little rebellion that had been suppressed in Sausalito or the secessionist thing in Walnut Creek would only be a bringdown, and bad for the digestion besides.

About half past eight he said, "You aren't going back to Monterey tonight, are you?"

"God, no! It's a five-hour drive, assuming no more troubles with the San Jose highway patrol. And the road's so bad below Watsonville that only a lunatic would drive it at night. I'll stay at the Claremont."

"Good. Let me put it on the imperial account."

"That isn't necessary. We—"

"The hotel is always glad to oblige the government. Please accept their hospitality."

Ms. Sawyer shrugged. "Very well. Which we'll reciprocate when you come to Monterey."

"Fine."

And then her manner suddenly changed. She shifted in her seat and fidgeted and played with her silverware, looking awkward and ill at ease. Some new and big topic was obviously about to be introduced, and Christensen guessed that she was going to ask him to spend the night with her. In a fraction, of a second he ran through all the possible merits and demerits of that and came out on the plus side, and had his answer ready when she said, "Tom, can I ask a big favor?"

Which threw him completely off balance. Whatever was coming, it certainly wasn't what he was expecting.

"I'll do my best."

"I'd like an audience with the Emperor."

"What?"

"Not on official business. I know the Emperor talks business only with his ministers and privy councilors. But I want to see him, that's all." Color came to her cheeks. "Doesn't it sound silly? But it's something I've always dreamed of, a kind of adolescent fantasy. To be in San Francisco, to be shown into the imperial throne room, to kiss his ring, all that pomp and circumstance—I want it, Tom. Just to *be* there, to *see* him—do you think you could manage that?"

He was astounded. The facade of cool, tough competence had dropped away from her, revealing unanticipated absurdity. He did not know how to answer.

She said, "Monterey's such a poky little place. It's just a *town*. We call ourselves a republic, but we aren't much of anything. And I call myself a senator and a diplomat, but I've never really been anywhere—San Francisco two or three times when I was a girl, San Jose a few times. My mother was in Los Angeles once, but I haven't been anywhere. And to go home saying that I had seen the Emperor—" Her eyes sparkled. "You're really taken aback, aren't you? You thought I was all ice and microprocessors, and instead, I'm only a hick, right? But you're being very nice. You aren't even laughing at me. Will you get me an audience with the Emperor for tomorrow or the day after?"

"I thought you were afraid to go into San Francisco."

She looked abashed. "That was just a ploy. To make you come over here, to get you to take me seriously and put yourself out a little. The diplomatic wiles. I'm sorry about that. The word was that you were snotty, that you had to be met with strength or you'd be impossible to deal with. But you aren't like that at all. Tom, I want to see the Emperor. He does give audiences, doesn't he?"

"In a manner of speaking. I suppose it could be done."

"Oh, would you! Tomorrow?"

"Why wait for tomorrow? Why not tonight?"

"Are you being sarcastic?"

"Not at all," Christensen said. "This is San Francisco. The Emperor keeps weird hours just like the rest of us. I'll phone over there and see if we can be received." He hesitated. "It won't be what you're expecting."

"In what way?"

"The pomp, the circumstance—you're going to be disappointed. You may be better off not meeting him, actually. Stick to your fantasy of imperial majesty. Seriously. I'll get you an audience if you insist, but I don't think it's a great idea."

"Can you be more specific?"

"No."

"I still want to see him. Regardless."

"Let me make some phone calls, then."

He left the dining room and, with misgivings, began arranging things. The telephone system was working sluggishly that evening and it took him fifteen minutes to set the whole thing up, but there were no serious obstacles. He returned to her and said, "The ferry will pick us up at the marina in about an hour. There'll be a car waiting on the San Francisco side. The Emperor will be available for viewing around midnight. I tell you that you're not going to enjoy this. The Emperor is old and he's been sick and he—he isn't a very interesting person to meet."

"All the same," she said. "The one thing I wanted, when I volunteered to be the envoy, was an imperial audience. Please don't discourage me."

"As you wish. Shall we have another drink?"

"How about these instead?" She produced an enameled cigarette case. "Humboldt County's finest. Gift of the Free State."

He smiled and nodded and took the joint from her. It was elegantly manufactured, with fine cockleshell paper, gold monogram, igniter cap, and even a filter. Everything else has come apart, he thought, but the technology of marijuana is at its highest point in history. He flicked the cap, took a deep drag, and passed it to her. The effect was instantaneous, a new high cutting through the wooze of bourbon and wine and brandy already in his brain, clearing it, expanding his limp and sagging soul. When they were finished with it, they floated out of the hotel. His driver and hers were still waiting in the parking lot. Christensen dismissed him, and they took the Republic of Monterey car down the slopes of Berkeley to the marina. The boat from San Francisco was late. They stood around shivering at the ferry slip for twenty minutes, peering bleakly across at the glittering lights of the far-off city. Neither of them was dressed for the nighttime chill, and he was tempted to pull her close and hold her in his arms, but he did not do it. There was a boundary he was not yet willing to cross. Hell, he thought, I don't even know her first name.

It was nearly eleven by the time they reached San Francisco.

An official car was parked at the pier. The driver hopped out, saluting, bustling about—one of those preposterous little civil-service types, doubtless keenly honored to be taxiing bigwigs around late at night. He wore the red-and-gold uniform of the imperial dragoons, a little frayed at one elbow. The car coughed and sputtered and reluctantly lurched into life, up Market Street to Van Ness and then north to the palace. Ms. Sawyer's eyes were wide and she stared at the ancient high-rises along Market as though they were cathedrals. When they came to the Civic Center area she gasped, obviously overwhelmed by the majesty of everything, the shattered hulk of Symphony Hall, the Museum of Modern Art, the great domed enormity of the City Hall, the Hall of Justice, and the Imperial Palace itself, awesome, imposing, a splendid many-columned building that long ago had been the War Memorial Opera House. A bunch of imperial cars were parked outside. With the envoy from the Republic of Monterey at his elbow, Christensen marched up the steps of the palace and through the center doors into the lobby, where a great many of the ranking ministers and plenipotentiaries of the Empire were assembled. "How absolutely marvelous," Ms. Sawyer murmured. Smiling graciously, bowing, nodding, Christensen pointed out the notables, the defense minister, the minister of finance, the minister of suburban affairs, the chief justice, the minister of transportation, and all the rest. At midnight precisely there was a grand flourish of trumpets and the door to the throne room opened. Christensen offered Ms. Sawyer his arm; together they made the long journey down the center aisle and up the ramp to the stage, where the imperial throne, a resplendent thing of rhinestones and foil, glittered brilliantly under the spotlights. Ms. Sawyer was wonderstruck. She pointed toward the six gigantic portraits suspended high over the stage and whispered a question, and Christensen replied, "The first six emperors. And here comes the seventh one."

"Oh," she gasped—but was it awe, surprise, or disgust?

He was in his full regalia, the scarlet robe, the bright green tunic with ermine trim, the gold chains. But he was wobbly and tottering, a clumsy staggering figure, gray-faced and feeble, supported on one side by Mike Schiff, the imperial chamberlain, and on the other by the grand sergeant-at-arms, Terry Coleman. He was not so much leaning on them as being dragged by them. Bringing up the rear of the procession were two sleek, pretty boys, one black and one Chinese, carrying the orb, the scepter, and the massive crown. Ms. Sawyer's fingers tightened on Christensen's forearm and he heard her catch her breath as the Emperor, in the process of being lowered into his throne, went boneless and nearly spilled to the floor. Somehow the imperial chamberlain and the grand sergeant-at-arms settled him properly in place, balanced the crown on his head, stuffed the orb and scepter into his trembling hands. "His Imperial Majesty, Norton the Seventh of San Francisco!" cried Mike Schiff in a magnificent voice that went booming up into the highest balcony. The Emperor giggled.

"Come on," Christensen whispered, and led her forward.

The old man was really in terrible shape. It was weeks since Christensen last had seen him, and by now he looked like something dragged from the crypt, slack-jawed, drooling, vacant-eyed, utterly burned out. The envoy from Monterey seemed to draw back, tense and rigid, repelled, unable or unwilling to go closer, but Christensen persisted, urging her onward until she was no more than a dozen feet from the throne. A sickly-sweet odor emanated from the old man.

"What do I do?" she asked in a panicky voice.

"When I introduce you, go forward, curtsy if you know how, touch the orb. Then step back. That's all."

She nodded.

Christensen said, "Your Majesty, the ambassador from the Republic of Monterey, Senator Sawyer, to pay her respects."

Trembling, she went to him, curtseyed, and touched the orb. As she backed away, she nearly fell, but Christensen came smoothly forward and steadied her. The Emperor giggled again, a shrill horrific cackle. Slowly, carefully, Christensen guided the shaken and numbed Ms. Sawyer from the stage.

"How long has he been like that?" she asked.

"Two years, three, maybe more. Completely insane. Not even housebroken anymore. You could probably tell. I'm sorry. I told you you'd be better off skipping this. I'm enormously sorry, Ms.—Ms.—what's your first name, anyway?"

"Elaine."

"Elaine. Let's get out of here, Elaine. Yes?"

"Yes. Please."

She was shivering. He walked her up the side aisle. A few of the other courtiers were clambering up onto the stage now, one with a guitar, one with a juggler's clubs. The imperial giggle pierced the air again and again, becoming shrill and rasping and wild. The royal levee would probably go on half the night. Emperor Norton VII was one of San Francisco's most popular amusements.

"Now you know," Christensen said.

"How does the Empire function, if the Emperor is crazy?"

"We manage. We do our best without him. The Romans managed it with Caligula. Norton's not half as bad as Caligula. Not a tenth. Will you tell everyone in Monterey?"

"I think not. We believe in the power of the Empire and in the grandeur of the Emperor. Best not to disturb that faith."

"Quite right," said Christensen.

They emerged into the dark, clear, cold night.

Christensen said, "I'll ride back to the ferry slip with you before I go home."

"Where do you live?"

"The other way. Out near Golden Gate Park."

She looked up at him and moistened her lips. "I don't want to ride across the bay in the dark alone at this hour of the night. Is it all right if I come home with you?"

"Sure," he said.

She managed a jaunty smile. "You're straight, aren't you?"

"Sure. Most of the time, anyway."

"I thought you were. Good."

They got into the car. "Frederick Street," he told the driver, "between Belvedere and Cole."

The trip took twenty minutes. Neither of them spoke. He knew what she was thinking about—the crazy Emperor, dribbling and babbling under the bright spotlights. The mighty Norton VII, ruler of everything from San Rafael to San Mateo, from Half Moon Bay to Walnut Creek. Such is pomp and circumstance in imperial San Francisco in these latter days of Western civilization. Christensen sent the driver away and they went upstairs. The cats were hungry again.

"It's a lovely apartment," she told him.

"Three rooms, bath, hot and cold running water. Not bad for a mere foreign minister. Some of the boys have suites at the palace, but I like it better here." He opened the door to the deck and stepped outside. Somehow, now that he was home, the night was not so cold. He thought about the Realm of Wicca, far off up there in green, happy Oregon sending a hundred fifty thousand kindly Goddess-worshiping neopagans down here to celebrate the rebirth of the sun. A nuisance, a mess, a headache. Tomorrow he'd have to call a meeting of the cabinet, when everybody had sobered up, and start the wheels turning, and probably he'd have to make trips to places like Petaluma and Palo Alto to get the alliance flanged together. Damn. Damn. But it was his job, wasn't it? Someone had to carry the load.

He slipped his arm around the slender woman from Monterey.

"The poor Emperor," she said softly.

"Yes. The poor Emperor. Poor everybody."

He looked toward the east. In a few hours the sun would be coming up over that hill, out of the place that used to be the United States of America and now was a thousand, thousand crazy fractured fragmented entities. Christensen shook his head. The Grand Duchy of Chicago, he thought. The Holy Carolina Confederation. The Three Kingdoms of New York. The Empire of San Francisco. No use getting upset—much too late for getting upset. You played the hand that was dealt you and you did your best and you carved little islands of safety out of the night. Turning to her he said, "I'm glad you came home with me tonight." He brushed his lips lightly against hers. "Come. Let's go inside."

We hope that you enjoyed this title and look forward to many more to come. Please, leave us a review! Reviews matter to all of our authors.

Take a look at some of our other award-winning series at https://threeravenspublishing.com/series-universes/

Visit us at https://www.threeravenspublishing.com and sign up for our newsletter for the latest and greatest news on upcoming titles and events.

Other series and titles you might enjoy.

DECLAN FINN
DECLAN FINN
DECLAN FINN
DECLAN FINN
Demons Forever
Honor at Stake
LOVE AT FIRST BITE ONE
Live & Let Bite
LOVE AT FIRST BITE THREE
Good to the Last Drop
LOVE AT FIRST BITE FOUR
The Dragon Award Nominated Series
FREE on Kindle Unlimited!

MYSTERY, MAGIC & MAYHEM
WITH A TWIST OF ROMANCE
J.F. POSTHUMUS
ON AMAZON
FIND ME

B.E.N.T.
BIOLOGIC   ENHANCED   NASCENT   TALENT

THE RAVEN AND THE CROW
MICHAEL K. FALCIANI
FIND ME
ON AMAZON

STARFLIGHT

IT CAME FROM THE
TRAILER PARK

You can also keep up to date with our latest release announcements on Scifi.radio and get some of the best fandom programing on the planet.

Scifi for your Wifi

And don't forget to check out our other Sponsors and Affiliates

A southern Appalachian jewel for craft beer lovers, Buck Bald Brewing offers something for everyone. With delicious, locally brewed beverages from across the spectrum, Buck Bald Brewing offers craft brews that are consistently amazing.

From the dark and smooth Shesquatch Scottish ale, to the intense hops of Hippibilly IPA, to the puckering sour of the blackberry and cinnamon in Berry My Heart at the Trailer Park, and more than 60+ rotating brews, you'll find what you're looking for and more.

With smiling faces behind the bar ready to help you find your next favorite brew, a constantly rotating selection of delicious craft beverages, toe-tapping tunes always playing, and the biggest games on TV, you can kick your feet up in either Copperhill, Tennessee or Murphy, North Carolina and immerse yourself in the Buck Bald Brewing experience. So, come out, fill a pint, fill a growler, and fill your mind at your new favorite family-owned craft brewery.

To discover more visit us at buckbaldbrewing.com or follow us on Facebook @buckbaldbrewing and @buckbaldbrewingmurphy.

Vesper Wren's
TRAILER PARK
PIXIE
PUNCH
· A PEACH STRAWBERRY SELTZER ·
BUCK BALD BREWING

And don't forget to check out the latest edition of ***Car Wars***

http://www.sjgames.com/car-wars/

Or the other amazing titles from
Steve Jackson Games

http://www.sjgames.com

…or the latest in the Car Warriors: Autoduel Chronicle fiction series.
https://threeravenspublishing.com/car-warriors-autoduel-chronicles/

Comprised of active or retired servicemen and civilian volunteers, Shepherd's Men enthusiastically raises awareness and funds for the SHARE Military Initiative (SHARE) at Shepherd Center in Atlanta, GA.

This nationally renowned program focuses on assessment and treatment for American military veterans who have sustained mild to moderate Traumatic Brain Injury (TBI) and Post-Traumatic Stress Disorder (PTSD) during post-9/11 service.

Find out more at: https://www.shepherdsmen.com/